Your valentine: Justin

WON'T YOU BE MINE?

Will you be my Daddy?
Mommy wishes
you were....

Katy

Dear Reader,

It's the beginning of a new year, and Intimate Moments is ready to kick things off with six more fabulously exciting novels. Readers have been clamoring for Linda Turner to create each new installment of her wonderful miniseries THOSE MARRYING McBRIDES! In *Never Been Kissed* she honors those wishes with the deeply satisfying tale of virginal nurse Janey McBride and Dr. Reilly Jones, who's just the man to teach her how wonderful love can be when you share it with the right man.

A YEAR OF LOVING DANGEROUSLY continues to keep readers on the edge of their seats with *The Spy Who Loved Him,* bestselling author Merline Lovelace's foray into the dangerous jungles of Central America, where the loving is as steamy as the air. And you won't want to miss *My Secret Valentine,* the enthralling conclusion to our in-line 36 HOURS spin-off. As always, Marilyn Pappano delivers a page-turner you won't be able to resist. Ruth Langan begins a new trilogy, THE SULLIVAN SISTERS, with *Awakening Alex,* sure to be another bestseller. Lyn Stone's second book for the line, *Live-In Lover,* is sure to make you her fan. Finally, welcome brand-new New Zealand sensation Frances Housden. In *The Man for Maggie* she makes a memorable debut, one that will have you crossing your fingers that her next book will be out soon.

Enjoy! And come back next month, when the excitement continues here in Silhouette Intimate Moments.

Yours,

Leslie J. Wainger
Executive Senior Editor

Please address questions and book requests to:
Silhouette Reader Service
U.S.: 3010 Walden Ave., P.O. Box 1325, Buffalo, NY 14269
Canadian: P.O. Box 609, Fort Erie, Ont. L2A 5X3

My Secret Valentine

MARILYN PAPPANO

INTIMATE MOMENTS™

Published by Silhouette Books

America's Publisher of Contemporary Romance

Special thanks and acknowledgment are given to Marilyn Pappano for her contribution to the 36 Hours series.

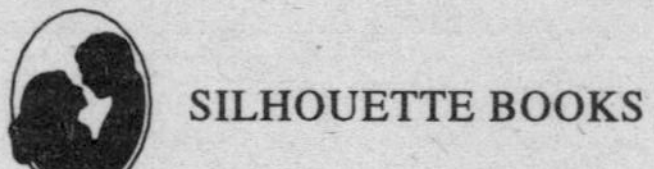

ISBN 0-373-27123-9

MY SECRET VALENTINE

This edition published by arrangement with Harlequin Books S.A.

Visit Silhouette at www.eHarlequin.com

Printed in U.S.A.

Books by Marilyn Pappano

Silhouette Intimate Moments

Within Reach #182
The Lights of Home #214
Guilt by Association #233
Cody Daniels' Return #258
Room at the Inn #268
Something of Heaven #294
Somebody's Baby #310
Not Without Honor #338
Safe Haven #363
A Dangerous Man #381
Probable Cause #405
Operation Homefront #424
Somebody's Lady #437
No Retreat #469
Memories of Laura #486
Sweet Annie's Pass #512
Finally a Father #542
**Michael's Gift* #583
**Regarding Remy* #609
**A Man Like Smith* #626
Survive the Night #703
Discovered: Daddy #746
**Convincing Jamey* #812
**The Taming of Reid Donovan* #824
**Knight Errant* #836
The Overnight Alibi #848
Murphy's Law #901
†*Cattleman's Promise* #925
†*The Horseman's Bride* #957
†*Rogue's Reform* #1003
Who Do You Love? #1033
"A Little Bit Dangerous"
My Secret Valentine #1053

Silhouette Special Edition

Older, Wiser...Pregnant #1200

Silhouette Books

Silhouette Christmas Stories 1989
"The Greatest Gift"

Silhouette Summer Sizzlers 1991 "Loving Abby"

36 Hours
You Must Remember This

*Southern Knights
†Heartbreak Canyon

MARILYN PAPPANO

brings impeccable credentials to her career—a lifelong habit of gazing out windows, not paying attention in class, daydreaming and spinning tales for her own entertainment. The sale of her first book brought great relief to her family, proving that she wasn't crazy but was, instead, creative. Since then, she's sold more than forty others, and she loves almost everything about writing, except that she would like a more reasonable boss to work for, which is pretty sad, since she works for herself.

She writes in an office nestled among the oaks that surround her home. In winter she stays inside with her husband and their four dogs, and in summer she mows the yard that never stops growing and daydreams about grass that never gets taller than two inches. You can write to her at P.O. Box 643, Sapulpa, OK 74067-0643.

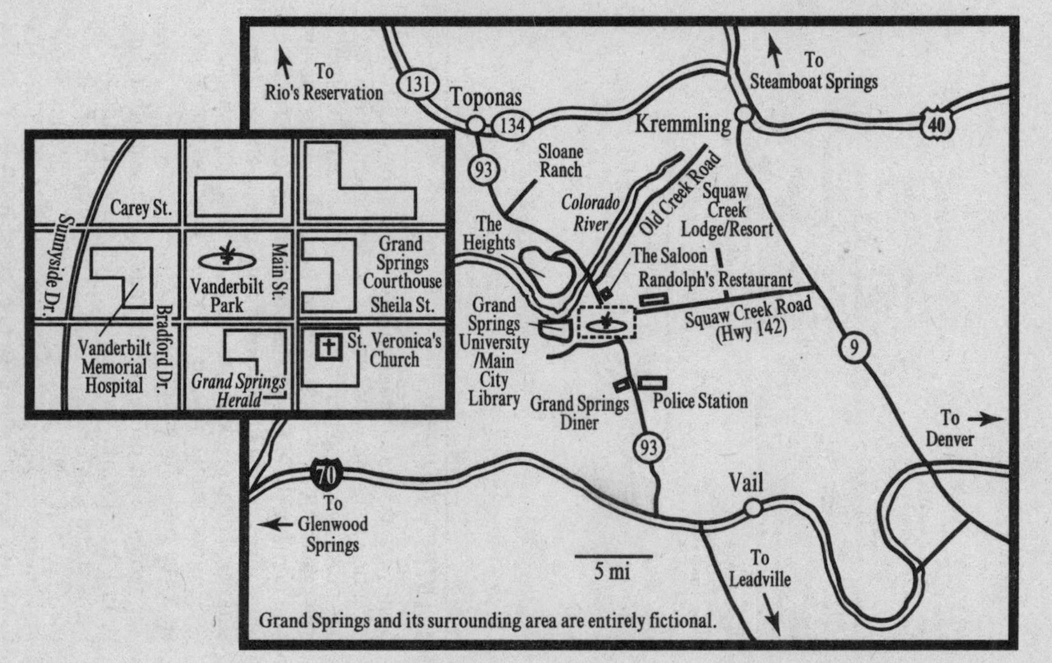

Grand Springs and its surrounding area are entirely fictional.

Chapter 1

It was ten minutes after two when Justin Reed slipped into his seat at the weekly squad meeting and opened the file in front of him. Though his supervisor didn't look up or miss a beat in his conversation, there was no doubt he knew that Justin had been late—again—and no doubt he would have something to say about it—again. He'd intended to be on time this afternoon—in fact, had started to leave his office five minutes early—but as he was walking out the door, the phone had rung. He could have left anyway, but he'd been playing phone tag with people all week and he wasn't about to miss the chance to actually connect with someone.

And so he was late. Again.

At least he wouldn't be put on the hot seat. His current caseload was nothing special, and everything was progressing steadily. Of course, there would be the perpetual question—Anything new on the Watkins case?—and the usual answer. *No, nothing.* One of these days, he'd promised himself, he was going to have an entirely different answer. *Yes, sir, we apprehended Patrick Watkins this week.*

Hey, a man could dream, couldn't he?

His boss worked his way around the table, reviewing cases, asking for reports. He'd made it halfway when the door opened and his secretary stepped inside. "Excuse me, sir. Special Agent Reed has an emergency call."

All eyes turned his way as his boss nodded toward the door. The muscles in his stomach tightening, Justin left the conference room and followed the secretary to her desk down the hall. The Bureau of Alcohol, Tobacco and Firearms wasn't quite like the police. They didn't get many emergency calls. Maybe Patrick Watkins had struck again, or something had happened to his mother in London or his father in Paris. That was about the extent of what he would consider an emergency in his life.

Picking up the phone, he tersely said, "This is Special Agent Reed."

"Mr. Reed—Special Agent Reed, this is Roger Markham. I'm an attorney in Grand Springs, Colorado."

Justin's stomach knotted, and his fingers clutched the receiver so tightly his knuckles turned white. He had only two connections to Grand Springs, Colorado, and he didn't want to hear bad news about either of them. He wished he could hang up, walk away and forget the call had ever been made, but of course he couldn't. All he could do was take an unsteady breath and ask, "What can I do for you, Mr. Markham?"

"I'm calling about your aunt, Golda Reed. She— I'm sorry, Mr. Reed, but she died a short while ago. As far as the doctors can tell, her heart gave out on her. She fell asleep and just didn't wake up. I'm sorry."

So was Justin, sorry and filled with regret. He hadn't been the best nephew Golda could have had, though he had been her favorite. He'd visited her a few times and called her when he thought about it, but…well, after his last visit nearly six years ago, there had been complications that made maintaining the relationship difficult.

His smile was thin and bitter. *Complications.* Yes, that was a good word to describe Fiona Lake and the way she'd made him feel. Trouble, decked out with red hair, hazel eyes, a sprinkling of freckles across her perfect little nose and a passion that could make a man weak.

Although he sometimes had trouble remembering. Had he been at his weakest with Fiona? Or when he'd dumped her?

"Mr. Reed?"

Giving a shake of his head, he focused his attention on the conversation. "I'm here. I just... Had she been sick?"

"The usual aches and pains you'd expect in a woman her age. But she was prepared for it. She had her funeral planned right down to the songs and the singers, and she reviewed her will regularly. The service is scheduled for Friday afternoon. Will you or anyone else from the family be able to attend?"

Justin gave a moment's thought to his caseload, though it wouldn't have changed his answer. "I'll be there, and I'll notify the rest of the family."

"Good. If you'd like, we can go over her will on Saturday. Golda always impressed upon me what a busy young man you are."

Yeah, sure, too busy to spend time with her. Too busy—and too afraid of running into Fiona. And if he'd gone to Grand Springs, he would have undoubtedly run into Fiona. After all, she lived right next door to Golda. They chatted on their porches in the evenings and shared flowers from their gardens.

At least, they used to.

"Of course, you're welcome to stay in Golda's house while you're here, or, if you'd prefer, we could make reservations for you at one of the local hotels."

"I'll—I'll figure that out before I get there." Stay in Golda's house without Golda? With Fiona next door? With powerful memories and more powerful guilt for company? An anonymous hotel would suit him just fine.

"I'm looking forward to meeting you, Mr. Reed, though I'm sorry it's under these circumstances. If you need anything between now and Friday, feel free to call me." The lawyer gave his number, then hung up.

After a long, still moment, Justin hung up, too, and found the secretary watching him sympathetically. "I'm sorry about your aunt," she murmured, then explained. "When I told Mr. Markham you were in a meeting, he told me why he was calling."

"Thanks."

"Can I do anything for you?"

His first impulse was to refuse. On second thought, he asked, "Could you get me round-trip reservations to Grand Springs, Colorado? I need to get in by noon Friday and leave late Saturday night."

"I'll take care of it."

He didn't return to the meeting but went to his office instead. He'd been sitting there, numbly staring out at the city, for some time when his supervisor knocked at the door, then came in.

George Wallace had been with the ATF since Justin was a kid. He'd sought a job in law enforcement because he figured carrying a gun and a badge might stop the endless teasing his name subjected him to, or so he claimed. He knew more about explosives and the people who tended to use them than all the other agents on their squad combined, and he wasn't at all shy about sharing his knowledge.

He sat down in front of Justin's desk. "The secretary told me about your aunt. I'm sorry."

Justin acknowledged him with a nod.

"You need some time off?"

"Just a day. The funeral's Friday afternoon, the reading of the will Saturday. I'll come back that night."

"You can take a couple extra days."

"There's no need to." Golda had told him many times that she was leaving the bulk of her estate to him, but he couldn't do anything with it until the will had been probated. That would give him at least a few weeks to consider it.

"Were you close to her?"

"She was my dad's sister, older by about eighteen years. She helped raise him. After my folks split up, she helped raise me, too. I didn't see her as often as I should have, but I liked her. I liked her a lot."

"Why don't you go on home? You must have people to notify."

There was his mother in London, who would be too busy playing hostess to her latest husband the earl to feel much more than a twinge of regret. His father, living in Paris with *his* latest spouse—a twenty-something poster girl for eating disorders—probably wouldn't even feel a twinge. He might have better luck with his father's two older brothers, their wives and children, though he wouldn't swear to it. With little chance of being included in Golda's will, there was little chance they would care she was dead.

The Reeds were nothing if not greedy, he thought with a cynical smile.

Fiona would care. Whether she profited or not, she would be sorry that Golda was gone. She would miss her, and know life was poorer without the old lady in it.

"Justin?"

He gave George a weak smile. "Yeah, I need to call the family. It's already evening in London and Paris. If I don't get my mother and father before they go out, I may not get them."

"Go on home. Take tomorrow off if you need it. And if you want a few extra days when you get there..."

"Thanks." As his boss left, Justin packed the papers he wanted to take home in his briefcase, then signed out. By the time he got to the apartment he called home, the news had sunk in, and he was feeling less dazed and more regretful. He should have been a better nephew, should have made more of an effort to keep in touch with Golda. He never should have let fear compromise the one healthy lifelong relationship he had.

But it was too late for regrets now.

When he reached his mother in London, she was dressing for a party. She said all the right words, but, as usual, they lacked sincerity. And she wondered why her marriages never lasted.

It was 10:00 p.m. in Paris and his father, surprisingly, was in. He said the right words, too, but when Justin asked if he would return for the funeral, he sounded genuinely perplexed. "It's a hell of a long flight to Colorado, and what would be the point?"

"I don't know, Dad. What *would* be the point of showing up for your only sister's funeral? Maybe showing that you cared about her? That you respected her? That at least you were grateful for everything she'd done for you?"

"What did she do for me?"

Justin bit back an obscenity. "Forget I even asked. I've got to go—"

"Don't you want to say hello to Monique? Talk about respect… Calling halfway across the world, then hanging up without even saying hello to your stepmother is a fine way to show your respect for her."

"Give her my best. I'll talk to you soon." Justin hung up before his father could say anything else, before he could blurt out what he really wanted to say—that Monique wasn't even old enough for him to lust after, so she for damn sure wasn't old enough to be his stepmother. That he felt little respect for her and none for his father. That with Golda gone, so was the Reed family's last chance at decency, generosity and humanity.

Without Golda, the entire rest of the family was nothing but a bunch of coldhearted, self-absorbed bastards.

Himself included.

Next he talked to his uncles and five of his six cousins, leaving a message for the last one. There might have been one or two genuine *I'm sorrys* in their responses, but he couldn't say for sure.

After the last call, he took a beer from the refrigerator and went to stand at the balcony door. As the sky darkened and lights came on across the city, he lifted the bottle in a salute to the west. "The family's gonna let you down again, Aunt Golda. But that doesn't surprise you, does it? We always disappointed you while you were alive. Why should it be any different now that you're dead?"

Unexpectedly his throat tightened with more emotion than he'd felt in years. "I'm sorry, Aunt Golda," he murmured as his eyes grew damp. "I loved you...and I'm so damned sorry."

"He's coming back."

Fiona Lake looked up from the table she was polishing to meet her mother's gaze. Delores looked both regretful and triumphant. The triumph came from her success in finding the answer to the question that had haunted them both since learning of Golda's death two days ago. Her regret came from the answer itself.

So Justin was coming to Golda's funeral.

He had every right to be there. He was her nephew, and she'd loved him like a son. It was only fitting that he honor her one last time by being present for her funeral. If he hadn't come, Fiona would have hated him for it.

Oh, but she didn't want to see him!

"How did you find out?" Fiona asked as if it wasn't important.

"I asked Roger Markham. He was Golda's attorney, you know. He called Justin at work Wednesday to tell him that she'd passed, and Justin said he would be here."

How many times had Fiona tried to call Justin at his Washington office six years ago? Eight? Ten? And yet he'd always been conveniently out. Now she knew she should have asked Roger to call for her—or anybody else in the world whose name wasn't Lake.

"What are you going to do?"

"Nothing. I'm going to Golda's funeral, and I'm going to pretend that Justin and I have never met."

Delores snorted. "Oh, yes, I can see you pulling that off. And what about after the funeral? When you go home and he's right there next door?"

"I'll be home. He'll be next door."

"What about Katy?"

Fiona's hand trembled at the mention of her daughter. Almost five years old, Katy was the light of her life. She loved her daughter more than she'd known she was capable of loving—more than she'd ever loved Justin, more than she'd ever hated him. She'd needed all that love to make up for the father who'd never given a damn that Katy existed, to atone for her sin of falling in love with a man who could be so coldhearted and selfish.

"What about Katy, Mom? He didn't care about her before. He's not going to care now."

"Are you going to let him see her?"

"I'm not going to hide her away like something to be ashamed of. But no, I'm not going to make a point of bringing her to his attention." She wasn't going to do anything to bring herself to his attention, either. Golda had had hundreds of friends. The church would be packed to overflowing this afternoon, and virtually all of them would want to express their regrets to Golda's only relative in attendance.

All of them except her.

"Nice table," Delores said as Fiona stepped back to study its shine. "What is it?"

"Rosewood. Mrs. Owens picked it up on her last trip to Europe, paid a fortune to have it shipped here, then decided it really didn't *go*. She traded it to me for that armoire that had been collecting dust in the corner for two years." Fiona looked around for something else in need of cleaning, but she'd been dusting and polishing practically nonstop since hearing about Golda's death. Everything in the shop looked fine.

Laying the cloth aside, she walked behind the counter and sat down in a circa-1920 oak desk chair. Nearly an hour remained before they had to leave for the church, and she had nothing left to do but think. Remember.

And she didn't want to remember.

Her mother came to stand behind her and gave her a shoulder rub. "You'll get through this, darlin'. I know it's tough, losing Golda and having to see Justin again at the same time, but you're strong. You'll survive."

"I know I will, Mom. It's just..." *Hard.* Hard saying goodbye to her good friend and neighbor, and even harder having to do it with *him* there. Hardest of all was having to face him, remembering his sweet words of love, his solemn promises to come back to her, his long years of silence. Sometimes she'd thought it would have been easier if he'd simply told her it was over. But how much clearer could a message be than no message at all?

Lord, she wished things were different! This wasn't at all where she'd thought she would be at the age of thirty. Not that she didn't have a lot to be grateful for. She owned her own house. Past Times, her antique shop, was well established and provided her with a comfortable living. She had family and friends, and best of all, she had Katy. In fact, the only thing she'd thought would be different was her lack of a husband. She'd assumed she would become a wife before becoming a mother. She'd thought her life would be more traditional, like her parents' and sisters' lives.

Of course, when she'd made those assumptions, she hadn't counted on falling in love with a man like Justin Reed. She hadn't known she could misjudge someone so badly.

He'd come to spend two days with Golda before continuing his vacation out west. Instead he'd stayed ten days, and she'd known before the first one was over that she'd met the man she was going to marry. They'd gone from strangers to lovers in the space of a few hours, had fallen head over heels in love soon after.

At least, *she* had. He'd told her he loved her, told her she was the most special woman in his life and talked of their future together—of the places they would go, the things they would see, the babies they would have. When his job cut his vacation short and called him back to the East Coast, he'd sworn he would come back as soon as he could. He'd asked her to visit him in Washington, had promised he would love her forever and told her he already missed her.

She had believed everything he said, and it had all been lies. Wonderfully romantic, just-what-she'd-wanted-to-hear lies. Carefully-calculated-to-seduce lies.

Seeing him would be hard, all right, but she would manage. As her mother said, she was strong. She would survive. But, please, God, she hoped there was a limit to how many times she was expected to survive Justin's intrusion into, then disappearance from, her life.

"We'd probably better go," Delores said, bending to give her a hug. "I told your sisters we'd pick them up on the way to the church. You don't mind, do you?"

"Of course not." Fiona switched on the answering machine, got her coat and purse from the back, then flipped the Open sign on the door to Closed. After locking up, she followed her mother to her car and settled in the passenger seat.

Though the day was cold—after all, it was January in Colorado—the sun was shining brightly. She was glad for that. Golda hadn't minded dreary, gray days, but she'd absolutely reveled in sunny ones, no matter what the temperature. It was only right that she be laid to rest on a bright sunshiny day.

Her mother chatted idly, requiring no response from Fiona, on the way to first Kerry's house, then Colleen's. Her sisters lived three blocks in opposite directions from their parents' home, while Fiona's house was two blocks north. Unlike Justin's family, the Lakes stayed close to home and liked it—though five years ago, she would have moved away with him if he'd asked, and been happy to do so. She would never consider such a move now. Family, she could count on to always be there for her. Justin had taught her that she couldn't count on a man for anything besides heartache.

And the most beautiful little girl in the entire world.

When they reached the church, space was at a premium, both in the parking lot outside and in the pews inside, seating them much closer to the front than Fiona wanted. Given the opportunity, she would have escaped to the standing-room-only crowd at back, but with her mother on one side and Kerry and Colleen on the other, she didn't get the opportunity.

Kerry squeezed her hand and gave her a smile. "It's all right. We'll stick close."

"It's silly to be so nervous."

"I'd worry if you weren't nervous. If you could see him for the first time since he—"

Betrayed her, Fiona filled in when her sister hesitated. Abandoned her. Broke her heart.

Kerry settled for a shrug. "—and not be nervous, then you'd be colder-hearted and more unfeeling than he could possibly be."

Fiona would bet Justin wasn't nervous about the prospect of seeing her again. For all she knew, he might not even remember her. And to be able to turn his back on his baby, he was definitely colder-hearted and more unfeeling than she could ever be.

The time for the funeral drew nearer, and the front row, reserved for family, remained empty. Just when Fiona was beginning to wonder if he hadn't betrayed Golda, too, Delores bent close and whispered, "Take a deep breath, darlin'. There he is."

Fiona didn't have to turn her head more than a few degrees to see the man she'd loved and hated and prayed to never see again, walking down the aisle alongside the minister. He wore a steel-gray suit with a shirt and tie in softer dove-gray, and his black hair was trimmed short enough to control its wavy tendencies. His gaze was directed to the floor as he ignored the hundreds of people around him, and his jaw was set so tightly that she could see the tension from where she sat.

Colleen gave a sigh as the two men passed their pew. "He's still handsome."

Of course he was—possibly the handsomest man Fiona had ever met. Years ago she'd figured she thought that because she was so much in love with him, but no, she admitted regretfully. It was the truth. She certainly didn't love him now, but he was still gorgeous.

And that was all right. Finding him handsome didn't mean she was still a sucker for his lies. It didn't mean he had any effect at all on her. She could admire the package without caring what was inside, because she knew what was inside—nothing worth having.

The service started promptly at two. Fiona listened to the eulogy, the prayers, the songs, and said a silent, final goodbye to her friend. With some bitterness, she hoped to soon do the same to Justin, who sat stiffly on the front row. He didn't bow his head for the prayers, showed no emotion during the songs. He reminded her of nothing so much as a statue.

For the first time in five years, she felt truly relieved that he wasn't a part of Katy's life. Her daughter might need a father, but she didn't need her own father. She was better off without him. So was Fiona. And so was Golda.

After the final prayer, Delores leaned across. "I'm going to pay my respects."

Kerry and Colleen looked at Fiona, who shrugged. "Go ahead. I'll wait here."

She followed their progress part of the way up the aisle, then went to study the nearest of a dozen stained-glass windows that stretched the length of the church. She was restless, impatient to leave, to collect Katy from the baby-sitter, take her home and shut themselves off from the rest of the world until Sunday. Maybe they could go somewhere for the weekend—pack their bags, get in the car and head off on an adventure. Or maybe they could go to Denver—

''Fiona.''

Tension streaked through her body, clenching her muscles and bringing a sick feeling to her stomach. She said a quick prayer that she would turn and find her friend Rebecca's husband Steve, or maybe Juliette's husband Colton, but she knew Steve's and Colton's voices. More importantly, she knew *his* voice. It had seduced her, haunted her, taunted her...and then gone silent on her. No, *It's over.* No, *Goodbye.* No, *I don't want you anymore.* Just silence.

Forcing all emotion from her expression, she slowly turned to face him. Watching him walk past at a distance was nothing compared to seeing him up close. Handsome? Try *incredible.* This close she could see the deep blue of his eyes, the straight line of his nose, the perpetually stubborn set of his jaw.

She could see the resemblances to Katy that she'd conveniently persuaded herself weren't there.

She thought of all the things she'd promised herself she would say to him if she ever saw him again. Every sentiment, every accusation, could be condensed into two harsh words—*Damn you*—but she didn't say them. She didn't say anything at all.

He shifted in a manner that should have screamed *He's nervous!* Of course, it didn't. It just seemed natural. Calm. ''I wondered if you were going to speak to me.''

''Actually, no. Speaking to you makes it harder to keep up the illusion that I'd never met you.''

"And you like pretending you never met me."

She smiled coolly. "I'd like it better if I really had never met you, but this is the next best thing."

A faint hint of bitterness came into his eyes, and his mouth formed a thin line. After a moment, he flatly said, "I'm sorry about Golda."

"Everyone here is sorry about Golda." But in some tender place inside, she was touched by his acknowledgment that losing Golda was a bigger loss to her than him. After all, she'd seen the old lady every day. He'd stayed away for six years.

Because of her? Or because he hadn't cared any more about his aunt than he had about Fiona?

He shifted again, and this time he did look… Not nervous. Uncomfortable. As if he wasn't at all accustomed to the position he found himself in—the grieving nephew, the polite ex-lover. "I understand your being here has nothing to do with me, but…thank you anyway."

"You're right. Nothing in my life has anything to do with you." Hoping her hand wouldn't tremble, she gestured toward the center of the church. "You should probably get back over there. There are people waiting who actually *want* to talk to you."

With a solemn nod, he turned and walked away, leaving her feeling… Edgy. Guilty. Ashamed. She wasn't a rude person, and had never been cruel a day in her life. She could blame it on Justin. She hadn't been a lot of things until she'd met him—easy, foolish, careless, dreamy, gullible, brokenhearted, pregnant. She hadn't been so strong until she'd loved him and lost him. She needed that strength now to get through the next thirty hours.

She needed it desperately.

Justin turned onto the three hundred block of Aspen Street and slowed to well below the speed limit. The houses on the block were moderately sized, reasonably priced and in good shape considering they were nearly double his age. Golda's was in the middle of the block on the left side of the street. Fiona's was one closer.

It looked the same as it had six years ago. It wore a fresh coat of white paint on the siding, dark green on the shutters and door. The same car she'd driven then was parked in the driveway in front of the two-car garage, and what appeared to be the same lace curtains hung at her bedroom windows on the second floor.

But there were a few differences. A bike with training wheels was parked at the bottom of the steps. A kid-size basketball goal stood in the driveway next to the car. A red wagon on the porch held a soccer ball and a basketball among other toys. A remote-control Jeep lay upside down near the curb.

Maybe the toys belonged to her nieces and nephews, he reasoned, or maybe she'd been baby-sitting a friend's children. But the cold, hard place that formed deep in his gut said otherwise. Fiona had a child.

Which meant she also had a husband.

He wondered how long she had waited for him before moving on. A few months? Six, maybe eight? And then she'd replaced him, gotten married and started the family she'd promised *him.* She was another man's wife, raising another man's child. Damn her.

And damn him. He'd promised he would come back, but he never had. He hadn't written, hadn't called, had ignored her calls. Plain and simple, he'd been afraid. All the intense emotions she roused in him had seemed perfectly normal when he was with her, but with distance had come doubt.

His parents had seen to it that he'd grown up with little belief in love and no faith at all in marriage. Their own marriage had been a mistake, and so had the ten or so they'd made since their divorce from each other. They'd acted on impulse every damn time, completing the meeting, lust, so-called love and marriage in record time, only to wake up with strangers they neither knew nor liked. Within a year, often less, the divorce was in the works and they were looking for the next person willing to make a fool of them.

He'd watched it happen time and again, often from the same household, usually from a distance, and he'd sworn it would never happen to him. If he ever married, it would be to someone he'd known a long time, someone he considered a friend, someone who didn't believe in fairy tales of love and romance any more than he did. And if the marriage ended, he wouldn't be so emotionally vested in it that it disrupted his life. He would deal with it like a mature adult and move on. He'd been so confident, so determined.

And yet the first time he'd mentioned marriage to Fiona, he'd known her all of seventy-two hours. After only three days, he'd been willing to tie the knot with a woman he hardly knew merely because she made him feel things he'd never felt before. He'd been not only willing but eager to follow in his parents' footsteps, and that had scared the hell out of him.

So he'd cut her out of his life. Refused her calls at work. Let the machine pick them up at home. Ignored her quiet pleas. With eighteen hundred miles separating them, he'd convinced himself that Fiona had just been a fling, that the affair had been about sex and not love, that nothing so hot and intense could last. It hadn't been difficult. He came from a long line of emotionally-stunted bastards. He'd had excellent role models.

Just past Fiona's house, he pulled into Golda's driveway and shut off the engine. He'd intended to spend the night at a motel, but his timing wasn't the greatest. There was no room at the inns, and so the wayward nephew was left with no choice but to stay at Golda's. Next to Fiona.

The lawyer had given him the key at the funeral—just in

case. Taking his bag from the trunk as well as his briefcase, he let himself into the quiet, old house.

The parlor opened off the foyer and was filled with mementos of Golda's life. He walked around the perimeter of the room, touching nothing, gazing at countless photographs of himself, from first grade through graduation, both prep school and college. His mother had missed one, and his father had missed both, but Golda had been there both days.

There were other photographs, mostly of people he didn't know, as well as some childish drawings that had been framed and hung as if they deserved it. He assumed they were the work of the pretty little dark-haired girl whose photos on display numbered second only to his own, and wondered who she was.

A framed portrait on the piano answered that question. It was the same girl snuggled on her mother's lap while they read a children's book. She looked sleepy, contented, and her mother… Fiona looked happier, more beautiful and more in love than he'd ever had the fortune to see her.

Angrily he turned away from the picture. He *didn't* care. Their affair never could have been more than it was, and it had ended six years ago. She felt nothing but contempt for him, and he…he felt nothing. He was just tired from the flight, worn-out by the guilt, depressed by the funeral and the graveside service. He needed sleep, then food, then more sleep, and he needed to get the hell out of Grand Springs, which he would do tomorrow immediately following the meeting with Golda's lawyer. Once he was back in D.C. and at work, he would be all right.

He carried his garment bag upstairs, chose the guest room where he hadn't once made love to Fiona, stripped off his clothes and crawled into bed. Sleep came easily, but it wasn't restful. Too many memories, too many dreams.

When he gave up and got up, it was nearly eight o'clock, the sky was dark, and his stomach was rumbling. He dressed in jeans and a sweater, grabbed his coat and headed for the car. He got so far as unlocking the door before some impulse he didn't understand and couldn't resist drew him away, across the yard next door and up the steps. It was incredibly stupid, he told himself as he crossed the six feet to the door. She'd made it clear at the church this afternoon that she wanted nothing further to do with him. He had nothing to say to her. Her husband certainly wouldn't appreciate him stopping by.

But none of that stopped him from ringing the doorbell or waiting impatiently in the thin glow of the porch light.

Through the curtained side lights that flanked the door, he saw a shadow approach the door. The long moment's hesitation that followed told him it was Fiona, debating whether to answer the door or leave him standing there like the idiot he was. If asked to guess, he would have put his money on the latter, but he would have been wrong.

She opened the door only halfway and blocked it with her socked foot. Hugging her arms to her chest, she fixed a slightly hostile, mostly blank look on him and waited for him to speak.

"Hi." Brilliant opening. Worthy of a door slammed in his face. "I was wondering..." About a lot of things, but the growl deep in his stomach gave him a topic to discuss with her. "Where can I get a decent burger around here?"

She looked suspicious of his question, but answered as if it were legitimate. "We have the usual fast food places. The diner downtown might still be open. Randolph's definitely is, though I don't know if they have hamburgers on the menu. The Squaw Creek Lodge restaurant, but it's a bit of a drive."

"Which one's your favorite?"

"We like McDonald's Happy Meals," she replied with a hint of sarcasm, then grudgingly went on. "The Saloon. It's a bar downtown that serves greasy burgers with fried onions and a side of heartburn. They're the best around."

"Any chance I could persuade you to keep me company while I eat?"

Her eyes darkened, and her mouth thinned into a prissy straight line. "No. None."

Of course not. What man would want to stay home and baby-sit while his wife went out to the local watering hole with her ex-lover? "I…I just thought maybe we could talk."

"What could we possibly have to talk about?"

He shrugged awkwardly. "Golda."

For a moment, she stood motionless. Then she pushed the door up, not quite closing it. Justin wasn't sure whether she'd changed her mind or was dismissing him, until she returned, wearing shoes and carrying a thick blanket. She slipped outside, closed the door, wrapped the blanket around her, then sat down on the top step.

He stayed where he was a moment. It was twenty degrees, and neither of them was dressed to spend any amount of time outside. Her warm house was a few steps away, and Golda's was thirty feet away. There was no reason for them to freeze outside.

Except that she obviously didn't want him inside her house, and he wasn't even sure he wanted to be alone with her.

He sat at the opposite end of the same step and rubbed his hands together before sliding them into his coat pockets. As the silence between them extended, he reminded himself that he was supposed to talk about Golda, but he couldn't think of anything he wanted to say—not now, not with Fiona still obviously hostile.

Gazing at the house across the street, brightly lit in the night, he finally asked, "How have you been?"

Fiona slowly turned her head to look at him. He felt it. "You're a little late asking, aren't you?" The voice he remembered in his dreams as sweet, warm, tender, was as cold as the frigid air that surrounded them. "You said you wanted to talk about Golda. Do it or leave."

Now it was her turn to stare across the street while he looked at her. The past six years had left him looking six years older and ten years wearier, but they'd simply left Fiona more beautiful. She'd always been pretty, with her red hair, hazel eyes, freckled nose, fair skin and exceedingly kissable mouth, but now she was lovelier, softer, more desirable, in a womanly sort of way. Was it motherhood that had brought about the change?

Or the man she'd married?

He couldn't ask. He had no right. She had the dubious honor of being part of the single most important relationship in his entire life. He'd seduced her, and been seduced by her. He'd wanted to marry her, to spend the next fifty years at her side. He'd even imagined himself in love with her—him, a Reed, when everyone knew that Reeds were capable of many emotions, but love was not one of them.

And he had no right to ask her anything. What was wrong with this picture?

Golda, his conscience reminded him when Fiona shifted impatiently on the step. Turning so the railing was at his back, he went straight to the heart of what troubled him most about his aunt. ''Did she ever forgive me?''

Chapter 2

Underneath the heavy comforter, Fiona was trembling, but it had nothing to do with the cold. Ask me if *I'll* ever forgive you, she wanted to demand. *Not in this lifetime.* But she wasn't Golda. She'd loved him in an entirely different way, and while he'd betrayed *her,* he'd merely neglected Golda. He'd broken Fiona's heart and cheated his daughter of a father, but he'd deprived Golda of nothing more than a few visits.

Not that he cared if Fiona and Katy ever forgave him. He hadn't even asked about her, hadn't shown any interest at all in her existence. For all practical purposes, for him, she *didn't* exist.

Someday, if there was any justice in life, he would come to regret the way he'd treated Katy. Someday it would be her turn to walk away from him, to abandon him and make him feel unwanted and unloved.

Fiona hoped she was around to see it.

"What is it you'd wanted her to forgive you for?" she asked. For failing to come and see the woman who'd put her life on hold from time to time to make his a little easier? For putting his own needs ahead of an old woman who loved him dearly and would forgive him anything?

Or for refusing to acknowledge his daughter? Not many people outside her family knew he was Katy's father, but Golda had known from the instant she'd heard about Fiona's pregnancy. She'd welcomed her grandniece, and Fiona, too, with all the love and acceptance Justin had refused to offer. She'd made them feel as if they'd mattered.

To him they never had. He'd had his fun—livened up a dull vacation with a steamy affair—and he'd never given a damn how much pain he'd caused. But Golda had.

"I—I didn't see her as often as I should have. I didn't write, didn't call..."

"Oh, gee, so it's a habit," she said sarcastically. "And here I thought I'd been singled out for shabby treatment. But you weren't being cruel. You were just being *you.*"

It was difficult to tell with so little light, but she thought he might have winced. "Fiona—"

Holding onto the comforter, she stood up and gazed down at him. "She kept pictures of you all over the house. She told everybody how proud she was of her nephew, the ATF agent. She said you were the only Reed besides her that had ever amounted to anything." She drew a deep breath and unwillingly softened her voice. "She loved the cards you sent, and the flowers on her birthday, and the roses on Mother's Day. She loved the phone calls, and the postcards, and the little gifts, and every minute of every visit. She loved *you.*"

After a moment, she went to the door. She turned back to say... What *could* she say? Clenching her jaw tightly, she went inside, locked the door, then leaned against it for a few deep breaths.

There. Two encounters down. There would be only one more—the reading of the will in Mr. Markham's office the next day—and Justin would return to Washington. She would never see him again.

The thought should make her happy. It *did* make her happy. So damned happy she had tears in her eyes.

After a while, she risked a peek out the window just as Justin got into his rental car. He was off to the Saloon, no doubt, where he'd get his burger and probably find a pretty little thing to keep him company while he ate. He might even take her back to Golda's house, the way he'd once taken Fiona there.

And she didn't care if he did. He was no longer a part of her life.

He was just a part of her daughter, who *was* her life.

Draping the comforter over the banister, she climbed the stairs to Katy's room. Her daughter's crib had been an antique, handed down through generations of the first family to settle in the Grand Springs area, and her cradle at the shop had come to America from Britain nearly two centuries ago, but her bed these days was a tree house. It filled half her room with one platform in the branches for a bed, another for a reading spot and a third one for a play area. The fat fake trunk had shelves inside to hold toys and books, stuffed squirrels and birds sat on the branches, and the felt leaves formed a canopy that reached up to the blue-sky-studded-with-fluffy-white-clouds ceiling.

It was an extravagance, built by Fiona's father and decorated by her mother, and it had made Katy the envy of the kindergarten class at Jack and Jill's Day Care. Fiona had thought it was much too indulgent, but she'd given in. After all, the kids at Jack and Jill's had teased Katy one time too many about not having a father. Fathers were a dime a dozen—all the teasing kids had them—but there was only one fabulous tree-house bed in all of Colorado, and Katy had it.

Fiona reached through the railing to smooth her daughter's dark hair from her face. The night-light—a string of white Christmas lights woven through the branches—cast a soft glow on her chubby cheeks, her long lashes, her full mouth. Asleep in an old T-shirt of Fiona's that slipped off one shoulder and twisted around her sturdy little body, she looked sweet, angelic, so utterly perfect that Fiona's heart ached.

Whatever sins Justin had committed, whatever lies he'd told, he'd given her the most precious gift she ever could have wished for. She might hate him. She might pray to never see him again. But she owed him her life. She should remember that the next time she talked to him.

In her bed, Katy rolled onto her side and her eyes fluttered open. "Is it time to get up?" Her voice was sleepy, baby soft, and never failed to brighten Fiona's heart.

"No, babe, not yet. Go back to sleep."

"Okay." In an instant, her eyes closed and she was snoring softly.

Fiona gave her hand a kiss, then wrapped her arm around her favorite teddy bear. Then, with a weary sigh, she returned downstairs, wishing it wasn't too early for her to go to bed, too. The sooner morning came, the sooner the appointment with Mr. Markham would come, and Justin would leave.

She *really* wanted Justin to leave.

After picking up the few toys Katy had left on the living room floor and rinsing their supper dishes to stack in the dishwasher, she couldn't find anything else to do. The nervous energy that had kept her busy at the shop had done the same here at home. Everything was cleaned, polished, vacuumed and laundered within an inch of its life. She fixed a cup of hot cocoa, grabbed the comforter from the stair railing and settled in the living room with all the lights off and the television on, and with a nice view of Golda's house. Not that she was keeping tabs on Justin, of course.

Though she did notice when he pulled into the driveway about the time she finished her cocoa.

And that he was alone in the car.

And that he hadn't been gone long enough for anything besides a burger at the Saloon.

He got out of the car, stretched as if he were stiff, then, for a time, simply stood there, gazing first at Golda's house, then at hers. With his hands in his pockets and his shoulders hunched against the cold, he looked…forlorn.

Sympathy she hadn't let herself feel for him earlier welled inside her. Maybe Golda hadn't been a regular part of his life, but she'd been the only person in his entire family to care about him. He'd never had brothers or sisters and apparently hadn't mattered much to either parent. It was Golda who'd loved him, encouraged him, advised him and was there for him, and now she was gone. He was alone.

Except for Katy, the daughter he'd wanted no part of, just as his own parents had wanted no part of him. It was bad enough that he could ignore her so thoroughly, doubly bad that he could do so when he knew from experience how much it hurt.

Fiona's sympathy died a quick death, and she resolutely turned away from the window and back to the television. He was alone, but that was his choice.

Let him live with it.

Still on East Coast time, Justin was up early Saturday morning. He finished his usual run before the sun came up, and was showered, dressed and eating breakfast by seven. His appointment with the lawyer wasn't until eleven, and then he was heading for Denver. Much better to hang around the airport with nothing to do than to stay in Fiona's territory.

He couldn't help but notice when he left on his run that her car was still the only one in the driveway. Maybe her husband parked in the garage—not very gentlemanly of him, Golda would have said with a sniff—or they were a one-car family. Maybe he was out of town on business.

Why hadn't Golda told him she'd gotten married and had a child? he wondered, then immediately answered. Because the one time she'd brought Fiona into the conversation, he'd been defensive and rude. She'd offered her opinion—*You owe her an explanation*—and he'd responded that it was none of her business. He'd given her two choices—she could talk about Fiona or she could talk to him. She'd chosen him and never mentioned Fiona again.

But it wouldn't have hurt her to mention something as significant as getting married.

Scowling because he felt like a petulant child, he carried his cereal bowl and spoon to the sink and washed them, then stood there with his coffee, staring out the window. Golda's yard, always her pride and joy, looked as good as was possible in the middle of winter. The grass was cut short, the flower beds mulched, the rosebushes protected from the cold. Fiona's backyard had once been as neat, but now there was a swing set firmly planted in the grass, along with toys scattered around.

And a kid.

She was so bundled against the cold that her arms stood out from her sides and her walk was nothing so much as a lumber. Halfway across the yard, she looked back at the house, then yanked off the knitted cap that covered her dark hair. It landed on the grass at her feet. A moment later, the bright yellow mittens followed, and soon the blue parka was on the ground, too. A pair of sweatpants hit next. Wearing jeans, a shirt and a heavy sweater, she skipped to the back third of the yard, where a fleet of toys, a dump truck and bulldozer among them, waited.

From this distance it was impossible to tell whether she resembled her mother at all, though the hair color had definitely come from her father. It would be a shame to have a daughter with Fiona who looked nothing like her. Beauty like that should be passed down through the generations.

Absently rubbing an ache in his chest that had come from

nowhere, he watched the girl fill the bulldozer scoop with dirt, empty it into the dump truck, then return for more. After the third load, he was about to turn away when a sharp report broke the quiet and the girl crumpled to the ground.

Apprehension tightening his chest, Justin set his coffee cup down, paying no attention when it slid into the sink, and started for the back door. When he opened the door to the sound of childish screams, he leaped over the steps to the ground and vaulted the chain-link fence into Fiona's yard.

The girl was curled in a tight ball, wailing for all she was worth. Justin glanced at the hole she'd been digging, caught a glimpse of a green box inside and drops of bright red on the yellowed grass. As he crouched beside her, from the house behind them came a panicked cry.

"Katy? Oh, my God, Katy!"

His heart pounding, he gently touched the girl with a shaking hand and spoke her name. "Katy? Are you okay? Are you hurt anywhere?"

At his touch, she launched herself into his arms with enough force to push him off balance. She clung to him, her thin arms wrapped around his neck in a choke hold, her trembling body pressed so tightly to his that he couldn't have peeled her away without help. Quickly getting to his feet, he headed for Fiona's back door and met her halfway, coatless, shoeless and damn near hysterical.

"Katy? My God, is she all right? Is she hurt?" she demanded, keeping pace when he didn't slow down.

"I don't know. Call 911. Get an ambulance and the police."

She ran ahead into the kitchen and was stammering on the phone when he got there. He set the girl on the counter, or tried to, but she refused to let go. She held onto him as if he could keep her safe, but it was too late for that.

"They're on their way." Shaking as badly as her daughter, Fiona joined them. "Katy, baby, come to Mama. Let me look at you. Let me see… Oh, God, Justin, she's bleeding."

He'd seen the blood before she plastered herself to him, but not where it was coming from. Her hands, most likely, since her digging had apparently triggered the blast, and her face. God, he hoped she hadn't lost any fingers! He'd seen it before with blasting caps, and experience suggested that was what she'd unearthed.

With Fiona's help, he gently forced Katy's hands from around his neck. Though her hands were, in fact, the source of at least some of the blood, he counted all ten fingers and gave a quick prayer of thanks. In the seconds before the still-wailing girl grabbed hold of her mother, he saw cuts on her hands and face, none that looked serious.

"It's okay, baby," Fiona crooned, holding her daughter tightly and rocking her side to side. "Everything's going to be all right. Don't cry, baby doll." Sparing a steely glance for him, she asked, "What the hell was that?"

"I don't know—a blasting cap, I think. I'll find out." But instead of heading outside, he went down the hall to the front door, reaching it just as an ambulance screeched to a stop at the curb. Two police cars were only seconds behind. He unlocked the door and left it standing open, then returned to the backyard. He was kneeling beside the hole in the ground when the two cops joined him.

"What happened here?" the taller of the two asked.

Justin automatically reached for his credentials, then realized they were locked in his bag in Golda's guest room, along with his weapon. Getting to his feet, he offered his hand. "Justin Reed, ATF."

"Colton Stuart, chief of police. You're Golda's nephew. I'm sorry about her death. We'll miss her a lot."

Justin nodded in acknowledgment.

"What happened?"

"The little girl was digging in the yard when she hit something." He gestured to the hole. "It's an old ammo can. I'd guess it had at least two blasting caps inside, maybe more. They must have been pretty unstable. When she hit the can with her shovel, they went off.'' He glanced back at the house. ''Is she okay?''

''She seems to be, except for getting the scare of her life.'' Stuart combed his fingers through his hair. ''Couldn't ask for better luck than to have an ATF agent next door when something like this happens. Do you happen to work on the explosives side of the house?''

Justin nodded.

''You have any suggestions on how to proceed?''

''You have a camera I can use? And an evidence form?''

Stuart gestured to the officer with him, who immediately left.

Once more Justin knelt a few feet away from the hole. There were bits of shrapnel on the ground—probably the cause of Katy's cuts—as well as pieces of twisted metal. The blast had been powerful enough to raise the lid on the steel can a few inches, until its hinge caught, but fortunately the can had contained much of it. If not… As close as she'd been, Katy could have suffered some damned serious injuries.

''Any ideas how the can got here?'' Stuart asked, crouching on the opposite side.

Justin gave the area a critical look. ''This used to slope down, and there was an alley separating these houses from those.'' He nodded toward the houses on the back side of the block. Come to think of it, Golda's yard had had the same slope. She'd complained that run-off from rain and snow created problems with erosion and kept her yard from being perfect. ''You have any idea when it was filled in, by who and why?'' The box could have been buried elsewhere, dug up and hauled in here. If it had been a few years, the caps wouldn't have been so unstable then. It was possible they could have survived the move, possible the can could have gone unnoticed with a ton or two of topsoil.

"Three years ago," Stuart replied. "The area had some major mudslides, and this was one of them. The city hauled out what it could and spread the rest around."

Justin looked up at the mountains that rose around the city. The ammo can could have been buried anywhere from the next block to the tops of any of a half-dozen peaks miles away. Finding its original resting place and the person who'd put it there would be tougher than identifying a single grain of sand at the bottom of the ocean.

The young cop returned with the equipment Justin had requested. "Chief, the paramedics want to know if they can go ahead and take Katy and her mom to the hospital."

"Sure. We'll talk to her later, after she's been checked out by the doctors and calmed down. Poor kid. She'll never enjoy the Fourth of July after this."

As Justin set up the thirty-five-millimeter camera, he casually asked, "You know Katy and her mother?"

"Sure. We just live a couple blocks away. We go to the same church, and our kids go to the same day care. Fiona watches our son, Martin, from time to time, and we keep Katy sometimes. Martin thinks of Katy as the big sister he never had. She thinks of him as a baby doll that won't stay put when she's tired of him."

Smiling faintly, Justin snapped a few shots of the area, followed by several of the can still in the hole. Laying the camera aside, he lifted it out, then opened the lid. "Holy..."

"What is it?" Stuart looked over his shoulder but didn't seem impressed. And why should he be? He'd never seen the carved wooden boxes before. He'd probably never heard of John Blandings, who'd celebrated his fifth wedding anniversary by giving his wife Anita an exquisite, one-of-a-kind, damn near priceless necklace and bracelet, each in its own hand-carved, ivory-inlaid wooden box. He'd probably never heard of Patrick Watkins, either, who'd relieved Mrs. Blandings of her jewels and, on his way out, left the garage in shambles with two well-placed explosives.

Quickly, Justin took several more pictures, then laid the camera aside and reached for one of the boxes. The lid was damaged, with flash burns and shrapnel embedded in its surface, but the gems inside…

All the Reed women—except Golda—loved flashy jewelry. They'd never seen a necklace too gaudy, a ring too ostentatious or a stone too big. Even so, not one of them had a piece that could compare to this. The emeralds were top quality, rich, deep, dark, damn near glowing inside, and the diamonds were as good or better. He'd estimate the smallest stone at three or four carats, the largest probably three times that.

Stuart gave a long, low whistle. "That must be worth—"

"One point two million. The matching bracelet—" Justin pointed to the other box "—is another half mil. It was stolen from a couple in the D.C. area four years ago. The thief slipped right through their elaborate security system, pocketed these and left another couple million dollars worth of jewels in the safe. Presumably they didn't meet his standards."

"And you know this because…?"

"To ensure that his cleverness didn't go unnoticed, as he was leaving, he blew up their garage. Did close to a million dollars damage there, including the Rolls, the Ferrari and the limo that went up with it." Justin shook his head wonderingly. "I've been after this guy for eight years. These were his fourteenth robbery and bombing. We're up to twenty-four now. I cannot believe he's been in Grand Springs."

Quickly he checked the other wooden box, then the velvet boxes underneath. He recognized every piece—knew who it had been stolen from, how much it was worth and what kind of blast had accompanied the theft. For years, he—and the owners, the insurance companies and other law enforcement agencies involved in the cases—had wondered what Watkins had done with the gems. Very few had been recovered, apparently fenced when he needed money, but the really exquisite pieces had never shown up on any market. Everyone had had their theories, but no one had ever suspected they were buried in an ammo can somewhere in the Colorado Rockies.

An ammo can containing blasting caps that had been guaranteed to become unstable and go off at the slightest disturbance—or, hell, no disturbance at all. Static electricity in the air could have caused them to detonate, and the damage could have been much worse than a petrified kid.

Though that was bad enough, he thought grimly, hearing in his mind Katy's hysterical tears and the panic in Fiona's voice. It was past time to put a stop to Patrick Watkins's games.

And he had a pretty good idea how to do it.

Fiona stood beside Katy's hospital bed, watching her daughter sleep, thanks to the sedative they'd given her. Her injuries had been relatively minor—cuts on both hands and her face from flying shrapnel, a few bruises from both shrapnel and small rocks blasted loose by the explosion. She'd been incredibly fortunate, the ER doctor had stressed, and Fiona had given thanks for it repeatedly.

Now that she knew Katy was safe, she was feeling the aftereffects of the day's emotional overload. The temptation to lower the side rail, crawl into bed with Katy and fall asleep holding her tight was strong, but she remained where she was, watching her, savoring the mere sight of her.

When the door opened, she didn't look up. Her parents had spent several hours at the hospital, as well as her sisters and several of her friends, and the hospital staff had been in and out. Whoever it was could take care of business, then leave them alone. She didn't want to talk, didn't want food, didn't want anything but to watch her daughter and make sure she remained safe.

The visitor stopped just inside the door. Fiona had pulled the shades to block the afternoon sun and turned off all but one dim light over the bed, so he stood in shadow, but she knew who it was. "She's asleep," she said quietly. "You won't wake her."

Justin came forward until he stood opposite her. "How is she?"

"Just bumped and bruised." That was Katy's favorite description for all the little injuries she suffered in her tomboy play. Smiling at the memory of the phrase in her little girl's voice, Fiona rubbed her arm, found it cool to the touch and gently tucked it under the sheet. "They had to put a few stitches in the worst cuts on her face, but she'll be fine. They'll hardly even leave a scar."

"How long are they keeping her?"

"Just until tomorrow. Her injuries are minor, but she was so upset..."

"She's lucky."

"I know." Fiona rested her arms on the rail and finally looked at him. He still wore jeans, but he'd changed from the shirt that had been splattered with their daughter's blood. Now he wore a leather jacket open over a dark blue dress shirt that brought out the color of his eyes—of Katy's eyes. He looked handsome, tired, serious—and just a bit excited. Because his uncomfortable duty trip to Colorado had turned into the work that meant so much to him?

Her resentment skyrocketed. Their daughter was lying sedated in a hospital bed, and he was happy to have a case to occupy his few remaining hours in town. But when she spoke, she kept the anger and shock out of her voice. "What happened? What exploded and how did it get in my yard?"

"It was an ammo can, a small steel case the military uses to store ammunition. Chief Stuart's theory on how it got there is the mudslides a few years ago that leveled off your yard."

Fiona was puzzled. "You mean, the military's responsible for this?"

"No. Ammo cans are sold at surplus stores all over the

country. This one held some stolen property, along with a couple of blasting caps. Katy must have uncovered the can while digging, and they detonated.'' Withdrawing a notebook and pen from his jacket pocket, he gave her an uncomfortable look. ''I need some information for my report—just basic stuff. Is that okay?''

She shrugged.

''What is your full name?''

''Fiona Frances Lake.''

His gaze lingered on her face a moment before he wrote it down. ''And Katy's?''

''Kathleen Hope.''

''Hope's her last name?''

''Middle name,'' she said impatiently. ''Her last name is Lake.''

''But— Why doesn't she have your husband's name?''

His question sent a stab of pain through Fiona. He was the only man she'd ever wanted to marry, the only one she'd wanted to spend the rest of her life with, and he'd claimed to feel the same about her. It had taken her years to stop wanting him, and she hadn't yet found a way to want anyone else. It had taken him only a few days, maybe even hours, to forget her.

''I don't have a husband,'' she said stiffly, ''so it would be difficult for her to take his name.''

Justin stared at her across the bed, obviously surprised. ''You're not married?''

''No.''

''Have you been?''

''No. I had plans once, but it turned out, the offer was just part of the joke.''

He had no reaction to the jibe. He simply continued to look surprised, with some confusion thrown in for good measure. ''But—Katy— Who is her father? Where is he? Why didn't you marry him?''

Fiona went cold inside. This wasn't funny. Pretending ignorance when she'd delivered the news of her pregnancy herself was *not* the best path to choose. He'd known he was going to be a father, and he hadn't cared enough to even acknowledge it. He'd ignored her message and ignored their daughter for her entire life, and now he was pretending he didn't know? Was he such a self-centered bastard that he possibly could have forgotten? Or merely a coward who couldn't own up to his failings?

Or...was it possible he truly didn't know? He sounded sincere—but he'd sounded sincere when he'd told her he loved her and wanted to marry her, and he'd been lying then. He could well be lying now.

She hadn't actually delivered the news to him herself, a sly voice reminded her. She'd left the message on his answering machine—the only way she could make contact, since he'd refused to take or return her calls. When he'd never responded, she had assumed that he'd gotten the message and just didn't give a damn about the baby. It had been so easy to think when he'd made it abundantly clear that he didn't give a damn about *her*.

But what if he hadn't gotten it? An accidental erasure, a tape malfunction, hitting the wrong button by mistake... Oh, God, what if he'd never known?

Her palms damp, her stomach queasy, Fiona turned away from the bed and walked to the window, where she lifted one corner of the shade. The sun was setting, turning the western horizon shades of pink and purple, and darkness was quickly settling in. Already the streetlights were on, and as she watched, lights flickered on in nearby houses. She raised the shade, then folded her arms across her chest as she stared out. "I thought you were leaving this afternoon."

"That was my plan, before this happened."

"There's an ATF office in Denver." Six years ago he had talked about trying to get a transfer there. Obviously that plan had changed, too. "Surely they can handle this."

"They could, but it's my case." His voice was closer,

though she hadn't heard him move. She felt, then saw his approach from the corner of her eye as he passed, then turned to lean against the windowsill. With his hands in his pockets and his ankles crossed, he looked more relaxed than he had a right to be. It was an illusion, though. There was tension in his jaw, in his eyes.

So much about him was an illusion.

"You can do that?" she asked as if she cared. "Claim a case as your own just because you have the dumb luck to be around when it happens?"

"No. Denver has jurisdiction, but they agreed to let me work it."

Wonderful. So he'd be in town longer than she'd planned. How much longer? she wanted to ask. How long would she have to cope with the fact that he was living right next door? To know that every time she left her house, she risked running into him? How long would she have to tell him the truth...or do her damnedest to hide it?

"So...about those questions... Who is Katy's father, and why didn't you marry him?"

"I don't see how either of them matters."

"This is a federal crime, Fiona, and unfortunately, Katy is the victim. I need identifying information on her."

"She's the only Kathleen Hope Lake in all of Grand Springs, and I'm the only Fiona Lake. You have our address. I'll give you our phone number and her social security number. I'll even show you the scar on her leg where she slid into home plate last summer. That's more than enough to identify her. As for why I didn't marry her father—" How could that possibly have any bearing? But what was the alternative? That he was asking out of personal interest? Equally impossible. His personal interest in her hadn't even survived the trip back to Washington. It certainly hadn't survived the six years since. "He didn't want to be married—didn't want to be a father." Maybe. Unless he truly hadn't known.

Forcing a chilly note into her voice, she asked, "Any other questions?"

He looked as if he didn't want to back down, but after a long, still moment, he shook his head. "Not at this time." He pushed away from the window, then stopped right beside her. "I'll be in touch," he said quietly.

"I hope not."

His smile was thin and thoroughly unamused. "I'm sure you do."

She watched him leave, then returned to Katy's bedside. Emotion tightened her chest and dampened her eyes as she gazed at her. Her daughter was the best, most wonderful thing to ever happen to her. She couldn't imagine life without her—couldn't imagine having a child somewhere and not knowing it, not being given the chance to love him or her.

So did Justin deserve to know about Katy? Would it make any difference? Would it turn him into father material, or would he walk away from her, the way he'd walked away from her mother? Would he want to spend time with her, be a part of her life, or would he reject her the way his parents had rejected him?

What if, God help her, he decided he wanted custody? Katy had never been away from Fiona for more than a night, and even then she hadn't gone farther than her grandparents' or a friend's house. Could Fiona bear to send her halfway across the country? To not be able to kiss her and tuck her into bed, to not be there in case she woke up in the night or got sick or scared? Could she trust the most important treasure in her life to the care of a man who'd already shown his lack of trustworthiness?

She couldn't. Wouldn't. Katy was *her* daughter. Simply providing the sperm didn't make a man a father, and that was all Justin had done. It wasn't an act that should be rewarded now with the privilege of having Katy in his life.

But what if that was all he'd done because he hadn't

known? What if he would have been as thrilled with the prospect of parenthood as she'd been—if he would have loved Katy dearly from the moment he'd learned of her existence?

Hiding her face in her hands, she groaned aloud. She wanted to be fair to Katy, to herself—even, reluctantly, to Justin. All her life she'd made a point of doing the right thing...but she'd never faced a decision in which the right choice could cost her dearly. Not only might she bring this man, who'd broken her heart, back into her life, but she could conceivably lose her daughter. If he was angry or felt cheated, he could make her life—and Katy's—miserable.

She groaned again, then gave a start when a voice came from the shadows near the door. "Is that shorthand for I'm tired, This day has been too much, Idiots shouldn't be allowed blasting caps, or a prelude to tears?" Steve Wilson, surgeon and husband to one of her best friends, came into the light, carrying Katy's chart. He laid it on the bedside table, then enveloped Fiona in a hug. "How're you doing?"

It had been the worst thirty-six hours of her life, but she kept that answer to herself. "I'm tired. This day has been too much. Idiots with blasting caps should be locked away forever." She smiled wanly. "No tears." Not yet, at least.

"How's Katy?"

"Sleeping peacefully."

"Rest is the best thing for her. It's best for you, too. It's not the most comfortable bed in the world, but that chair in the corner reclines, and you can get a blanket and a pillow from the nurses' station. Have you had anything to eat?"

"I'm not hungry."

He gave her a critical look, then said, "I'll have them bring you a tray when they serve dinner. You've got to keep your strength up. Katy's going to be pretty clingy the next few days. You'll need all your energy and then some."

Remembering the way she'd hung on to Justin that morning, and then the strength with which she'd grabbed hold of *her,* Fiona nodded. ''Other than that, she'll be all right, won't she?'' she asked, hearing the pleading in her voice and not the least bit ashamed of it.

''As far as we can tell. She might overreact to loud noises, have a few bad dreams, be afraid to leave your side, or she might bounce right back. You never know with kids. However she reacts, you'll have plenty of help dealing with it. You won't even have to ask.''

With a grateful nod, she rested her head on his shoulder as her gaze was drawn back to Katy. She'd practically forgotten what it was like to have a shoulder to lean on, to feel a man's arm around her, to feel safe and secure in the way only a man could make a woman feel. The feminist in her rebelled at the thought—she'd been perfectly happy, safe and secure the last six years without a man—but the realist admitted it was true.

And the woman wondered how much truer it would be if the man wasn't married to her friend and the closest thing she'd ever had to a brother.

If it was someone like Justin.

Speak of the devil... Once more the door swung open, and Justin made it halfway to the bed before abruptly stopping. He looked from her to Steve, and a curiously frosty look came into his eyes. ''Sorry to interrupt,'' he said, though clearly he wasn't. He offered her purse to her across the bed. ''I locked up your house when we finished there this afternoon. I forgot to bring this in earlier. Your keys are inside.''

''Thank you.'' Feeling something oddly like guilt, she moved out of Steve's embrace to take her bag. ''Steve Wilson, this is Special Agent Reed with the ATF.''

The chill in his eyes dropped a few more degrees as he extended his hand. ''Justin.''

''Golda's nephew. I'm very sorry about your aunt. I was one of her doctors and one of her admirers.'' Steve nodded toward Katy. ''I hope you catch the man who did this.''

"I intend to."

He'd always been so damned confident, and he'd always had reason before. Fiona hoped he did this time, too. She hoped he was the best damn special agent the ATF had ever seen and that he buried the man responsible for hurting Katy under the tallest mountain in the state.

After a moment, Steve broke the strained silence that had settled. "I'm heading home, Fiona. Rebecca's waiting for me. If anything comes up, don't hesitate to call. And eat the meal they bring you. You can't live on nerves alone. Justin, nice to meet you."

"Thanks, Steve." Fiona watched him go, then turned to put her purse on the nightstand.

The silence settled again, heavy, tense. It crawled along her skin and made the hair on the back of her neck stand on end. She was on the verge of snapping at Justin to say something or get out when he spoke. "A married man. I'm surprised. I never figured you for that type."

"We both know what 'type' you figured me for, don't we?" The easy type. The love-her-and-leave-her type. The gullible believe-all-the-sweet-lies type.

He ignored her comment. He was so damned good at ignoring anything he didn't want to notice. "Is that why you wouldn't tell me Katy's father's name? Because he's married?"

Too angry to face him, she went to the corner to move the recliner closer to the bed. Unfortunately, even angry, she didn't budge it more than a few inches.

Justin came across the room and easily slid the chair exactly where she wanted it, where she could lean back and still touch her daughter. "No answer prepared, Fiona?"

Her fingers gripped the back edges of the chair tightly. Her voice was equally tight when she spoke. "Not that it's any of your business, but no, Steve isn't Katy's father. He's a very good friend. I'm sure that's a concept you don't understand, but it's true all the same. I don't tell anyone Katy's father's name because I'd rather forget he exists, just as he forgot we existed.''

Forgot *her,* her annoying little voice whispered. *Never knew about Katy.*

She took a few deep breaths to ease the panic rising in her chest, to control the emotion in her voice. ''I appreciate your bringing my purse and keys. Now I'd appreciate it if you would leave.'' *And not come back.* She bit back the words, but he looked as if he heard them anyway.

Lines bracketed his mouth, and tension gave his face a hard, shuttered look. ''I'll be around.''

Was that a promise? she wanted to call out as the door closed behind him.

Or a threat?

Chapter 3

Justin felt like hell when he left the house Sunday morning. His night had been restless—dreams of Fiona interrupted by nightmares of explosions and a crying, bloodied, dark-haired child. He'd seen kids injured far worse than Katy before, had helped dig tiny broken bodies out of the rubble after a bombing. It was the toughest aspect of his job. He hated it and hoped each time would be the last time.

But those kids had been strangers. He hadn't made love to their mothers, hadn't planned a future or kids with them, or imagined himself in love with them. Maybe Katy's injuries weren't serious, but the fact that she was Fiona's daughter—that, if he'd been a braver man, she might have been *his* daughter—made them seem deadly serious.

And he wanted Patrick Watkins to pay for them.

After a fast-food breakfast and a stop at the hospital gift shop, he took the elevator to Katy's floor and went down the hall to her room. The door was open a few inches. He tapped on it before pushing it wider and stepping inside.

The room was brightly lit, and flowers, balloon bouquets

and gifts covered most of the flat surfaces. Counting a half-dozen stuffed animals, he looked wryly at the polar bear he'd bought. Looked like he could have saved his money and the gesture.

Katy was sitting up in bed, pillows behind her back, and Fiona sat facing her, coaxing her to eat her breakfast. He knew from the photos in Golda's house that she was fair-skinned, but she looked even paler today with the bruises and the lines of stitches across her cheek and jaw. With her dark gaze locked on him, she opened her mouth automatically for a bite of eggs, chewed, then opened it again for more. She showed no interest in him, no recognition, no curiosity at all.

After taking one last bite, she refused to open her mouth again, no matter how Fiona prodded. With a sigh, Fiona pushed the tray away and brushed Katy's hair back, then turned to see what had caught her attention.

Her clothes were rumpled, her hair mussed, her face free of makeup. There were shadows under her eyes and a tight set to her mouth, along with an overall tension that gave her a brittle air. She looked tired, worried, worn down…and beautiful. No matter what had changed between them, that hadn't. He'd always thought she was one of the most beautiful women he'd seen, and he still did.

Beautiful, and not happy to see him. Surprise, surprise.

Justin moved closer to the bed. "Hi, Katy. How do you feel this morning?"

After a moment in which the girl continued to treat him to that steady stare, Fiona replied with some strain in her voice, "She doesn't feel like talking yet."

"Is that—" Not *normal.* That would raise her hackles. Though, hell, his merely being there raised her hackles. "—expected?"

"The doctor said to give her a few days. She was traumatized by the blast. She just needs a little time. You don't have to question her, do you?"

He shook his head. If he hadn't been watching from the kitchen window, he might need to hear whatever Katy could tell him, but he had been watching, and it was doubtful she could add anything to what he already knew.

"Then...not to sound rude, but...why are you here?"

"I brought her this—" he held up the bear "—and I thought you might need a ride home. They said last night she would be released around ten, barring any complications. Is not talking a complication?"

"Not enough of one to keep her here." She didn't say anything about the ride home—didn't point out that she had family and friends in town willing to provide more rides than she could possibly accept. No doubt, someone was already on his way over, someone she'd be happy to see. "Have you found out anything?"

"An agent came in from Denver to pick up the evidence we'd collected. It'll be sent to our lab in Maryland for examination. The stolen property that was in the can is locked up at the local police station. It will eventually be returned to its owners."

"And you don't have a clue who's responsible?"

Justin's fingers tightened in the bear's fur. "Actually I do. I told you last night, it's *my* case. I've been after this guy for years."

She stared at him as if she was having trouble understanding. "Someone you were already investigating before you came here buried that can with blasting caps and it wound up in *my* yard?"

"Quite a coincidence, huh?" His smile felt sickly, and it faded quickly. "His name is Patrick Watkins, and he has a fondness for exquisite jewels, adrenaline highs and explosives, though not necessarily in that order. To date, he's responsible for twenty-four jewel thefts, along with twenty-four bombings. He's a thrill-seeker. He steals the gems to prove he can, and he sets off the bombs afterward as..." He shrugged. ''A signature. And a celebratory thing. Like spiking a football in the end zone after a touchdown.''

''A *celebratory* thing? He sets off bombs *for fun?* My daughter could have been—'' Realizing that Katy was listening, she clamped her jaw shut, but that didn't stop a shudder of revulsion from rippling through her.

''We're going to stop him.'' It sounded lame, small comfort to any mother who'd been through what she had in the last twenty-four hours, but it was all he had to offer. Beyond that, he didn't know what else to say, whether he should repeat the offer of a ride or just leave. Before he could decide, he became aware of tentative touches brushing his fingers where they burrowed into the bear's fur. Looking down, he saw Katy stroking the fur. ''It's soft, isn't it?''

Her only response was a wide-eyed look.

''Do you like polar bears?''

Nothing but the same look.

''I see you've got a lot of stuffed animals here, but maybe you can find room for him, too. Do you think so?''

For a long time she remained motionless, but when he offered her the bear, she took it, wrapping her arm around its neck and holding it close. She was a pretty little girl, with her mother's delicate bone structure, with the same fragile air that belied the strength underneath. He would guess she was about four, though he would find out for sure before he filed his report.

He would also find out who her father was, if for no other reason than to satisfy his own curiosity.

He was about to make an excuse and leave when a nurse came in, followed by an aide pushing a wheelchair. ''Are you ready to get out of here, Katy-bug?'' she asked cheerfully, pretending not to notice that the girl didn't answer. ''Fiona, do you have some clothes for her?''

''No. I—I didn't think...''

''That's okay. She can go home in her gown and take a

blanket. We'll trust you to return them,'' the nurse said with a wink. ''You've signed all the paperwork, haven't you?''

Fiona nodded.

''So all you need is your ride. Do you have your car here?''

''No. I…'' She looked at Justin, silently asking if the offer still stood.

He didn't renege. ''I'm taking them home.''

''You're Golda's nephew, aren't you? I'm sorry about her death.'' The nurse gave him an appraising look that turned into an appreciative smile. ''We all thought she exaggerated about her nephew the ATF agent. Now I see she didn't tell the half of it.''

Justin made a weak gesture that he hoped resembled a smile, then turned to Fiona. ''I'll get the car and meet you at the front entrance.''

He left the room and, too impatient to wait for the elevator, took the stairs to the lobby. It was cold outside, the air fresher, sweeter, than it ever smelled in D.C. He filled his lungs, replacing the hospital smells, as he crossed the lot to his rental.

By the time Fiona approached the entrance with Katy in her arms, he was parked out front and leaning against the car. The nurse had ditched the aide and the wheelchair and instead pushed a cart filled with flowers, balloons and gifts. ''I offered them both a ride in the wheelchair,'' she said as Justin opened the car door, ''but they turned me down. Maybe I could interest you instead.''

Justin caught the mocking look that stole across Fiona's face as she bent to slide Katy into the middle of the back seat, and tried to ignore the heat that crept into his own face. ''Not right now, I'm afraid. Sorry.''

With a good-natured laugh, the woman picked up an armful of the cart's contents. ''Want these in back with you, Katy-bug?''

Fiona tried to straighten, but with a wail, Katy grabbed

hold tightly. "I'm going to sit beside you, babe," she assured her, "but I can't get in if you don't let go."

Hiding a vague disappointment, Justin circled to the driver's side. Over the roof of the car, the nurse grinned and gave him a sly wink. "Guess all the cuddly creatures get to ride up front with you. That would certainly be *my* first choice."

Smiling weakly, he slid inside and helped her arrange flowers, plants and stuffed animals in the seat and floorboard. In back, Fiona fastened her seat belt, then wrapped her arms around Katy. Immediately the wails quieted, and the girl settled contentedly against her.

And no wonder. He knew from past experience that in Fiona's arms was a damned sweet place to be.

Not that he was likely to ever be there again.

"Do you need to stop anywhere? Grocery store? Pharmacy?" he asked as he pulled away.

"No. We just want to go home." In a voice not intended for his ears, he suspected, she added, "We should have gone to Denver."

"You had plans to be in Denver this weekend?"

"No. But I thought about it at the church Friday—about picking up Katy from the baby-sitter and going off to the city until—"

Until he was gone, he silently finished for her. Then Katy wouldn't have been digging in the yard and he never would have known that Watkins had been in the area. It would have been too bad if he'd never known, but it certainly wasn't worth Katy getting hurt.

She didn't say anything else, and neither did he. Within minutes he was pulling into Golda's driveway. Fiona got out with Katy and started for her door. He filled his arms with flowers and animals and followed. By the time she'd juggled daughter and purse to find her keys, he'd joined them on the porch. He waited until she'd opened the door, then set everything on the hall table before returning to the car for more.

When he brought the last load in, they were standing in the living-room doorway, watching. Katy reached out as he passed, snatching the polar bear and making her mother's jaw tighten. Did she hate him so much that she couldn't bear to see her daughter with the toy he'd bought?

Not that she didn't have good reason to hate him.

He set down the last of the vases, then shoved his hands into his pockets. "About…what happened before…" Bitterness flared in her eyes, and he felt a corresponding surge of guilt. "I—I'm sorry. I never meant…"

"A word you said." Her smile was cold, a world apart from the sweet, sexy smiles she'd once given him, and it was edged with hurt. "I figured that out."

That wasn't true. When he'd talked about marrying her, he'd really wanted to. When he'd told her he loved her, he'd meant it with all his heart. Unfortunately, back at work, in the real world and too far from her, it hadn't seemed such a sure thing. Reality had set in. Doubt. Fear.

"I handled things badly—"

"No kidding."

"—and I'm sorry. You deserved better than that."

"And I still do." She moved past him to open the door, then pointedly waited for him to leave.

He had no choice but to go. But he felt empty as he walked out the door. As if he might have lost more all those years ago than he could afford to lose.

Fiona awakened Monday morning with the weight of the world on her chest. Breathing was difficult, and there was a distinct pain in her ribs. But when she opened her eyes, her first response was a smile. It wasn't the weight of the world. It was merely Katy, stretched out on top of her, head tucked under her chin, knee pressing against her ribs. She freed one arm from the covers, then stroked her daughter's silky hair.

She had crawled up in the tree-house bed with her last night, had told her stories, sung her songs and held her until she was sound asleep. She'd hoped Katy would stay there, sleeping through the night, but obviously not.

As she eased out from under her daughter, the doorbell rang. A glance at the clock showed that it was barely daytime—only seven thirty-five—and far too early for visitors, which meant it was probably her mother. Delores had a key and would ring only once before letting herself in. If it was anyone else, they could wait until a decent hour, and if it was Justin… When hell froze over sounded reasonable.

The front door creaked, then footsteps sounded on the stairs. A moment later, Delores came through the door. "Hey, sleepyhead. How's my baby?"

"She's okay." Fiona scooted up to lean against the headboard, then dragged her fingers through her hair. "What are you doing out and about so early?"

"Roger Markham called. He didn't want to call here in case you and Katy were resting. He's rescheduled the reading of Golda's will for ten o'clock this morning, and he'd like you to be there."

Fiona had been more than willing to go Saturday, but today it just didn't seem important. She'd rather spend the day in her pajamas and in bed with Katy, watching TV, eating junk food and sleeping whenever the urge hit. She didn't want to take a shower, comb her hair or put on clothes, especially since she hadn't yet managed to take three steps without Katy right behind her.

And the biggest reason—she didn't want to be in the same state as Justin, much less the same room.

I'm sorry, he'd said yesterday, as if that would make everything all right. He'd deceived her, betrayed her, abandoned her. He'd broken her heart and left her with little trust and no faith. He had emotionally devastated her, and that was nothing compared to what his abandonment of Katy had done to her. And he thought *I'm sorry* could make a difference?

"Come on, darlin', you have less than two and a half hours to pull yourself together." Delores gave her an assessing look and bluntly added, "And you're going to need every minute. You jump in the shower, and I'll wait here in case Katy-bug wakes up."

"I don't want to go, Mom. I'm really tired, and it's not as if my presence is necessary, and I'd just rather stay here—"

"Now you listen to me, darlin'. You are *not* going to start shirking your responsibilities just because Justin Reed is in town. You've never been a coward before. You didn't crawl into bed and pull the covers over your head when he left, and you're not going to do it now just because he's come back."

"Actually," Fiona pointed out, "that's exactly what I did once I realized that he hadn't left only Grand Springs—he'd left *me*. I stayed in bed for two days." And when she'd found out she was pregnant, she'd spent another two days there, and when she'd finally accepted that it was over, she'd thought she just might curl up there and die.

"Well, if I'd known, I would have hauled you out by your hair. No daughter of mine is going to take to her bed and get all weepy over a man, of all things."

"I'm not weepy," Fiona said crossly. "And this isn't about Justin. I've just had the worst weekend of my life. I'm recuperating."

"You're hiding. You're letting him make your decisions for you, and no daughter of mine does that, either." Delores leaned across to pull back the covers. "Go on. Get in the shower."

She went only because she did happen to need a shower, and she didn't want to tackle shampooing her hair and shaving her legs with Katy hanging on for dear life. But she wasn't going to Roger Markham's office, wasn't dealing with a single problem outside her bedroom for the rest of the day.

So how was it that, a few minutes before ten, she carried a silent Katy into Markham's conference room while her mother left to open the shop?

The lawyer sat at the head of the long oval table. The pastor from Golda's church sat at the opposite end, and Golda's weekly card group sat two on his left, two on his right. The college boy who'd helped her around the house was present, as well as the director of the homeless shelter and the president of the local animal aid group.

And, of course, Justin. He sat on the lawyer's right. The only empty chairs were beside him and across from him. She opted for distance and sat across from him.

Once everyone expressed their concern for Katy, Mr. Markham got down to business. He explained that his father, also a lawyer, had prepared Golda's will and that the elder Markham had reviewed it with her only a week before her death. His father, unfortunately, was out of town and Roger was handling it in his place.

Somewhere along there, Fiona stopped listening and let her attention wander—and despite her best efforts, where it wandered was Justin. He sat with his hands folded at the edge of the tabletop, his gaze directed at a point somewhere between them. His suit was the same gray one he'd worn to the funeral, this time with a white shirt and burgundy tie, and he wore the same impassive expression. He was incredibly handsome in an unfeeling-statue sort of way.

What had happened? When she'd met him, he'd been full of passion. Had he really become so cold and emotionless, or was this a mask to hide his true feelings from the world?

She preferred to think it was a mask. If he'd ever loved anyone, surely it was Golda. Maybe he hadn't been as attentive as he could have been, but Golda had understood. He'd done his best, she'd said, and considering that he was a Reed, it had been pretty darn good. Neither she nor Justin had held the rest of their family in high esteem. Not being close to family was, for Fiona, unimaginable. She talked to her mother virtually every day, saw her sisters multiple times each week and joined them all at their parents' house for dinner practically every Sunday. Golda had once told her that she hadn't seen Justin's father in over ten years. Amazing.

Unexpectedly Justin looked up, and in the moment it took Fiona to gather her wits, her gaze locked with his. Was there a slight softening in his dark blue eyes? A hint of regret? The memory of better times and more tender feelings? Or was she merely seeing what she wanted to see?

She didn't have time to decide as Mr. Markham discreetly coughed. "Just a few minutes more, folks," he said. "We're down to the last three bequests. 'To my dear friend Fiona Lake, I leave the mission style chairs in my attic and the Gustav Stickley table, chairs and sideboard in my dining room. And to her daughter, Kathleen Hope, my grand—'"

Fiona's gaze jerked to the lawyer's face. His eyes were wide with surprise, leaving no doubt in her mind what Golda had written. *My grandniece.* Everyone knew Katy had called her Aunt Golda, but they'd assumed it was merely a title of respect. No one had known that Golda called Katy grandniece—as in great, wonderful, positively grand, she'd always added.

Markham gave Fiona a disbelieving look, and she tried her best to warn him, plead with him, with nothing more than her own look. She wasn't sure he'd gotten the message until he cleared his throat and went on.

"'And to her daughter, Kathleen Hope, my grand…little friend, I leave all the jewelry I've accumulated over the years. I hope she'll think of me when she wears it.'"

Fiona darted a look around the table. Golda's fondness for jewels had led to quite a valuable collection, and everyone seemed to think giving such a gift to a five-year-old tomboy who was nothing more than a neighbor's child was the reason for the lawyer's surprise. Please, she silently prayed, let them continue to think it.

"'The remainder of my estate, I leave to my nephew Justin, the only other Reed to ever amount to anything. I also leave my dearest wish for him—that he learn these lessons well—mistakes can be set right, forgiveness is vital, and love *is* possible. Forget our disreputable family and trust yourself. Trust your heart. I know you have one.'"

Fiona smiled faintly. Golda had had an endless supply of faith. That last line proved it.

Mr. Markham looked up from the pages and shrugged. "That's it. Any questions?" When no one spoke, he gestured to Justin. "Mr. Reed will be in town indefinitely, staying at Golda's house. Those of you whose bequests are property—teapots, jewelry and so forth—can make arrangements with him to pick them up. And that takes care of it. Thank you for coming."

Fiona tried to lower Katy to the floor, but the child refused to go. With a deep sigh, she settled her on her hip as she stood and left the office before anyone could delay them. When they reached the top of the stairs, she shifted Katy to her other hip. "How about a deal, sweet pea? I'll carry you down the stairs, and then you can carry me to the door. Sound fair?"

Katy's only response was to lay her head on Fiona's shoulder. The only verbal response came from behind them.

"Maybe she'll let me carry her," Justin said. "Hi, Katy. Remember me? I'm Justin."

She hid her face, then peeked at him.

"You're the shy type, huh? Cat got your tongue?"

After another quick look, she stuck her tongue out at him.

"Kathleen Hope," Fiona admonished. "Get that tongue back inside your mouth."

"She's just showing me that she's still got it," he said, his manner easier than she would have thought possible.

''Aren't you?'' He lifted Katy's chin with one finger—a surprise—and she let him—another surprise.

As they started down the stairs, he asked, ''How is she?''

''Still clinging. Still not talking.''

''Any problems sleeping?''

''I put her to bed in her room last night and woke up this morning with her snuggled on top of me. If she had a bad dream, it didn't wake me, but obviously something woke her.''

''I wish this hadn't happened.''

Fiona looked sidelong at him. His expression was grim, the set of his features hard. For six years, she'd believed he was coldhearted, but not even she could think he would wish harm to a child, even if it did give him another chance to catch the man he'd been investigating for years.

In the lobby, she stopped at the bench that flanked the door to help Katy into her coat. It wasn't easy when she refused to stand on her own feet and clutched Fiona's hands tightly in her own.

''How did you manage to drive over here with her?''

''I didn't. My mother brought us. She's at the shop. We're meeting her there.''

''Want a ride?''

She glanced out the glass door. It was bright, chilly, sunshiny—a good day to be out. ''No, thanks. We'll walk.''

''Mind if I walk with you?''

Yes, she minded. She minded tremendously. But she didn't say so, maybe because he'd given her that regretful look in Mr. Markham's office. Maybe because Golda had loved him, and *she'd* loved Golda. Maybe because he was a part of the daughter she also loved.

With a shrug for an answer, she picked up Katy again and waited for him to open the door.

''Whenever you're ready to take Golda's jewelry, let me know.'' He spoke casually, as if they weren't discussing a small fortune in gems, some that were family heirlooms, others that he'd given Golda himself. She knew people who would fight over a loved one's prize ring, and yet he didn't seem to care about these family diamonds at all.

"You don't mind her leaving it to Katy?"

"It was her jewelry. She was free to leave it to anyone she chose."

"Will the rest of your family see it that way?"

"The rest of my family will think you exerted undue influence on Golda in her doddering old age, but she never cared what the rest of them thought. As far as she was concerned, they could go to he—" With a glance at Katy, he bit off the word and substituted a shrug instead. "I have no doubt she made certain her will was airtight, just for their benefit."

"I was sorry she couldn't be closer to her family."

He gave her a wry look as they waited for a car to pass before crossing the street. "You don't get close to that bunch. Trust me, she was better off without us."

"You..." Fiona drew a quick breath that smelled of Katy's baby shampoo and warned herself that getting personal wasn't a good idea. With Golda dead and her decision whether to tell him about Katy still unmade, the only connection between them was his investigation. It was purely professional, and she'd be a fool to change that in any way.

But she'd been a fool before. "You never talked about your family much." He'd mentioned that his father lived in New York at the time, his mother in Monaco, that he rarely saw either of them and was an only child. He'd never actually admitted they were wealthy, but she knew from other things he'd talked about—prep schools, summer homes, winter homes, drivers and servants. She'd learned from Golda that his parents were self-centered and not fit to be parents, that the only fights they'd had over Justin weren't to decide who *got* to have him but rather who *had* to take him. Other than a few disparaging comments about the family, as if neither of them were a part, they'd ignored them.

"They're not exactly people you point to with pride and say, 'That's my mom and dad.' Between them, my parents have been married eleven times and had plans to marry another dozen or so times. All my life one of them has been leaving someone or looking for someone else to eventually leave. My mother is currently married to an earl in London, though that could change any day. He's about twice her age, rich as God and with any luck, she can force herself to stick around until he dies, leaving her with enough money to attract husband number seven. My father is living in Paris with his latest wife, Monique. She's twenty-two, she eats nothing but lettuce, and when he brought her to the States on their honeymoon last fall, I went home from work one night and found her naked in my bed. She wanted to be 'close' to her stepson."

Fiona couldn't resist a smile at his very dry tone of voice, but it faded quickly. With the example his parents had set for him, the wonder wasn't that he'd gotten cold feet about his relationship with her as soon as he'd left town, but that he'd been able to have a relationship with her at all. She tried to imagine stepparents coming and going with great regularity, or parents who took marriage vows so lightly, or fell in and out of love so easily. Her own parents had been married nearly forty years, and they were still deeply, passionately in love. They were committed to each other, their marriage and their family, and they'd passed on that same sense of commitment to their daughters.

Not that his parents' example excused what he'd done to her.

"So what happened with you?"

The look he gave her was sharp, defensive. "What do you mean?"

"Thirty-four and not married even once. Unless..." He'd gotten married since leaving her. For months she had tormented herself with thoughts that he'd met someone else when he returned to Washington, or that he'd already been seeing someone. She'd wondered if he'd avoided her because he was in love with another woman, if he'd wanted no part of their baby because this other woman wasn't the forgiving type. She'd never found the courage to ask Golda, and then Katy had been born and the demands of running a business and raising a baby alone had pushed everything else to the back of her mind.

As a gust of wind whipped down the street and sent a shiver through him, Justin buttoned his overcoat, then reached across to tug the hood of Katy's coat over her head. She was resting against her mother's shoulder, contentedly watching him. With her big eyes, chubby cheeks and pouty mouth, she looked like a dark-haired cherub, too sweet, too solemn—and too heavy for Fiona to carry endlessly. "Katy," he said, gently tugging a curl that escaped the hood. "Why don't you give your mom a break and let me carry you?"

"She's all right," Fiona said. "She wouldn't even let her grandma take her downstairs this morn—"

As if oblivious to the excuse her mother was providing her, Katy leaned across the space that separated them, reaching for him. Surprised into silence, Fiona let go, and he settled her against his chest. Immediately she laid her head on his shoulder and slid one small hand between the buttons and inside his coat.

Justin swallowed hard. He'd never had much exposure to kids, certainly not to fragile little girls, and had never been offered such trust. It made his chest tighten and raised a lump in his throat. Stupid responses, he told himself. She was just a little girl, the victim in his investigation.

No, she was Fiona's little girl, and if he were a better man, she might have been *his* little girl. If he'd had the courage to do what Golda recommended—forget their family and trust himself. He'd never done much of that, and it had cost him.

With a glance at Fiona, he amended that. It had cost him dearly.

With another hard swallow, he forced his thoughts away from what might have been and focused on retrieving the thread of the preceding conversation. She'd been waiting for a response from him—*So what happened with you? Thirty-four and not married even once. Unless…* He cleared his throat and breathed deeply to force the tightness from his chest.

"No, not married even once. What happened with me was mostly Golda. She did her best to give me values, morals, a sense of honor." He gave her a sidelong look and saw that she was looking in the windows of the stores they passed. "I know you think she failed miserably, but she didn't. What I did with you, the way I ended it—those were *my* failings. I knew it was cowardly, but…" He'd also known he couldn't talk to her—had known that hearing the pleas in her sweet voice, not on a tape but directed to *him,* would undo all the rational, logical decisions he'd made—and he couldn't put in writing words he couldn't give voice to. He couldn't have risked any contact with her at all, no matter how big a bastard it made him.

She remained silent for half a block before looking at him. "If that's my cue to say, 'It's all right, don't worry about it, I got over it'…it isn't all right and it never will be. But there's no reason to worry about it. It took me a long time, but I did eventually get over it, and I learned a few lessons. I know better than to trust you again. I know better than to believe a man who has proven himself a liar. I know that, in the long run, we were lucky you left when you did, because I would have married you, given the chance, and you would have left me at the first chance. That's what Reeds do, isn't it?"

There was no accusation in her voice—just a quiet acceptance of the facts—and it cut him deeper than the coldest anger or the cruelest insults. He couldn't even defend himself. He *had* lied to her. He *had* left her. He *was* a Reed, in every disreputable aspect.

"Fiona—" How many times could he say he was sorry when the words clearly meant nothing to her? Apologies couldn't undo betrayals. They couldn't heal broken hearts. They couldn't make a reasonable person forgive and forget. They were just words. Empty. Worthless. But he offered them anyway, because he had nothing else. "I'm sorry."

"Yeah. So am I." She stopped and faced him, and he realized they'd reached her shop. The lights were on inside, and through the glass he could see her mother talking on the phone. "Come on, Katy. Let's go in and see Grandma."

When she reached for her, Katy brushed her hands away, then twined her arms around Justin's neck. There was a definite strain in Fiona's voice when she said, "Come on, Katy. Mr. Reed has to go."

Her next effort to reclaim her daughter resulted in an angry shriek right in Justin's ear. He winced, then awkwardly patted the girl on the back. "Want me to take you inside?"

Katy nodded vigorously.

"And then you'll have to let go, okay?"

Another nod.

Though Fiona clearly would have preferred that he not set foot inside the shop, she grudgingly opened the door for him. The air inside was warm and smelled of oil, wood and potpourri. She'd made a few changes in the last six years. The old vinyl floor was gone, with gleaming wood in its place. The white walls had been painted deep red with a stenciled border near the top, and the drywall ceiling had been replaced with pressed tin.

The merchandise hadn't changed, though. It was still top-quality antiques. No junk or reproductions here.

Delores Lake met them in the central aisle, giving her daughter a reassuring pat. "Hi, darlin'. Hey, Katy-bug, when am I gonna get my sugar?" The warmth disappeared the instant she looked at him and the air turned frosty. "Mr.

Reed. Or, since you're here only on *business,* should I say Special Agent Reed?''

''You used to call me Justin,'' he said evenly.

''I used to think I knew you. But I was wrong.'' Once again becoming the Delores he remembered, she bent to bring her face close to Katy's. ''Want to come with me, darlin', and get some hot chocolate? I'll hold you *real* tight.''

For a time, Justin thought the kid would refuse, but finally she reached for her grandmother. As they walked away, Delores called over her shoulder, ''Don't be long, Fiona. You've got a dozen things to do.''

Once they were out of earshot, Justin asked, ''Is there anyone in the Lake family who doesn't hate me?''

Fiona pretended to consider it. ''Only Katy. But then, she doesn't know you.''

The ache in his chest made his smile grim. New rule for his remaining time in Grand Springs—never ask a question if he wasn't prepared for the answer. He put it into effect immediately. ''If you'd like to come over this evening to get Katy's jewelry...''

''No.''

His jaw tightening, he nodded once, then turned away. Some part of him stupidly hoped she would say something before he reached the door, but she didn't. She didn't even wait to make certain he left. When he looked back, she was already halfway to the storeroom where Delores had taken Katy.

Straightening his shoulders under the weight of regret, he returned the way they'd come, but he didn't stop to retrieve his car from the lawyer's parking lot. Instead he walked one block farther to the Grand Springs Police Department. Colton Stuart had offered him an office and the use of their resources for the duration of his investigation. Local cops weren't always so cooperative with the feds, but Stuart was a former fed himself—Drug Enforcement Administration. That made things easier for Justin.

Inside he asked to see the chief and was directed to an office at the back. Through the open door, Justin saw Stuart sitting behind the desk and a pretty and very pregnant blonde leaning against it. His hand rested familiarly on her stomach until Justin knocked.

"Hey, Justin." Stuart got to his feet. "We've got you set up in one of our interrogation rooms. It's right back here."

He led the way, the blonde followed and Justin brought up the rear. The room was in the back corner and contained a scarred desk, an equally scarred table, a broken-in chair, a computer, a telephone and both Grand Springs and Denver phone books.

"Juliette— Oh, sorry," Stuart said. "Justin Reed, Juliette Stuart. She's our records supervisor, computer guru and my wife. If you have any problems with the computer or need anything for it, she'll take care of it."

Justin shook the hand she offered.

"I'm sorry about your aunt," she said with a hint of a Texas drawl, "but I'm glad you're here. I hope you catch whoever did this to Katy."

"I intend to." Not that it would make up for anything with Fiona. She might be perfect in damn near every other way, but forgiveness wasn't her strong suit.

"My office is over there—the one with the big window," Juliette went on. "If we can do anything for you, just ask. The fax machine is right out there—the numbers are taped to the phone—and the coffee machine is next to it, and…let's see…the bathroom is at the end of this hall." She took a few steps toward the door, then turned back with a warm smile. "Oh, yes… In case you're wondering, I was records supervisor before Colton came to work here."

Justin had to admit, the question had crossed his mind. She certainly didn't look like any records supervisor or computer geek he'd ever known, and if a small-city police chief couldn't get his wife on the payroll, he wasn't trying hard enough. It was good to know that wasn't the case here.

"Can you think of anything you need?" Stuart asked.

Just privacy, so he could get to work. He thanked them both, told Juliette it was nice to meet her, then closed the door behind them and sat down at the computer. His first task was to put his notes on the computer. Seeing them neatly typed, spelled correctly and in order always helped him organize his next step in the investigation.

And he reached the next step before he'd typed more than a few lines. Reaching for the phone and the Denver directory, he placed a call to the Vital Records Division of the Department of Public Health, identified himself and asked for the information he wanted. She would get back to him just as quickly as she could, the clerk promised.

He hung up the phone feeling guilty. Fiona had her reasons for withholding the name of Katy's father, and he didn't *really* need it for his report. Sure, if the information was readily available, he would include it, but as long as he had one parent's name and a good address…

The simple truth was, he wanted to know. Needed to. And he wanted more than insignificant details like a name or address. He wanted to know where Fiona had met the bastard, whether she'd loved him as much as she had once loved *him,* how long it had taken her to get over loving him and whether she might ever get over hating him. He wanted to know what other man out there was as big a fool as he was and what she'd done to deserve two such losers in her life.

While he waited for a callback, he finished his report, called his supervisor in D.C., checked in with the Denver office and turned down two invitations to lunch. When two o'clock came with no call, he accepted the third invitation.

When he returned forty-five minutes later, Colton was talking to the dispatcher. He gestured for Justin to wait, then, when he was finished, turned to him. "You just missed a call from Vital Records in Denver. The clerk had her information a bit confused, so she's going to pull the birth certificate and fax it to you.''

''All I asked for was the father's name. What's so tough about that?''

''Whoever wrote it down put your name in both places—as the person requesting the information and as the father. She'll get it cleared up. In fact—'' as the fax machine began printing, Stuart glanced that way ''—that's probably it now.''

Justin approached the machine as it spit out the cover sheet, addressed to him. The birth certificate was slower to print. Rocking back on his heels, he studied the announcements and posters on the bulletin board above, but with little interest.

It was obviously a mistake. There was no way he could be Katy's father. She was too young. They'd taken precautions every single time. Golda would have told him. Hell, Fiona would have told him. No matter what she thought of him, she had to know that he wouldn't turn his back on his own child. His parents had done that to him. He knew the rejection firsthand, and he would never subject a child of his own to it.

The printing stopped, and he snatched up the page, skimming over the blocks until he came to the one he wanted. *Name of father.* As he read, his hands began to tremble and dark, cold anger clouded his vision.

Katy *wasn't* too young.

Their precautions hadn't been foolproof.

Golda hadn't told him.

And Fiona believed his daughter was better off never knowing him.

Chapter 4

"What's bothering you, darlin'?"

Fiona gave her mother a weak smile. "What makes you think anything's bothering me?"

"Because you've been chewing that fingernail for two hours. Tell Mama and let her make it better."

After a look at her index finger, Fiona pushed her hands into her pockets and walked over to the sofa where Katy was sleeping. She lay on her back, her mouth open and snoring softly, with the polar bear Justin had given her tucked in the crook of her elbow. Of all the animals in her stuffed menagerie, the bear was her new favorite, and the new target for Fiona's resentment. She wanted to drop it in the Dumpster out back, toss it off one of the two-thousand-foot drops that lined the roads out of town or throw it in the street in front of a convoy of heavy, muddy eighteen-wheelers. Of course, she couldn't do anything.

"Isn't she beautiful?" Delores joined her in simply looking for a moment, then looped her arm around Fiona's waist and drew her to a delicate little tea table with two equally delicate little chairs. "Let's sit down here as if we're two ladies of leisure having a spot of tea, and you tell me what's going on in that pretty little head of yours."

"Don't you think everything that's happened in the past few days is reason enough to be bothered?"

"Of course it is. But I think this is something else, and it has to do with Justin."

"Great guess, Ma." Normally "Ma" was enough to rile her mother so much that she'd forget what they were talking about by the time she stopped ranting. This afternoon it didn't work.

"Do you still have feelings for him?"

Oh, she had feelings—more than she wanted. Cold ones, dark ones, angry ones. Confusing ones.

With a deep breath, she answered. "I loved Justin more than I'd ever loved anyone, and I hated him more than I'd ever hated anyone. He's a selfish bastard...and he's Katy's father. I wanted to never see him again, but now that I have..." She didn't finish, didn't even allow the thought to form.

Delores laid her hand over Fiona's. "When are you going to tell Katy he's her father?"

"I don't know. Maybe never."

"Fiona, you can't—"

"I can't tell her until...unless I tell him."

Delores drew back, sat straighter. "I thought you told him five and a half years ago!"

Heat flushed Fiona's face. "I thought so, too—at least, I tried. I left a message on his machine, and I always believed he got it and just didn't care."

"And now?"

"Now...I have reason to believe he didn't get the message."

"What reason?"

Fiona shrugged guiltily. "He needed information on Katy for his report, and he asked for her father's name."

"And he was serious? Not just playing innocent?"

Fiona thought back to those few tense moments in Katy's hospital room—his surprise and confusion and, later, his hostility when he thought Steve Wilson might be the father. "He was serious. He doesn't know."

"Well…that changes everything, doesn't it?"

"Does it?"

Delores's expression shifted from confusion to understanding to dismay. "Yes, it most certainly does! It was one thing when we thought he wanted nothing to do with Katy, but to not even know…! You can't keep that from him, Fiona. He has a right to know!"

"Yes, he does. And he has the right to see her. To spend time with her. To have her with him in the summer and on holidays. He also has the right to go to court and seek custody of her. Could you bear that, Mom—your only granddaughter living halfway across the country? Because I couldn't."

Turning in her chair, Delores gazed at Katy for a long, still moment before facing Fiona again. "No," she agreed quietly. "I couldn't bear that. But…this isn't your decision, Fiona. You can't play God. *You* can't decide to remove Justin from Katy's life."

"He's never *been* a part of her life—and that was his choice, not mine. Even if he never knew she existed, he chose to cut *me* out of *his* life, and he chose to do it by breaking off all contact with me. If he hadn't done that, he would have known about her."

"But you can't use that to justify keeping her from him now. It's wrong, Fiona, and you know it."

She did know. That was why she hadn't reached a decision yet. If only she could convince herself that it was all right to lie, to keep Katy for herself, she would do just that and not give it another thought. But every time she made that decision, the guilt started building, along with the nagging voice whispering, This is wrong. *You have no right.*

"You have to tell him, darlin'. Who knows? Maybe he'll prove himself to be the cold, unfeeling man we all thought he was. Maybe he won't want anything to do with her. Or maybe he'll be the best father that little girl could ask for. Either way, he has to know." Delores came around the table, gave Fiona a hug, then pressed a kiss to the top of her head. "I'm going to head home. Want me to take Katy with me?"

Katy had been better this afternoon—not back to normal, but better. If she was willing to spend a few hours with her grandparents, Fiona could certainly use the break. "Let's wake her and see what she says."

Katy was sleepy and dazed, but she understood Delores's question. Her answer—holding out her arms to her grandmother—was pretty clear, too.

"I love you, babe." Fiona kissed Katy goodbye, watched from the front window until they were out of sight, then took a long look around the shop. Delores had sold a set of chairs that morning, so a little rearranging was in order. There were a half-dozen pieces in the storeroom in need of cleaning before coming out onto the floor, and there was always paperwork to be done. Because manual labor left her mind free to wander, she chose the paperwork and settled in at her desk. Before she'd done more than turn on the computer, though, she leaned her elbows on the desk and hid her face in her hands.

She wanted this whole mess over. She wanted to open her eyes to find that six months had passed, that Katy was completely recovered and Justin was a fading memory. She wanted him to be totally indifferent to the fact that he had a child, wanted irrevocable promises that he would stay out of their lives forever.

And she wanted him to be as awed and amazed and thrilled with their daughter as she was. She wanted him to look at her with wonder, with love, and be humbled by the fact that he'd played a part in giving her life. She wanted—

The hairs on the back of her neck stood on end, and she

felt a faint disturbance in the air. Moving her hands from her eyes, she watched a piece of paper flutter to the desktop in front of her. She stared blankly at it, registering that it was a birth certificate—Katy's birth certificate—before realizing its significance.

It took forever, it seemed, to force her gaze from the paper upward to Justin's face. His eyes were shadowed, his jaw taut, his features expressionless. The anger radiating from him made her mouth go dry and brought a guilty flush to her face.

When he spoke, his voice was icy, unsteady with all the emotion he wouldn't allow on his face and the effort to control it. "Were you ever going to tell me?"

All she could manage was a weak whisper. "I tried."

"No. Uh-uh. 'Hey, Justin, say hello to your daughter.' 'Katy, this is your father.' 'You want to know who Katy's father is, Special Agent Reed? Why, you are.' I would have remembered any one of those."

"What about 'Justin, what's wrong? Please call me. Please let me know what's going on. I love you, and I'm scared I'm losing you.' Do you remember that?"

Now it was his turn to look guilty, to flush a deep crimson. It was the only response she waited for.

"All those pathetic little calls ended with one last message on your machine. I told you I was pregnant, that I didn't want anything from you, that I just thought you should know." She had lied. She'd wanted *everything*—love, marriage, happily-ever-after. But she would have settled for nothing more than an acknowledgment of their daughter's existence. And she hadn't even gotten that. "I asked you to call me if you had any interest at all in your child. And I never heard from you."

"I never got any message like that."

Reaching into the bottom desk drawer, she thumbed through a sheaf of papers before pulling one out and offering it to him. It was a phone bill, and all the calls she'd made to Washington were highlighted in yellow. "The last one. August, six years ago."

When he looked at the page, the color in his cheeks heightened, presumably because most of the page was marked in yellow, each slash representing one failed attempt to reach him. If it made him uncomfortable, wonderful. It showed he'd developed something of a conscience. Too bad he couldn't have done it soon enough to save her some heartache.

"August 17," he mumbled. "The seventeenth. Why does that date seem important?"

"Maybe because it was the day you decided to pretend your child didn't exist."

He gave her a sharp, angry look. *"I didn't get that message."*

In spite of her jibe, she believed him. "Why not? Because you'd started erasing my messages without listening to them?"

His response was quiet, subdued. "I listened to them."

She remembered the tears, the pleading, the shameless begging, and felt a rush of embarrassment. She was older now, more mature and valued her dignity. She would never again beg for anything less than Katy's life. But back then, she hadn't known what else to do, short of getting on a plane to Washington and confronting him in person. Fear had kept her away—fear that she would find him with another woman, that a face-to-face rejection would be more cruel than she could bear, that he would callously confirm that she'd been nothing more than a vacation fling.

And so she'd called, and she'd begged, and he'd listened and said nothing. Done nothing. Felt nothing.

He shook his head as if to clear it and looked at the phone bill again. "Can I keep this?"

"No." She tugged it from his hand, then returned it to the bottom drawer. "It's one of my souvenirs of you. If I find myself getting weak or lonely or wondering why I'm still single, I pull them out and they remind me how much better off I am alone.''

''Why didn't you call again? When you didn't hear from me, why didn't you try one more time?''

Unable to sit still a moment longer, she jumped to her feet and hugged her arms to her chest. ''I tried two dozen times! And you refused to speak to me two dozen times. How many chances was I supposed to give you?''

''This was different. It was about a *baby.* It was *important.*''

Hurt more than she could say, Fiona stared at him for a time before finally swallowing over the lump in her throat. ''And I wasn't.''

''That's not what I—''

''It's exactly what you meant, Justin,'' she said quietly, hating the tears that clouded her eyes but making no effort to wipe them away. ''You had already decided to dump me. I didn't matter anymore. I never really did. You'd had your fun, and it was over. You were just waiting for me to get the message.''

He rubbed one hand over his eyes. When he lowered it, he looked both physically and mentally exhausted. ''It wasn't like that, Fiona.''

''You told me in the airport that you loved me, that you would come back to me, that you wanted to marry me. And then you got on the plane, and I never heard from you again. Were you locked in a cell the next six years? Did terrorists threaten to blow up the White House if you had contact with me? Did you bump your head on the overhead bin and cause amnesia that lasted six years but magically disappeared last week?'' She wiped her eyes before the tears could start falling, then sadly finished, ''It was exactly like that.''

He looked away, rubbed his neck awkwardly, then looked back. ''Is that why you hate me? Because you thought I didn't want Katy?''

''I hated you for not wanting *me.* For making a fool of

me. For betraying my trust and breaking my heart. I hated you for a dozen reasons, but, yes, not wanting Katy was the big one.''

''Does she know?''

Fiona shook her head.

''Are you ever going to tell her?''

This time she shrugged.

''Were you ever going to tell me?''

''Until Saturday, I thought you knew. Since then...I hadn't decided.''

''How could you believe I wouldn't care?''

Her laughter was choked. ''You lied to me, Justin. You proved two dozen times that you were not an honorable man. Based on my experience with you, how could I believe you *would* care?''

''Because...'' His voice trailed away, and a look of great regret settled over his features. He couldn't find a single argument to offer on his own behalf. She knew, because she'd had moments of weakness over the years when she'd tried to find some explanation that made him less a bastard.

He walked away a few yards and stared off into the distance. Facing the fact that he couldn't find one good thing to say for himself? Still trying to wrap his mind around the idea that he was a father? Or just making an effort to take it all in?

Fiona stayed where she was, watching him, wishing this scene had never taken place. Maybe she *should* have kept trying to reach him back then. Maybe news of a baby on the way was too important for only one attempt. Maybe she should have gone to D.C. or had someone else call him or left the message with the smug secretary at his office.

Better yet, maybe he should have acted like a man.

When he took a few more steps toward the door, she thought—hoped—he was going to leave without another word. She couldn't be so lucky, of course. He came back, resting his hands on the desk between them. ''How could you not tell Golda? You knew she didn't have any family worth a damn. How could you keep her greatniece a secret from her?''

''Golda knew.''

He shook his head emphatically. ''She would have told me. She knew how my parents treated me. She knew— She would have told me.''

Fiona shook her head, too, but with much less emotion. ''She guessed it the day I told her I was pregnant. Why do you think she had pictures of Katy all over the house? Why do you think she left a fortune in jewels, including family heirlooms, to a five-year-old girl? Why do you think she didn't make provisions for the jewelry you'd given her to be returned to you? Because she wanted Katy to have something of her father.'' She laced her fingers together to still the temptation, not to touch, but merely to reach out. ''Golda knew. She simply agreed it was in Katy's best interests to not discuss her with you. She—she felt it was in her own best interests to not confront you about her. She was afraid of—of what she might say.''

Moment after moment crawled by as he stared at her. The pain that came into his eyes was intense, breath-stealing, and was accompanied by regret, guilt, shame and something she'd never thought she would see Justin Reed wearing—defeat. It rounded his shoulders, aged his eyes ten years and gave him a lost look that tugged at her heart no matter how she resisted. He opened his mouth as if to speak, then changed his mind, turned and walked out.

Fiona lost track of how long she stood in exactly the same place—maybe ten minutes, maybe sixty. When she finally found the strength to move, she walked the few steps to the desk, sank down in the chair and pillowed her head on the desk.

And she wept.

* * *

Justin saw more of Grand Springs that afternoon and evening than he ever had before. He walked from one end of town to the other, crisscrossed back and forth on streets lined with houses ranging from shabby to middle-class, from understated old-money elegance to built-to-impress flash. He wasn't going anywhere or thinking about anything in particular.

Except that he had a daughter.

And his aunt had believed he'd abandoned her.

All his life Golda had been the one to love him and treat him as if he mattered. He'd thought of her as a surrogate mother, infinitely better than the mother he'd been born to…and she'd thought of him as not fit to be a father. Like his own father.

He *wasn't* like his father. He would never reject his own child, would never put his own selfish pleasure ahead of Katy. He would never make any kid feel as worthless and unloved as his parents had made him feel.

But that was exactly how he'd made Fiona feel. She thought he'd used her, thought he'd cared nothing for her. She couldn't begin to guess how wrong she was, and he couldn't begin to tell her. She wouldn't believe him even if he could.

Stopping on a corner under a streetlight, he checked his watch. It was almost nine o'clock. He'd been walking for hours, and the cold and hunger were starting to seep into the numbness. He was only a few blocks from the Saloon, where he could get a burger and enough beer to forget his sorrows, at least for a while. Or he could walk a few blocks in the other direction and go home, eat a bowl of cereal, go to bed and try to decide what to do.

He'd known from the instant he walked out of Fiona's shop what he *should* do—turn this case over to the Denver office. Go home to D.C. Make arrangements for Katy, and then forget her. Stay out of her life. Not burden her with him for a father and the Reeds for a family. That was what Fiona wanted. Judging by Golda's silence on the matter, that was what she had wanted, too.

He just didn't know if he could do it.

Feeling lower than he'd ever been, he turned toward Golda's house. Her block was quiet. Lights were on in most of the houses. The families inside were doing dinner dishes, helping kids with homework or getting them ready for bed—normal family stuff. Wherever he'd lived as a kid, there'd been kitchen staff to do the dishes and servants to help with homework and getting ready for bed. He'd never been read a bedtime story except when Golda came to visit—had never been tucked into bed and kissed good-night except by her. Every time she'd left to go home, he'd begged to go with her. He'd wanted desperately to live here in Grand Springs, even though he'd never been there, in her house that wouldn't be deemed suitable servants' quarters by either of his parents. He'd wanted to grow up like a normal kid.

What would it have been like—growing up with someone who cared, watching Fiona mature from a pigtailed tomboy to the most beautiful woman in the whole damn state? He had no doubt he would have had the same knock-him-for-a-loop reaction to her. The only difference was he would have known what to do about it. It wouldn't have scared him into some very stupid mistakes.

It would have been incredible.

His steps slowed until he was standing motionless on the sidewalk across the street from her house. There were lights on inside, but the blinds downstairs were closed and the curtains upstairs were drawn. He wondered if Katy was in bed yet, if she'd broken her silence. He wondered what she would think of him as a father, if she ever missed having a dad like the other kids or if she was perfectly satisfied with the status quo. He thought about Saturday morning in the backyard, when she'd shot into his arms and he'd seen the blood. What would he have done differently if he'd known she was his daughter?

He would have prayed harder. Would have been a hundred times more frightened. Would have held her tighter. And when he was certain she was all right, he would have tracked down Patrick Watkins and killed him.

But, according to Fiona and Golda, he didn't have the right to do any of that. He didn't even deserve to be part of her life.

Exhaling heavily, he crossed the street and started up the sidewalk to Golda's house. At the foot of the steps, he suddenly stopped and automatically slipped his right hand inside his coat to the weapon he wore underneath his left arm. Before he touched the grips, though, he recognized the figure sitting on the porch floor, huddled against the door.

Fiona.

He slowly climbed the steps, then sat down opposite her, a small square column at his back. She was wrapped in a comforter that covered her from her neck all the way down to house slippers that looked like fuzzy ski boots. In the dim light he could see how serious she looked—how troubled—and he regretted that it was his fault.

He'd been sitting there three or four minutes when she finally spoke. "I'm sorry."

What did she have to be sorry for? Trusting him? Making love with him? Having his baby? He didn't think he could bear a yes to any of those, so he didn't ask. Instead he laid his head back and focused on the stained-glass arch above the door. "I never knew Golda thought so little of me."

"She loved you."

"Yeah. And she thought I was a coldhearted, self-centered bastard. She thought having no father at all was better for Katy than having me." The words had been running through his head all evening, but their pain hadn't lessened. They left a raw, throbbing place deep inside that he wasn't sure would ever go away.

"She thought you'd turned your back on Katy. She believed you knew about her and didn't care, so, yes, she thought that no father at all was better than one who didn't give a damn."

"And she died, thinking I didn't give a damn." His smile felt bitter, and his words tasted it. "You and Golda knew me better than anyone else in the world. You're the only two people I can honestly say I meant something to, at least for a while. And you both found it so easy to believe I would abandon my own little girl. Doesn't say much for me, does it?"

"Maybe it doesn't say much for us," she murmured.

He shook his head in disagreement. They'd thought what he'd given them reason to think. The failings were his, and so was the fault. "What do you want me to do, Fiona?"

"About...?"

"Katy. Do you want me to go back to D.C.? Do you want me to sign away my parental rights and stay out of her life? Tell me. I'll do whatever you decide." Even if it might kill him.

She stared at him, speechless. Her mouth worked, but no words came out, not until she dragged in a noisy breath. "You can't put that decision on me. I can't— It's not right."

"You're Katy's mother. You know her. You know me. Who better to decide what's right for her?"

Drawing her knees up, she huddled deeper in the comforter and replied with some bitterness, "I don't know you at all, Justin."

"So you're going to leave it up to me. What if I want to stay here? Live next door? See Katy every day? You won't object to that?"

She didn't answer, but he could feel the tension radiating from her.

"What if I want to take her back to D.C. for a visit? How about having her this summer? For Thanksgiving and Christmas? Hell, Fiona, you know firsthand what a selfish son of a bitch I am. What if I want custody of her? You've had her all to yourself for five years. Isn't it only fair that I have her all to myself for the next five years?''

''You *can't*—'' She caught herself, took a couple of deep breaths, then tried again in a calmer, quieter voice. ''No, it isn't fair that you missed the first five years of her life, but that doesn't justify taking her away for the next five years. I tried to tell you I was pregnant. Leaving a message on your machine wasn't the ideal means, but you'd made it clear you wanted nothing to do with me. That machine was the only way I could reach you. You can't punish me now because you didn't get the message.''

''I don't want to punish you, Fiona. It was my fault, not yours. Everything is my fault.'' Sliding his hand inside his coat, he rubbed his chest. He'd like to believe the ache there was nothing more than indigestion that would go away as soon as he took some antacid, but he couldn't kid himself. It was sorrow that Golda went to her grave believing he would reject his own child far more thoroughly than his own parents had rejected him. Regret that Fiona, who'd once loved him with a passion, had learned to hate him so much more, and he'd given her every reason. Guilt that he'd disappointed his aunt, betrayed Fiona and cost himself five irreplaceable years of his daughter's life.

And hurt. Plain and simple, he was hurt. Though he had no right to be. He'd gotten exactly what he deserved.

And no antacid in the world could take all that away.

''Where is Katy?'' he asked after a time.

''In bed. Our neighbor, Anne, is sitting with her.''

''And why are you sitting out here in the cold when you could be inside with her?''

''I just wanted to say…I'm sorry.''

''You don't owe me an apology.''

Silence settled again. Every time she moved, he expected her to get up, walk away and leave him alone in the cold.

Every time she didn't, he was grateful. After a while, he hesitantly asked, "When is her birthday?"

"March 1st."

"Why did you name her Kathleen?"

"It was my grandmother's name."

"And Hope?"

She smiled just a little. It softened her face and made her look achingly lovely. "I—I was having a really hard time after—after you left. When I found out I was pregnant, I had a reason to go on, to deal with the hurt and get on with life. She gave me hope at a time when I needed it desperately." After a moment, she asked, "Why did you get a copy of her birth certificate?"

"I needed to know."

"For your report?"

He shook his head. "For me. When they called back and named me as her father, I thought it was just a clerical error. Someone had seen my name as the one requesting the information and mistakenly wrote it down again. Katy was too young, and we'd been careful, and surely you or Golda would have told me." He shrugged. "Then they faxed me the copy."

"She's small for her age," Fiona conceded. "She's like a puppy, though. She thinks she can run with the big dogs."

It wasn't easy to imagine the traumatized, silent child he'd seen as playful, running and acting like a normal kid. He wondered if he would ever see her that way—if, once this case was over, he would ever see her, period. His lifestyle—living in a small apartment, working long hours both in the office and in the field, being subject to recall at any time, no family and few friends to call on in an emergency—wasn't conducive to playing single parent, even if it was only summer vacations and occasional holidays. And, frankly, seeing her like that would be an unpleasant reminder of his own upbringing, when he'd gone weeks without seeing his mother or father, even though he was living in the same house with her or him.

What if I want to stay here? he'd asked Fiona earlier, and her only answer had been to stiffen with dismay. He could do it, though. Golda's house was his to do with what he wanted. He could quit his job with the ATF and apply to the Grand Springs Police Department or the sheriff's office. If they weren't hiring, he could be a stay-at-home father. Whatever failings the Reed family embraced, they'd always had a knack for making money, and he'd received a substantial share of it from his grandparents and now Golda. He'd always worked because he wanted to, not because he needed to.

He thought about quitting the ATF—turning in his badge and credentials, leaving the squad of agents who were the only real friends he had, giving up the investigations that had dominated his life for eight years. If anyone had suggested it six months ago, he would have laughed. He'd joined the ATF with the intention of staying there until he retired or they buried him. Any other life had been inconceivable.

But six months ago he hadn't known about Katy.

"She has my eyes," he remarked absently.

The look Fiona gave him was edged with surprise. "I didn't think you'd noticed."

"I noticed. It just didn't register until now. They're dark blue, like mine." It was a simple thing. Every idiot passed along the genes for his particular eye color, whether dominant or recessive, to his kids. Katy's blue eyes were no major accomplishment. Still, it made him feel just the slightest bit possessive toward her. It was tangible proof that he'd played a role in creating her. Not that he needed any further proof.

"I'd better get home." Fiona gathered the comforter close and started to stand. On his feet quicker, Justin extended his hand to her. She merely looked at it for a moment, then accepted it, wrapping her fingers around it.

He pulled her to her feet, bringing them face-to-face with mere inches separating them. Wishing the street lamps were a thousand watts brighter, he stared at her—at the soft waves of red hair framing her face, the creamy perfection of her skin, marked only by the sprinkle of freckles across her nose, the lush curves of her mouth slightly open as if she'd caught her breath and hadn't let it go. She was so damned beautiful, and once he'd loved her the best he was capable of. Too bad it hadn't been enough. How different the last six years of his life would have been if it had.

How satisfying. Hell, maybe even happy.

Her fingers flexed around his hand, but he couldn't tell whether she was trying to let go…or hold on. She looked so soft, so delicate—and afraid. He'd put that fear in her eyes, and the knowledge shamed him. She deserved so much better than he'd given her, and if he had another chance…

If he had another chance, he'd screw it up just like before. That was what Reeds did.

Easing his hand free of hers, he took a step back, then five or six more, until she had a clear path to the steps. Looking disconcerted, she walked to the bottom of the steps before turning back. Her voice was husky, sounded off balance. "Katy has an appointment at the hospital tomorrow morning with her pediatrician. If you want to be there…"

"As her father? Or as the agent investigating her case?"

She swallowed hard. "That's up to you. The appointment is at ten-thirty. You can meet us at the shop fifteen minutes before, or at the hospital."

He nodded.

She walked away again, and he turned to unlock the door. He'd just opened it when she spoke from the driveway. "Justin?"

Two strides took him to the top of the steps, where he could see her better.

"I would have told you about Katy. I know you don't believe me, but..."

He studied her in the thin light, so earnest, so honest, and smiled faintly. "You're wrong, Fiona. I do believe you. And I never would have turned my back on her if I'd known. Someday *you'll* believe *me.*"

Chapter 5

On Tuesday morning, ten-fifteen came and went with no sign of Justin. Fiona waited as long as she could, then turned the Open sign to Closed, locked up and clasped Katy's hand tightly for the short walk to the car. She belted her daughter in the back seat, then fastened her own seat belt before backing out of the space.

She'd given him the option of meeting them at the hospital, she reminded herself on the way. Heavens, she'd given him the option of not showing up at all. If you want to be there, she'd said. Maybe he didn't. Or maybe he did, but he was busy. Or maybe he'd be waiting at Vanderbilt when they arrived.

She glanced at Katy in the rearview mirror, so quiet and distant, and hoped the doctors could work some miracle cure. Normally her daughter talked to her, to her dolls and stuffed animals, to the television and her storybooks and herself. She read out loud and sang, and when she played, she provided appropriate sound effects. The house had been so quiet without her ongoing chatter. Fiona wasn't sure how much more of it she could bear.

At the hospital she found a parking space near the entrance and hustled Katy inside. They hadn't gone more than ten feet when Justin pushed away from the wall where he'd been leaning and met them. "You're late," he said without censure. "Some things never change." In jeans and a pullover, wearing a pleasantly open expression, he looked younger, less grim, less like a federal agent and more like the man she'd fallen in love with so long ago.

She preferred the somber suits and stuffy ties. The last thing she needed was him looking approachable. Likable. Forgivable.

"I wasn't always late," she said in guarded response to his comment. "Most of the time you were just early."

"Because I was always eager to see you."

But that certainly wasn't the case this time. The knowledge sent a small pang of regret through her, and that baffled her. He was out of her life. Any future contact they had would deal with Katy or his investigation and nothing else. There was nothing between them anymore, and never could be. Even if there could, she'd gotten over wanting him years ago—so far over it that she could never go back.

"The pediatrician's office is this way." She directed him to a wide corridor that connected to the doctors' building next door.

As they walked, he bent to tug the ear of Katy's polar bear. "Hey, Katy, does your bear have a name?"

Fiona watched as Katy glanced up, then solemnly nodded.

"Can you tell me what it is?"

She continued to look at him but offered no response.

"You want me to guess, huh? Is it...Bartholomew? No? How about Clementine? Aristotle? Zenobia? Xerxes?"

With each name, Katy shook her head, and with each shake, her solemnity gradually gave way to a smile.

"I know—I bet it's Ursula. You know what that means?

She-bear. That's a girl bear. I dated an Ursula back in college. She lived up to her name.''

''In what way?'' Fiona asked dryly.

''She was wild. She got me in more trouble than I could get out of.''

An unwilling smile curved Fiona's mouth as she tried to imagine Justin with some free-spirited wild child. The image wouldn't quite form. ''Here's Dr. Keaton's office,'' she said, gesturing to the next door.

Unless she was unusually sick, Katy always made a beeline for the play area in the doctor's waiting room. This time she stood quietly at Fiona's side, clutching her hand, and didn't so much as look at the playhouse or toys. The change in behavior made Fiona's chest tighten with despair, but she refused to give in to it. Katy would be all right. She *would* be.

The receptionist showed them to the doctor's private office. He stood up from his desk, said hello to Katy first, then Fiona, then waited for an introduction to Justin. Problem was, she didn't know how he expected to be introduced, so with a deep breath, she said, ''This is Justin Reed. He's...''

''Golda's nephew,'' Dr. Keaton said as they shook hands. ''I'm sorry about her death.''

''Thank you. I'm also—'' Justin glanced at her, and Fiona felt her face grow hot. She didn't know if that made him change what he was about to say, or if she'd worried for nothing. ''I'm a special agent with the Bureau of Alcohol, Tobacco and Firearms. I work arson and explosives cases, and I'm investigating Saturday's incident.''

''Are you here in an official capacity?'' the doctor asked.

''Yes.'' The grimness with which Justin spoke made the word flat and empty. Because he would have preferred to make his real connection with Katy known?

''Have a seat, will you?'' Dr. Keaton gestured to the chairs in front of his desk as he returned to his own chair.

As soon as Fiona sat down, Katy immediately climbed

into her lap, pulled Fiona's arm tight around her middle and leaned against her. Under normal circumstances, there was nothing Fiona loved more than cuddling with her daughter, but today she'd give a lot if Katy would revert to her exploring, getting-into-everything ways just for a minute.

"How are you doing, Katy?" the doctor asked. "You had a pretty big scare, didn't you?"

She looked at him but remained silent.

"What's that you've got?" When she thrust the animal toward him, he said, "That's a pretty neat bear. Where did you get it?"

She used the bear to point in Justin's direction, then hugged it to her chest again.

"How do those cuts on your face feel? Do they hurt at all?"

Once more she simply looked at him.

Dr. Keaton directed his next words to Fiona. "Obviously she understands quite well. She's just stopped talking. Is that right?"

Fiona nodded.

"Have there been other changes? Is she sticking closer to you? Is she eating all right, sleeping all right?"

"The first few days she wanted me to carry her everywhere. Yesterday she let Justin take her, then my mom. Now she's willing to walk, but she wants to hold my hand, and sometimes she clings to my leg. Her appetite's fine, except she won't ask for what she wants. As far as sleep... The first night she was home from the hospital, she woke in the middle of the night and got in bed with me. Last night I let her sleep with me all night. I know I probably shouldn't, but..."

"It's okay for a few times," the doctor said, brushing off her concern. "You've both had a tremendous scare. I imagine it's pretty comforting to not wake up alone in the dark. Are there any other changes? Is she fidgety? Irritable? Does she cry more than usual?"

"Some. Not too much."

"How does she play with her friends?"

"She hasn't seen any of them. She doesn't show much interest in playing. Mostly she sits quietly close to whoever she's with."

"Today I'm just going to tell you what you have to look forward to in the next couple of weeks, and then we'll have you back in tomorrow to begin the tests. First...what Katy has is called acquired aphasia. Aphasia is the loss of speech, and acquired means she had the ability to talk before the explosion but has lost it. In her case, it's most likely caused by the trauma of the blasting caps going off practically in her face, but we can't know that for certain until we rule out other possibilities, okay?"

Fiona swallowed hard and nodded.

"Now I've already gone over her history with Dr. Hunter—he's a neuropsychiatrist on staff here—and he wants her in tomorrow morning for a CT scan to rule out any organic cause for the aphasia. If everything's okay there, then we'll set up an appointment with a speech pathologist for a complete evaluation. We'll get an audiogram and a tympanogram to make sure her hearing's not affected, and we'll get a consult with an ear, nose and throat doctor. Dr. Hunter will do a neuropsychiatric evaluation, and he'll probably want an EEG, too."

CT scans, consults, EEGs... It all sounded too daunting to Fiona, as if something might be *seriously* wrong with her baby. That couldn't possibly be the case. She couldn't bear it if Katy's problem was more serious than an extreme reaction to a scare.

"If all the tests and evaluations are normal and she's still not talking, then what?" Justin asked.

"Then we'll probably be looking at a diagnosis of post-traumatic stress disorder. If that's the case, about the best we can do is give her time and a lot of TLC. If she were older, we would have a few more options, but she's just five, and a five-year-old's brain doesn't process information the way an adult does. Any questions, Fiona?''

She glanced at Justin, who looked as serious as she felt, then summoned the courage to ask the one—the only—important question in her mind. ''Is Katy going to recover fully from this?''

''Based on what we know right now, I would say her prognosis is very good. I can't give you any guarantees, of course, and I can't give you a timetable. She might start talking on the way home, or it might take a while. But I think the odds are definitely in her favor.'' The doctor looked from her to Justin. ''Any other questions?''

They both shook their heads.

''Okay. Glenda will set up an appointment for the CT scan on your way out. In the meantime, baby her a bit, talk to her, try to get her to talk to you, but keep things as close to normal as you can. And we'll see you back here tomorrow.''

Fiona stood up, cradling Katy against her, and numbly walked out of the office. She would have walked past the receptionist's desk if Justin hadn't stopped her. She talked to Glenda, agreed on an appointment time, took the reminder card and left the office, all without really noticing.

''She'll be all right.''

She looked sharply at Justin, then glanced around. They were outside in the parking lot, standing beside her car, with Katy buckled into her seat, and she hadn't noticed leaving the hospital. She took a deep, cold breath, then let it out, watching miniature clouds of fog form. ''What if she isn't?''

''She *will* be.''

''You don't know that. You're just guessing. Everyone's just guessing. What if she *isn't?*'' She looked through the window at Katy, sitting silently, gently stroking the bear's fur, looking so damn innocent and vulnerable, and the queasiness in her stomach began spreading, sending shivers through her, making her eyes fill with tears and her voice unsteady. "What if my little girl stays like this for the rest of her life?"

"Then you deal with it, Fiona. You do everything in your power to help her recover, and if she doesn't, then you do everything you can to give her what she needs to live a normal life." He combed his fingers through his hair, and his jaw tightened. "Not being able to speak doesn't even make the list of the worst things that could have happened to her. I told you this guy likes explosives. That's what he uses the blasting caps for. Instead of tossing a nearly empty tin of caps into the can, he could have just as easily tossed in a bomb capable of—"

He broke off abruptly, but Fiona could guess the rest—for three days had avoided even thinking of other scenarios. Capable of killing her baby. She stared at him, horrified, then burst into tears.

Hell, Reed, Justin thought with disgust. That was good. All she'd wanted was reassurance, and all he'd done was make her cry. He glanced around the parking lot, futilely wishing her mother would appear, or the soothing-voiced Dr. Keaton, or even the married-and-just-friends Dr. Wilson. But there was no one around. Today wasn't his lucky day.

Or was it? he wondered when he pulled her hands from her face and drew her into his arms. It felt so damn good to hold her—better than he'd remembered even in his loneliest moments. She fitted against him exactly the way a woman should, as naturally as if they'd been made for each other. He wrapped his arms around her, and she pressed her face to his chest and clung to a handful of his coat as she cried.

He didn't pat her, didn't tell her it would be all right, didn't make any promises he couldn't keep. He just held her, and remembered all the other times he'd held her, followed by all the times he'd held another woman and wished it was her. She had been the sweetest gift he'd ever had, and the cruelest. Their relationship had taught him two lessons—

that, contrary to his life experience, someone *could* love him…and, that fact aside, he didn't deserve to be loved.

Before long her tears subsided to an occasional hiccup. For a time, she stayed where she was, then—before he was ready—she freed herself from his embrace. She didn't turn away, but she didn't look at him, not until she'd pulled a tissue from her coat pocket and dried her eyes. When she did look, her eyes were puffy, her nose red, and her cheeks were flushed with embarrassment. "I'm sorry. I'm not normally a weepy person."

"Under the circumstances, I think you're entitled."

"Crying serves no purpose. It doesn't get anything done."

"It provides an emotional outlet. It keeps you from getting overstressed and self-destructing." He studied her a moment before asking, "Are you okay to drive?"

"Sure." She sounded confident, but her smile was fragile. "Driving's automatic, no matter what's going on. I drove myself to the hospital when I was in labor with Katy. At three in the morning. With snow on the ground."

"I wish I'd been here."

"So did I. I would have killed you."

Though he smiled faintly at her dry comment, his thoughts were on her first words. *So did I.* Past tense. As in, no longer wanted. He'd known that for a long time, so why did it sting to hear her say it now?

Rather than find an answer to that question, he opened the car door and unbuckled Katy before scooping her into his arms. He locked the door, closed it, then faced Fiona. "Come on. I'll take you to lunch, and then home."

When he took her arm, she didn't go along willingly but planted her feet instead. "I can drive. I'm fine."

"You don't even remember how you got from the doctor's office to the car, do you? Or unlocking the car, putting Katy inside and fastening her seat belt. I saw the look on your face when you realized where you were."

"I was just a little dazed. I'm fine now."

"Humor me, Fiona. Maybe you are fine, or maybe you're a little emotional. Is it worth taking a chance with Katy? With yourself?" He tugged her arm, and this time she grudgingly allowed him to guide her toward his car the next row over.

As he unlocked the door, she offered one last protest. "My car—"

"I'll bring you back later to get it." He settled Katy in the center of the back seat and secured the lap belt, then slid behind the wheel. "What do you want for lunch, Katy? How about some liver and onions?"

She screwed up her face in response.

"Fried frog legs? Turtle soup? Blackbird pie?"

When she said nothing, he glanced at Fiona. "Where should we go?"

"How about home? I have a pot of chili left over from last night's dinner. It's Katy's favorite."

He felt a moment's disappointment that she didn't name a restaurant and wondered if she didn't want to be seen with him. Was she afraid people would think there was still something between them? Or that they would look at him and Katy together, both with dark hair and unusually dark blue eyes, and realize the truth?

On the other hand, though, alone with Fiona and Katy seemed a good place to be.

Fiona's house was warm and welcoming in a way Golda's house wasn't. Of course, she was there to make it so, while Golda was gone and Justin knew zilch about making anything feel warm and welcoming.

Fiona hung their coats over the stair rail, then gestured toward the living room. "Have a seat. I'll put the chili on."

He watched until she disappeared into the kitchen, then went into the living room. Like a shadow, Katy followed. Virtually everything had changed in the six years since he'd last been in the room. Except for a table or two, the antiques were gone in favor of sturdy kid-proof pieces, the collectible Oriental rug where they'd made love the first time had been replaced by a reproduction, and photos of Katy were everywhere.

He picked up a framed portrait of the entire Lake family. Katy was flanked by two cousins and, behind them, Fiona stood between her sisters. Kerry and Colleen looked enough alike to be twins—both tall, slim, with dark red hair cut short and sleekly styled. If they had freckles, they covered them with enough makeup that no one knew. They looked like women he might work with in D.C.—confident, aggressive, sharp. In contrast, Fiona was shorter, her hair lighter in color, longer, more luxurious. She was more feminine, softer. Touchable. Desirable. Lovable.

His throat suddenly dry, he returned the photo to the mantel, then turned to find Katy watching him. His daughter. His chest tightened, and for an instant he thought he might give in to the same sort of emotional overload that had brought Fiona to tears in the parking lot. His *daughter*—the very best part of him, made much better by Fiona. Out of their passion and need and hunger, they'd created this delicate little girl in all her perfection. It was an incredible thought, and a humbling one.

Coming across the room, she tugged at his shirt, then returned to the doorway. With one look back to ensure he was coming, she shifted the bear to her left hand and gripped the rail with her right as she climbed the stairs.

"Where are we going, Katy?" he asked as he followed her upstairs and down the hall. They passed the guest room, the bathroom and Fiona's room before she skipped ahead into her own room. By the time he reached the door, she was scrambling up a ladder to a mattress-covered platform in the branches of a sprawling tree.

He stared—a reaction she was obviously accustomed to, because she knelt on the bed and grinned. "Wow. This is incredible. Okay, Katy, you win the grand prize for having the best bed in all the world. Did your mom do this?''

She shook her head.

''Your granddad?''

Vigorously she nodded, then scrambled along a bridge to another platform. There she picked up a book and held it out to him. He took the few steps necessary to accept it and flipped through the bright-colored pages. ''Can you read this book?''

She nodded.

''Really? And you're only five years old?''

Another nod.

''Show me. Read it to me.'' He offered the book, but she refused to take it. The pleasure was gone from her face, and the look in her eyes turned wary. ''Come on, Katy,'' he coaxed gently. ''I don't know any five-year-olds who can read a whole book, and nobody's read me a story in a long, long time. Can you read just one page for me?''

Leaning over the railing, she snatched the book, then threw it with all her strength. It narrowly missed him and bounced off a chair to the floor.

''Kathleen Hope,'' Fiona said sternly from behind him. ''We do not mistreat books in this house, do we? And we certainly don't throw things at people. Don't you ever—''

''Hey, it was my fault,'' Justin interrupted.

She turned the reproachful look on him. ''Your fault? I suppose you telekinetically made her throw the book?''

''I was trying to get her to read to me. I didn't know what I was doing, and it upset her.''

''Being upset is no reason to throw a book at someone. She knows that. Don't make excuses for her behavior.''

His gaze narrowed as he looked at her. ''She has a damn good excuse for her behavior, or have you forgotten?''

Fiona started to respond, then noticed Katy watching, one leg extended over the railing. ''Go wash up for lunch. *Now.* And don't jump.''

Grudgingly Katy drew her leg back, then climbed to the floor and left the room. A moment later the sound of running water came from the bathroom down the hall.

"I know this child, Justin. If you give her an inch, she's going to grab the entire mile. If I let her jump off her bed, the next thing I know, she'll be climbing out the window to jump off the roof, and she'll find a way to make it seem as if it's the next logical step after jumping off the bed. She needs consistent limits."

"The doctor said to baby her. That means cut her some slack."

"He also said to keep things as normal as possible, and normally, she doesn't get away with that kind of behavior."

He bent to pick up the book and returned it to the platform as he said stiffly, "Hey, she's your daughter. You get to make the decisions."

"Damn it, Justin—" Frustration tightened her features and sharpened her voice. "The chili's ready. Come on down whenever you are."

He resisted the childish urge to call that he wasn't hungry and then leave. While he wasn't hungry enough that eating later would be a problem, he didn't want to leave, not yet. He rubbed his temples where a headache was trying to take root, then, with a sigh, started toward the stairs—and got sidetracked at the open door leading into Fiona's room.

This was the room where he'd spent most of his time six years ago, and little had changed. The bed was still a four-poster rice bed that had come from the Carolinas, and the rest of the furniture a mismatch in styles, woods and finishes that worked together anyway. The walls were still pale green, the wood trim still white, and the cheval mirror they'd put to such good use still stood in the corner.

It was a world apart from his own bedroom in D.C., with its matched set of furniture, off-white walls, plain blue spread and blinds that were never opened. He used the room for sleeping, and the less time he spent there, the better. He rarely took women there, certainly none who mattered, and—

That last remark stopped him. It sounded cold, callous. He didn't mean to disparage the women he'd been involved with in the city. After all, he certainly didn't matter himself. They'd been willing to put up with him, which said a lot for their tolerance, and they'd been exactly what he was looking for at that time, but the simple truth was, not one of them had been what he'd needed.

Not one had been Fiona. The ten days he'd spent with her had been the best time in his life. He could have had more—months, maybe even a few years before the inevitable end—but he'd thrown it away.

And he'd been alone ever since.

Weighted with regret, he went downstairs to the kitchen. Three places had been set at the corner table, and Fiona and Katy were already seated. He took his seat and began eating as if he ate lunch in deafening, tension-filled silence every day. He awkwardly complimented Fiona on the food, and she just as awkwardly thanked him. The only one unaffected was Katy. She ate with one hand and drove saltine cars around her bowl with the other, pausing occasionally to eat the cracker, then reach for a new one.

They broke the silence at the same time. "Are you—" "How many—"

Justin gestured for her to go ahead.

"You said you don't know any five-year-olds who can read a whole book. How many do you know?"

He glanced at Katy. "One."

"That's what I thought."

"What gave it away?" he asked dryly. "The fact that I don't know nothin' 'bout kids?"

"You know how to talk to her, as if she's an intelligent person capable of understanding and responding to what you say. That's more than most adults with no kids of their own." Then she grimaced. "Well, you know what I mean."

Yeah, he knew. A father who missed the first five years of his daughter's life might as well have no children. He certainly wasn't fit to be a father.

"Have you learned anything—besides the truth about Katy—in your investigation?"

"I should get a preliminary report from the lab soon, but it'll just confirm what we already know. To be honest, it's been difficult to concentrate. I've had a few other things on my mind."

She followed his gaze to Katy, then looked back at him. "Isn't that a conflict of interest? Even if it's been your case all those years, now that your…child is involved, isn't that a problem?"

He liked hearing her refer to Katy as his child. He just wished she hadn't hesitated, as if she found connecting him to her daughter offensive. "Not for me. It's a damn good incentive to stop this guy once and for all. But my bosses wouldn't agree. If they knew our relationship, they would replace me in a heartbeat." He grinned weakly. "There's your chance. You want to get rid of me, call George Wallace in the D.C. office and tell him the truth."

"And it would be that easy? He would tell you to pack your bags and go home, and you would?"

"No. But I wouldn't be here in an official capacity, so you wouldn't have to deal with me if you didn't want to." He toyed with the spoon in his empty bowl while looking for the courage to ask a question. He really needed an answer to it, but if it was the wrong answer… He'd had enough disappointments in the last twenty-four hours. He didn't want another.

Finally, dropping the spoon in the bowl and pushing it away, he met her gaze head-on and asked, "Would you feel more comfortable if someone else took over the investigation?"

She carried their dishes to the sink, then returned with a pitcher of tea to refill their glasses. When she sat down, she chose the chair to his right instead of across the table. ''Even when I hated you, I never had any doubt that you were very good at what you did. You've been after this man a long time. Does anyone in your office know him and this case better than you?''

He shook his head.

''Would anyone in your office care more about what he did to Katy than you?''

''No.''

''Does anyone have a better reason for wanting to stop him than you?''

''No.''

She smiled tautly. ''So there you go. I want this man caught, Justin. I want him punished. I believe you can do it.''

Her vote of confidence meant more than he could say, so what he did say was inadequate. ''Thanks. I, uh...I'd better get to work. I'll come by this evening if you want to pick up your car.'' Rising from his chair, he bent to muss Katy's hair. ''See you later, Kate.''

She waved, scattering cracker crumbs over the table, then went back to her play.

Justin made it to the hallway, then turned back. ''About Katy's medical expenses...''

''I have good insurance.''

''But it won't pay everything, will it?'' He waited for her to shake her head. ''Let me pay whatever it doesn't cover.''

''I appreciate the offer, but—''

''I have money, Fiona, more than I can spend, and I have the right to help provide for her.'' When she started to protest again, he impatiently gestured. ''If it bothers you that much to accept money from me, you can consider it a down payment on the five years of child support I owe you.''

''You don't owe me anything, Justin. But thank you.'' She made an effort at a friendly smile. ''And the hospital and my shop thank you, too.''

With a satisfied nod, he left.

And before he'd backed out of the driveway, he was already looking forward to coming back again.

The waiting room in the radiology department was small and cramped, decorated with orange vinyl sofas, fake plants and a television with bad reception. The newest of the magazines on the table was more than six months old, and there was a water stain on the ceiling tile that resembled a triceratops from the right vantage point.

Fiona sat on one sofa, tapping her fingernails on the metal clasp of her purse. She hadn't asked Justin if he wanted to come with them this morning. He'd simply shown up as they were leaving the house. She was glad he had. She had no tolerance for waiting alone.

With a heavy sigh, she wished she'd asked how long these tests would take. She wished she'd taken Katy to Denver last Friday, or had sold the house after the mudslides three years ago when she'd considered it. She wished—

Justin reached across the corner table from the next couch and wrapped his fingers around hers. "Please stop doing that, or one of us is going to hurt someone. Let's talk."

Her expression turned suspicious. "About what?"

"How long were you in labor with Katy?" He rested his hand, still clasping hers, on his knee. She should pull away and fold her hands together safely in her lap, but for reasons she didn't care to examine, she didn't.

"Twenty-three and a half hours. It wasn't one of my better moments. I've been told I threatened harm to everyone working in labor and delivery, as well as someone who shall go unnamed, as he did that night."

His fingers tightened fractionally around hers. "How much did she weigh?"

"Seven and a half pounds. She was beautiful. She had all that dark hair, those eyes and the sweetest face."

"Did you hate me then?"

Fiona wanted to blow off his question, to make a joke of the answer. *I was in labor for twenty-three and a half hours. Of course I hated you. I'm only human.* But he looked so serious, as if the answer really mattered.

She thought back to that night, the most bittersweet of her life. She'd been exhausted, overjoyed, excited, scared and everything in between. She'd thought it was unbearably sad that Katy's father wasn't there to fall in love with her at first sight, but at the same time she'd been glad he wasn't. Her daughter deserved a better man than he'd proved to be, and so did she.

"I didn't hate you. If you had walked into that delivery room and said, 'I'm sorry, I'm back now, I want to see my baby,' I would have forgiven you everything. But you didn't come, and that night, you broke my heart for the second time." She smiled wanly. "I swore I would never let it happen again."

Sliding her hand free at last, she leaned back, propped her feet on the coffee table and gestured to his clothes. "Did you go shopping?"

He gave the navy suit and blue shirt a negligible glance. "No, I had my supervisor pack up some things and send them to me. Got 'em yesterday."

"I didn't think you'd had time to go to Denver, and you're not going to find suits like that on the racks in Grand Springs." The fabric, she knew from the time he'd held her hand on his leg, was fine, the cut exquisite, the tailoring superb. It made him look unbearably handsome—not that he needed any help in that department. "Can I ask you a personal question?"

"I think we've gotten personal before."

"How rich are you?"

Discomfort swept over him instantly. "Does it matter?"

"No. I'm just curious. Does it matter to most people?"

"Yeah, it does. You'd be surprised how many people

think your net worth is all they need to know about you to decide whether they like you or resent the hell out of you.''

''That rich, huh?''

He was silent a moment before responding. ''Before my parents divorced, we lived on a fifty-acre oceanfront estate in Massachusetts. The house had twenty-seven rooms, and there wasn't a single room where you couldn't hear them screaming when they fought. After the divorce, my father bought a place in Rhode Island. And one in Vail. And one in the Caribbean. He usually tried to be at whichever one I wasn't. When I was eleven, my mother went off to spend two weeks in Greece with the latest man in her life, and she gave the servants the time off. She forgot that I was there.''

Fiona felt heartsick for the boy he'd been. His parents should have been strung up. Instead of visiting for weeks at a time, Golda should have demanded custody of him, brought him here and raised him the way every child deserved to be raised.

''Point taken,'' she murmured. Money couldn't buy love, guarantee happiness or security, or stop people from leaving you. ''How do you get along with them now?''

''From a distance. If they come to Washington, I try to see them, usually for a meal. They've always got other things to do. Usually, so do I.''

''What will they think of Katy?''

The look he gave her bordered on startled. ''Actually, I hadn't given any thought to telling them. My father's married to a girl practically young enough to be *my* daughter. I don't think he's exactly anxious for someone to call him grandpa. My mother…I honestly don't know. She might be pleased to have a granddaughter…or she might not give a damn. I don't have a clue.''

''That's okay,'' she said, though in reality, she thought it was sad. Her grandparents had been an important part of her life, all four of them, and she wished Katy could be as lucky.

"My parents adore the ground she runs on enough for six or eight grandparents. What about the rest of your family?"

He picked up a magazine from the coffee table and flipped through the pages as if he found them interesting. "I have two uncles, who have each had three wives. I don't even know the current Mrs. Reeds' names. Each of the six wives provided me with one cousin. I last saw the cousins...probably four or five years ago. I assume some of them have children, but I don't recall ever seeing them. And there are probably some distant relatives out there, but I don't know for sure."

Even his closest relatives were distant, Fiona thought with...not pity. Sympathy. Maybe regret. Some people were perfectly suited for that kind of emotionally isolated upbringing, but Justin wasn't one of them. He must have been terribly lonely and hungry for affection growing up—which made it easier to picture him with Ursula the wild child.

"So Golda wasn't kidding when she said you and she were the only Reeds to amount to anything."

"She was only half kidding," he said just a little bitterly.

Fiona watched as an orderly brought in a patient in a wheelchair, then left with the same chair and a different patient. She'd never had any feelings about hospitals one way or the other before now. She was grateful the staff and equipment were there when needed, but she could easily come to dislike the place. She doubted she would ever set foot inside again without remembering these times with Katy.

In search of a distraction, she turned to face Justin again, tucking her feet beneath her. "With your family's fondness for weddings, why didn't Golda ever marry? She had so much to give. She was the perfect candidate to be a devoted wife, mother and grandmother, and yet she chose to remain single."

"My family likes its scandals as well as its weddings. Live a good life, and they'll forget you existed. Shock them, and they'll remember you forever.'' He grinned ruefully. ''To celebrate Golda's graduation from college, her parents sent her to Europe for a month. Upon her return, she was to marry a suitable young man whose family had even more money and influence than ours. But, when she came home, she brought a charming Italian husband with her. Unfortunately he was also penniless, pedigreeless and spineless. My grandparents wrote him a nice little check and put him on the next boat back to Italy. She refused to marry the suitable young man or anyone else, and she never forgave her parents.''

''My gosh.'' Fiona laughed softly. ''I'd known Golda all my life, and I'd never imagined...''

''Sometimes we think we know someone, but they surprise us.'' The somberness in his voice made her think he was referring to the fact that Golda had believed him capable of abandoning Katy. ''Take us.''

''Us?''

''You think I'm a thoroughly coldhearted bastard.''

Fiona's face grew uncomfortably warm. She wanted to squeeze his hand, to deny that she thought that—not anymore, at least. She wanted, God help her, to take that dismayed, hurt look from his face. Instead, her voice husky, she made a lame attempt to tease. ''And you're really just slightly coldhearted, right?''

Before he could respond, a woman in a white lab coat approached. ''Mrs. Lake? Mr. Lake? I'm Dr. Montrose, the radiologist.''

Anxiously she got to her feet. ''I'm Fiona Lake. This is Justin Reed.''

''Sorry,'' the doctor said to Justin. ''I assumed you were Katy's father. We're finished with Katy down here. I'll review the films and send a report to Dr. Hunter and also to Dr. Keaton. One of them will be in touch with you later today or tomorrow.'' As her pager beeped, she paused to check it, then continued. ''Because Katy was sedated for the

CT scan, now she's on her way to the outpatient recovery room. They'll keep an eye on her there until she wakes up, and once they're sure everything's okay, she'll be free to go home. Do you have any questions?"

When Fiona didn't speak, Justin did. "You can't tell us that everything is normal, can you?"

Dr. Montrose shook her head. "'Fraid not. Why don't you get some lunch, and when you get back, she should be ready to go."

"Thank you." Fiona picked up her coat, then slung her purse strap over her shoulder. As she and Justin left the waiting room, she asked, "Would you like to go upstairs to the cafeteria with me?"

"I've got to get some work done or my boss will be on the next plane out here. Call me when Katy's ready—here's my cell number—and I'll give you a ride home."

"Okay." She accepted the card he gave her, then stopped at the elevator and pressed the Up button. "Justin? Thanks for coming with us this morning—for being there."

For a moment he went still. Surprised that she could be gracious? she wondered regretfully. Then he nodded in guarded acknowledgment and walked away.

If she'd tried more than once to tell him about her pregnancy, if she'd succeeded, how different would their lives have been? Would he have *been there* for them all along? He insisted he would have, and she was starting to believe him.

Believing was all right, she counseled as she got onto the elevator. It was necessary for the nonadversarial relationship they needed to cultivate for Katy's sake. She could believe him all she wanted.

As long as she protected her heart. He'd broken it twice, and she'd sworn it would never happen again.

She had to remember that.

Chapter 6

After leaving the hospital, Justin stopped by his office at the police department to collect his messages, then knocked on Colton Stuart's open door. "How's the crime business?"

"Slow but steady. Come on in."

Justin took a seat, then glanced around the office. It was large, as befitted the chief's status, but plain. The furniture had seen better days, and hadn't been much when it was new, but he liked it. It suggested the chief spent his budget where it was needed.

"How's your case going?" Stuart asked.

A shrug was Justin's only response. As he'd told Fiona, he'd been distracted lately. The guys on his squad would be astonished by that. He had a reputation for being single-minded when on a case, like a hound on a scent.

He also had a reputation for having no life outside his work. He put in more hours than anyone else on his squad. If he wasn't in the office or out in the field, odds were he was at home, reviewing his case notes, looking for some fresh angle. It was the only life he'd ever had, and it had been enough.

Until the last few days.

"Mind if I ask you a question?" When Stuart gestured, he went on. "Was it hard leaving the DEA? Giving up the undercover work, the danger, the challenge?"

Stuart considered it a moment. "I liked the work. When I started, I honestly thought we were making a difference. I enjoyed the travel. I liked the game—being undercover, pretending to be someone I wasn't. But the job almost got me killed more than once, and by the time I quit, I knew we weren't making any difference. And I had Juliette. There's not a job around that can compete with her."

Justin didn't have a Juliette, but he had a daughter. He could spend the next twenty years in Grand Springs making up to her for the last five. He could get to know her, watch her grow up, protect her and be there when she needed him. And who knew? After enough penance, maybe he could have a Juliette all his own.

And maybe her name would be Fiona.

"You thinking about leaving the ATF?" Stuart asked.

"Not seriously," Justin hedged. "It just occurred to me that there might be more to life than investigating crazies who get their kicks blowing things up."

"There is, son. Trust me." Stuart turned a frame on his desk so Justin could see it. It was a picture of a pregnant Juliette and Stuart holding a little blond boy. Martin, who thought of Katy as the big sister he'd never had.

The photo gave Justin a funny ache in his gut. Hunger, he told himself, but he didn't believe it for a moment. This was a different kind of emptiness, one that all the food in the world couldn't fill.

But a dark-eyed little girl and her red-haired mother could. If they were willing to try. If he was able to let them.

Resolutely he forced his attention away from them and to

his real reason for coming by. "Can you direct me to the county clerk's office? I need to check some land records."

"It's in the courthouse annex. Turn right out the door, go to the third intersection and turn left. It's a two-story brick building in the middle of the block. You looking to see if your guy owns any property around here?"

"It'd be one hell of a coincidence, wouldn't it, for him to own land halfway across the country in the very county where my aunt lived. But he buried that can somewhere, someplace where he thought it would be safe, where he could retrieve it when he wanted. *If* he wanted."

"Unless he chose this county because of you." When Justin scowled, Stuart raised one hand to stall him. "You've been after this guy from the beginning. Outsmarting you could have easily become part of his game. Maybe he's been tracking you. Maybe he found out about Golda, and he appreciated the irony of hiding the gems in a place connected to you."

It was a freaky idea, one that made Justin's skin crawl, but it wasn't outside the realm of possibility. Though he avoided the papers these days, getting background information on him wasn't tough. His parents' lifestyle, money and frequent marriages and divorces had provided plenty of fodder for gossip columns over the years. And there were plenty of instances when a criminal developed some sort of bond with the cop who was after him. Still, Justin would prefer to find out that Watkins had other reasons for leaving the gems here.

"But, hell," Stuart went on. "Coincidences *do* happen. What are the odds of that can ending up in the yard next to your aunt's? Or of an ATF agent witnessing an explosion next door?" Stuart grinned. "Some people might call it karma."

"Or pure dumb luck," Justin retorted. He wasn't sure *what* he would call it. "I'd better get out of here."

Ordinarily, when his destination was only a few blocks

away, he would walk, but this afternoon he took his car in case Fiona called in need of a ride. He had to admit, he liked playing chauffeur and—what? Friend? Shoulder-to-lean-on? Concerned ex-lover, acquaintance, father of her daughter? Whatever the role, he could get used to it pretty easily.

The county clerk's office was on the second floor of the courthouse annex, and a sign outside the door directed him to the land records office. It was typical of most government offices he'd seen—nondescript, functional, cramped. And, at the moment, it appeared to be empty.

He leaned on the counter that stretched two-thirds of the way across the room and called, "Hello. Anyone here?"

"No need to shout, young man. I'll wager my hearing is as good as yours." The woman who'd come in silently behind him poured the water she carried into the coffeemaker, pressed the Start button, then came to stand in front of him. As she set a pair of glasses on the counter, she briskly asked, "What can I do for you?"

Justin couldn't help but look bemused. She was older than God, couldn't reach the five-foot mark without a stool and looked sharper than any number of people one-fourth her age.

"Don't just stand there, Mr. Reed. If you have a request, make it. If not, then kindly vacate my office."

"How is it you know my name when I haven't had the pleasure of learning yours?"

"I'm Millicent Peterson. My friends call me Millie. You may call me Ms. Peterson. I was a friend of your aunt Golda's, but that doesn't mean I will automatically be a friend to you. Friendship must be earned, you know."

"I understand." He took his credentials case from his pocket and flipped it open, but the woman didn't even look at it.

"Put that away. I *know* who you are, and I know why you're here. You think your suspect might own property in the area."

"You've been talking to Chief Stuart."

"Colton thought a phone call might speed the process along. *Hmph.*" She turned away, heading for a computer at a corner desk. Halfway there, she looked back. "Are you coming, Mr. Reed, or do you expect me to shout across the room to you?"

"You forgot your glasses," he said as he circled the counter.

She gave him a narrow look. "Those aren't mine. They belong to one of the girls who works down the hall. She's forever leaving them places. This time I found them in the bathroom. *I* have twenty-twenty vision, my hearing is acute, my health is good, and—"

"Your temperament is ever so sweet."

The look sharpened for a moment, as if she were debating giving him the boot. Then her features relaxed into what could almost be described as a pleasant set. "Pull up a chair and give me the name of this scoundrel."

He obeyed her, and she *hmphed* again. "Watkins. You couldn't suspect a man with a name likely to be uncommon in these parts, could you? Something like Giamarese or Baryshnikov. That would narrow the search."

She had definitely been friends with Golda, Justin acknowledged. Giamarese was the name of the weak-willed Italian she'd married, and it wasn't something she would have shared with just anyone.

"Sorry," he remarked. "I'm just grateful he's not named Smith or Jones."

When a search for Patrick Watkins didn't turn up anything, she repeated it with only the last name. It gave them a listing for every Watkins who had owned land in the county back as long as records had been kept. They could eliminate every property within the city limits and, with some confidence, each Watkins Ms. Peterson knew personally. That appeared to be most of them.

"What about his mother's maiden name?"

Justin opened his briefcase and took out the top file. It was marked with Watkins's name, two inches thick and the first of multiple files. He skimmed through the biographical information at the front of the file until he found what he was looking for. "Lafrannier."

Under the weight of her chastising gaze, he spelled the name. For a long time she continued to look at him, then slowly, with a great sigh, typed it in. "One entry. Claude Lafrannier. Sixty-one years ago he inherited a parcel of forty-five acres on Bear Creek Mountain. The family sold it ten years ago to a developer in Denver." Tapping her finger against her chin, she said thoughtfully, "I remember that. There were local people who would have been happy to make an offer on the land, but it was a done deal by the time we heard about it."

"Is there anyone around who would have known Claude Lafrannier?"

"Me—if he'd lived here, which he never did. Tax bill went to an address in Richmond, Virginia. If he ever even came here to see it, he kept to himself. You know, in the long run, I guess it's a good thing none of the local people did buy the place."

"Why is that?"

"Because it came down in the mudslides. Less than half of that forty-five acres is still up there on Bear Creek Mountain. The rest is on Little Mountain." She grinned wickedly. "And on Hickory Street. And Aspen. And Gum. I imagine part of it's in your own backyard."

Justin nodded with satisfaction. That explained how the ammo can wound up in Fiona's backyard. "Can I have a copy of the legal description, the map of the property and the deed?"

"You don't ask for much, do you?" she grumbled as she got up. "Anything else I can get you? A cup of coffee and a doughnut so you can sit back and relax while the old woman does your work for you?"

"No, thanks. The paperwork's enough." Justin grinned as she walked away, then he went to the window. He had no clue which of those peaks was Bear Creek, but he would find out, just as soon as he got a warrant.

It would be one hell of a coincidence for Watkins to own property in the county, he'd told Colton Stuart. It was a mighty big one that he had ties to the county, just like Justin. Karma, Stuart had suggested. Hell, maybe it was. Maybe, for some unknown cosmic reason, he and Watkins had been fated to begin their careers at the same time and fated to end them in the same place. Maybe *he* had been destined to come back here and discover the truth about Katy.

And maybe fairies existed and there really was a pot of gold at the end of every rainbow.

"Here you go, Mr. Reed." Millicent had sneaked up on him again and was holding out a file folder. "Is there anything else you need?"

"As a matter of fact..." After placing the file in his briefcase, he pulled out a county map. "Can you show me how to get to the Lafrannier place?"

She took the map, marked the route with a yellow highlighter, then handed it back. Folding her hands primly, she said, "I was truly sorry to hear of your aunt's passing. She was a good friend."

"And a good aunt, though I'm afraid I wasn't such a good nephew."

"Nonsense. She loved you very much, and she understood why you kept your distance from Grand Springs."

He believed the first part, but not the second. Golda never would have understood how a man could turn his back on his own child. She would have been sorely disappointed in him for not returning to Grand Springs and accepting responsibility for his daughter. But how could he accept responsibility for someone he hadn't known existed? And how could he redeem himself to someone who had died believing the worst of him?

By accepting that responsibility now. By being the best damn father any child could ever hope to have. It wasn't enough, but it was the best he could do.

If Fiona would let him.

"Thank you for your help, Ms. Peterson. It's been a pleasure meeting you."

Her mouth twitched before she controlled it in a stern expression. "I'm paid to provide assistance, Mr. Reed. If you need anything else..." Slowly the smile escaped and brightened her entire face. "Drop on by."

"I will."

He was halfway down the stairs when his cell phone rang. When he answered, there was a moment's hesitation, then, "Hi, it's me—Fiona."

As if he wouldn't recognize the voice that had intrigued him, seduced him, haunted him. "What's up?"

"They're getting Katy checked out now, so if the offer of a ride still stands..."

"Is she okay?"

"Yes. She's just a little drowsy. Cranky. If you're busy, I can call one of my sisters."

"No," he said hastily. "I'll be there in a few minutes."

"We'll be waiting at the front entrance."

He made it to the hospital in good time, stopping at the double doors as Fiona and Katy came out. It was such a normal family thing to do, he thought—picking up the wife and child from an appointment, taking them home, making certain everything was all right before returning to work. But if, by any stretch of imagination, they could be considered a family, it certainly wasn't a normal one.

But they could have been. Should have been. If he weren't such a coward. If he'd been willing to forget all the lessons his parents had taught him about love, commitment, marriage and self-worth, and put his faith in Fiona and himself.

No, not if he'd been willing, he amended in his own defense. He would gladly forget everything about his parents if he could, but it wasn't easy forgetting thirty-four years of neglect, aloofness and indifference. If he'd been *able.* That was more accurate.

Fiona buckled Katy into the back seat, then slid in beside him. "We appreciate this. I know you have more important things to do than chauffeur us around."

"Other things," he said absently. "Not more important." When she gave him a curious look, he realized what he'd said and felt the heat of a flush spreading across his face. But he didn't take the words back, didn't offer some lame explanation. He'd meant what he said. Let her make of it what she would. "Do you want to go home or to the shop?"

"Home. Mom's got everything under control at the shop, and I think Katy needs some quiet time at home."

The last thing Katy needed was quiet. She should be chattering, singing, talking back, arguing or throwing a temper tantrum—anything that involved noise and emotion and seemed halfway normal for a five-year-old. Instead she sat silently in the back seat, gazing out the window with no interest.

"Have you considered inviting some of her friends over to play?"

"I don't think that would be a good idea."

"Why not? She goes to nursery school, doesn't she?"

"She's in kindergarten half a day and at the day care center the other half."

"So she plays with kids every day. It's a normal part of her life. And the doctor said to keep things as normal for her as possible."

"Yes, but—"

"Maybe she'll feel safe with them. Maybe it'll help her relax. If you treat her like something terrible has happened, then she's going to believe it."

"Something terrible *did* happen."

"Yes, but she survived. She's alive and well, and in a

few more months it's just going to be a distant memory. The sooner life starts getting back to normal, the sooner that memory will become distant."

"Gee, thanks for the parenting advice," she said snidely. "And you gained this invaluable expertise where? Growing up in the Dysfunctional Family of the Year thirty-some years running?"

He didn't reply. Instead he clenched his jaw, tightened his fingers around the steering wheel and concentrated on driving.

After a few silent blocks, Fiona picked up the map on the console between them, saw Ms. Peterson's highlighted route and unfolded it. "You're going to Bear Creek Mountain?" She sounded awkward, embarrassed.

"Yes."

"Why? Is that where you think the jewels were originally buried?"

"I can't discuss the case with you." But that wasn't true. There was nothing inappropriate about telling her that Patrick Watkins's maternal grandfather had owned a parcel of land on Bear Creek. He just wasn't inclined to confide in her at the moment.

"'The case,'" Fiona said sharply, "is my daughter."

"No." He pulled into her driveway and shut off the engine before looking at her. "The case is *our* daughter. She's as much mine as yours."

"Really? Let's see... She saw you for the first time ever four days ago, and she doesn't have a clue who you are. I'm the one who raised her for five years alone. Who got up with her for 2:00 a.m. feedings and juggled work and caring for her. Who changed her diapers and rocked her all night when she was sick or teething. Who was there when she learned to walk, when she said her first word, when she had her first birthday and first Halloween and first Christmas. I was the one who taught her and worried about her and protected her and loved her. I was the one—"

"Who made only one token effort to let me know you were pregnant—or so you claim."

Catching her breath, she stared incredulously at him. "I showed you the phone bill!"

"That proves you called. It doesn't prove you left a message."

"*Why* would I lie?"

He looked away, wishing the conversation had never started. But it had, so, after staring at yellowed grass for a moment, he looked back. "I don't know. You already knew it was over between us. Maybe you decided I couldn't have her if I didn't want you. Maybe you wanted to bolster your status as the innocent victim by telling everyone I'd rejected our baby, too. Maybe you wanted to punish me by making Golda believe I was a coldhearted bastard, just like my father."

Her face was pale, her lower lip trembling. "You can't believe that," she whispered. "I would *never—*"

"I know. I don't believe it." He spoke firmly, flatly. "But you found it so easy to believe that I listened to your message, then erased it, and you and Katy, from my life without a second thought. You found it damn easy to believe I was that coldhearted." And that hurt, more than he could say.

For a time she didn't move, didn't even blink. Then abruptly she gave a shake of her head, unfastened her seat belt and said, "Come on, Katy, let's go in."

He got out and lifted Katy from the back seat, but before he'd fully straightened, Fiona snatched her away from him. He watched them walk away, then muttered a curse, slammed the door and started after them. As he reached the front door, Fiona took her chance to repeat his childish action, slamming it in his face.

He invited himself inside. Katy stood listlessly on the stairs while Fiona removed her coat and gloves. Without pausing, she coldly said, "Thank you for the ride. You can leave now, and don't bother coming back."

Ignoring her, he crouched in front of the girl. "Hey, Kate, can you go upstairs and play in your room for a minute while I talk to your mom?"

She leveled her identical blue gaze on him for a moment before solemnly nodding. He thanked her and brushed his hand over her hair before she left, then he watched until she was out of sight.

"I have nothing to say—" Fiona broke off when he raised one hand in warning. In the following silence, the *click* of Katy's bedroom door closing was clearly audible.

"I spent seven years listening to my parents scream at each other. We're not putting her through that." Hanging his overcoat on the railing with hers, he asked, "Why are you so angry?"

She headed for the kitchen, and he followed, figuring the more distance between them and Katy, the better. "Gee, you just called me a liar and accused me of deliberately trying to destroy your relationship with Golda. You're giving me advice on caring for my daughter as if you know something about it, you so kindly reminded me that when I was in love with you, you didn't *want* me, and you accused me of denying my baby a father, of sacrificing an important part of her life, just so I could play the poor, mistreated victim. You tell me, Justin. *Why* am I angry?"

"I told you, I don't believe—"

When the laundry room door blocked her way, she whirled around to face him. Mere inches separated them. "You thought it. You put it into the words. You never would have said it if you hadn't wondered, if you hadn't suspected..."

"I never 'suspected' anything. But, damn it, Fiona, you can't be so damn superior and claim you're more of a mother to Katy than I am a father because you were there for her. You *knew* she existed. I didn't."

Her answer came softly, in a deadly chilling voice. "So you claim."

Justin's fingers curled into a fist that hit the door beside her head with enough force to make her flinch. Feeling sick inside, he backed off a few feet, then bitterly said, "You were right the other night, Fiona. You don't know me at all. You never did."

Spinning around, he left the kitchen, grabbed his coat and stalked out the door. He headed for Golda's house, letting himself into the cool, dark quiet, leaning against the closed door and dragging in a shallow breath—all he could manage without intensifying the ache in his chest.

If she'd never known him, then she had never loved him. Maybe she'd been in love with the idea of love, but she hadn't loved *him.*

And at that very moment, he hated her for it.

Hated her.

Fiona awoke Thursday morning feeling as if she'd gone ten rounds with a fighter far stronger and more experienced than she. Her head ached. Her body ached. Mostly her heart ached.

She'd tried to call Justin last night at Golda's house, but had gotten only the machine. As if it wasn't disconcerting enough to hear her friend's voice on the tape, the call had reminded her too painfully of another such call five years ago. That time she'd left a tearful message. This time she'd simply listened to the hum of the telephone line before the machine disconnected—as he'd accused her of doing before.

She should have tried harder six years ago, should have tried until she got him on the phone, until she knew he was listening, until she heard him say, I don't care. *I don't want our child.* If she had forced the issue, they all could have been saved such heartache—the two of them, Katy, Golda.

Becoming aware of a solemn, unwavering gaze, she turned to find Katy sitting cross-legged on the bed in her pajamas. "Good morning, sweetie," she murmured, pulling her close for a kiss. ''Did you sleep in here with me last night?''

Katy shook her head.

''You stayed in your bed all night? That's good, baby. I'm proud of you.'' She ruffled Katy's hair, then sat up and combed her fingers through her own hair. ''Why don't you snuggle in here while I take a shower, then I'll get breakfast and we'll decide what we're going to do today.''

She'd thought about it all afternoon after Justin had left and all evening—had even called Elena Melendez, a psychologist at the hospital, to ask her opinion. Elena had agreed with Justin. Katy needed normalcy in her life, needed to understand that while her ability to talk had changed, nothing else had. Everything was the way it should be, and soon she would be, too.

But everything wasn't the way it should be in Fiona's life. Justin had created such turmoil and confusion. She didn't understand half her responses to him, didn't know why she'd reacted so hatefully to his suggestion about getting Katy together with other kids. Maybe because, in her heart, she'd known he was right and she hadn't wanted him to be. Because *she* wanted to be the one who helped Katy. *She* wanted to be the wise parent, the capable one, the one who knew what was best for her. After all, she knew Katy intimately. He didn't.

And whose fault was that? She'd left him a message that he claimed he never got. If he'd been willing to talk to her, like an adult, there wouldn't have been any message to miss. If she'd taken up Golda on her offer to talk some sense into him, he definitely would have known. If he'd told her from the beginning that all he wanted was a vacation fling instead of breaking her heart, she could have dealt with him more rationally.

All told, there was plenty of blame to share.

But only one Katy, and sharing her was tough. After five years of being unquestionably the most important person in

Katy's entire life, it was hard to back off and give someone else—even her father—an equal chance. Especially when he might take her halfway across the country.

Or he might not. She didn't know what his plans were. She didn't even know what she hoped they were.

She showered and dressed for work, helped Katy dress, then went downstairs. She kept up a steady stream of conversation, asking questions that got no answers, making comments that drew no response. By the time breakfast was over, her nerves were on edge.

"Come on, babe, let's go, or we'll be late for school," she said cheerfully.

Katy's only response was to wrap her arm around the spindles on the back of her chair.

"Come on, sweetie. You didn't think you were on vacation forever, did you? Grab your coat and your backpack and let's hit the road. Hustle, kiddo."

Grudgingly Katy released the chair and followed her down the hall to the coat closet. She didn't put her coat on, though, or scoop up her battered pack.

Fiona shrugged into her coat, then sat down on the steps. "Are you afraid of going to school?" At Katy's nod, she gently teased, "At least you won't get in trouble for talking too much, will you? Though I would give anything in the world to hear you say one word. Honey, I know what happened scared you badly, but you're going to be just fine. And the kids at school are your friends. They've been worried about you, and they'll be happy to see you. You'll get to play games and color and read stories, and when you go to day care, you'll get to see Martin. Won't that be fun? You've missed him, haven't you?"

With an unwilling nod, Katy put on her coat, picked up one strap of her backpack and dragged it across the floor to the door.

In the subfreezing cold, Fiona locked up, then walked briskly to the car with Katy, pretending not to notice how reluctantly her daughter was accompanying her. She got her settled in the back seat, circled the car—and looked up in time to see Justin walking out to his own car. Pretending not to notice him was impossible, and so she openly watched.

The look he gave her made the surrounding air feel like a balmy spring day. She'd never been on the receiving end of such frigid contempt before, and it cut through her. She took a few stunned steps toward him, wanting to ask him what she'd done to deserve such a look, but he got into his car, the engine already running, and drove away.

When his car was out of sight, she nervelessly got behind the wheel, started the engine and let it idle while she hugged herself tightly. It was because of the cold, she pretended. Not because of Justin. Certainly not because she felt as if that look might make her fall apart.

After a time, she backed out and drove the mile and a half to the elementary school. As she found a parking space, she felt a pang for the days—only a week ago—when she'd pulled up out front and Katy had jumped out of the car and raced for the doors with no more than a hasty wave goodbye. She'd loved school, seeing her friends, being the teacher's pet. This morning she dragged her feet and made the journey inside that much more difficult.

As they walked through the doors, the bell rang, and Katy cringed. Instantly her hand tightened painfully around Fiona's and she jammed her head against Fiona's ribs and clapped her free hand over her ear. At the same time, she gave voice to a low, pitiful wail.

"Katy, honey, it's all right." Fiona dropped to her knees and wrapped her arms around her. "It's okay, sweetie, it's just the bell. It's nothing bad. Don't be afraid. You remember—the bell rings twice every morning. That's all it is, sweetie. It's not going to hurt you."

Katy opened one eye, then the other, then swiped her hand across them. She was pale and trembling like a leaf, and

Fiona wanted nothing more than to scoop her into her arms and run all the way back home where she could keep her safe. But if she let the warning bell scare them both away from school this morning, how much harder would it be to try again tomorrow?

"It's okay, baby doll," she murmured, pushing Katy back so she could stand up. "When the next bell rings, you just cover your ears if you want, okay? Now let's hurry to Miss Lance's class so you won't be late."

Leaving Katy five minutes later in the care of her teacher was the hardest thing Fiona had ever done. She wanted to stand in the hallway out of sight and watch through the glass so she could go rushing in if needed, but she forced herself to return to the car, to drive to the shop and park out back.

Past Times wasn't scheduled to open for more than an hour. Normally she liked it when it was quiet and dimly lit, when she could work without interruption, but this morning she was grateful when a knock came at the front door only moments after she arrived.

It was Rebecca Wilson, bundled against the cold and carrying two steaming cups of coffee. Fiona let her in, then locked the door again behind her. "I come bearing caffeine and sugar," Rebecca said in greeting, handing over one of the cups, then pulling a paper bag from her shoulder bag. "Where shall we eat?"

Fiona led her to a rustic table in the back, pulled up two canvas chairs and sat down.

"I half expected to see your mom in here. She was prepared to fill in for you as long as you needed. Is she keeping Katy?"

"No, I dropped her off at school today. Elena Melendez thought it would be a good idea."

"I'm sure it is," Rebecca said as she tore open the bag to reveal two caramel-and-nut honey buns. "We missed you Tuesday."

"Tuesday..." Fiona flushed. Every Tuesday she met Rebecca and Juliette Stuart at a sandwich shop down the street, but this week she hadn't spared them a moment's thought. "We were at the hospital Tuesday morning. Believe me, I would rather have had lunch with you."

"Your mom says Katy's the same."

"Yeah. I used to get frustrated with her constant chatter and would send her over to Mom's just for a little quiet. Now..." Fiona's throat tightened, and tears filled her eyes. "I'd give anything to hear one word from her, one argument, one *I love you.*"

"Oh, honey, it'll happen. You just have to have faith. She's going to be fine. What do the doctors say?"

"We're supposed to get the results of the scan today, and if it's okay, then she'll undergo a— Oh, God, Rebecca, what if it's not okay? I hadn't even considered that. What if there's something wrong with her, and the explosion has nothing to do with her speech loss? What if—"

Rebecca leaned forward to give her a shake. "Hey, don't go borrowing trouble. The chances that it *wasn't* the explosion are minimal. She's a perfectly healthy, normal kid who got the scare of her life. There's not going to be any other problem."

"God, I hope you're right." Fiona's trembling settled enough that she could break off a piece of pastry and take a bite. Rebecca let her get that far before grinning.

"So...tell me about this gorgeous ATF agent. Since the explosion occurred in your backyard and involved your daughter, are you getting to see a lot of him?"

It seemed to Fiona that the more she chewed, the bigger the doughnut got. She finally managed to choke it down, then swallow a gulp of coffee. "I— He's been around."

"I hear he went to see Katy in the hospital."

"He needed information for his report."

"And that he went to her doctor's appointment with you

Tuesday. And kept you company during her CT scan yesterday.''

''How did you hear all this?''

''It's a hospital. The place exists to pass on gossip. Come on, Fi, give it up. Tell all.''

For one insane moment Fiona considered doing just that. As far as she knew, no one in town outside of Justin, Golda's lawyer and her own family had any clue who Katy's father was, and there was a need inside her to share the truth with someone. But she'd kept it secret so long, and now it was no longer her secret alone. She couldn't tell anyone without Justin's permission, not even one of her two best friends in the world.

''This case is very important to him,'' she said lamely. ''He's being very thorough.''

''Yeah,'' Rebecca agreed with a wicked grin. ''I understand he's checking out the victim's mother quite thoroughly.''

''Justin and I have known each other for years. We met when he was visiting Golda a while back.''

The disappointment that crossed Rebecca's face was comical. ''And you didn't hit it off?''

''Not so you'd notice.''

''Why not? He's gorgeous, and you're gorgeous. Were you blind?''

''I noticed,'' Fiona said awkwardly. ''He...he's a federal agent in Washington, D.C. His family's filthy rich, and he meets all kinds of beautiful, wealthy, sexy women. Whatever I could have offered couldn't even have begun to compete with them.''

''Hey, I *know* filthy rich, and I can tell you, this man is *not* your typical rich guy. He's worth going after.''

It wasn't common knowledge around Grand Springs that Rebecca's maiden name was Wentworth, of the Denver Wentworths. At one time they'd owned half of the state and controlled the other half, and they'd managed to alienate their only daughter so completely that she'd had no contact with them for years. Of all the people Fiona knew, Rebecca was the only one who could relate to Justin's upbringing because her own had been similar.

"Worth going after based on what?"

Rebecca shrugged. "He has a job—a difficult job—in public service that probably pays less in a month than his trust fund earns in a day. He cares about something other than making money and spending it. He's dedicated to something besides his own pleasure."

He was certainly dedicated to his job. Fiona hoped he would prove to be equally dedicated to Katy…as long as that didn't mean having her in Washington with him.

"So…what's he like?"

He could be incredibly charming, funny, tender and passionate. He was the best lover she'd ever had in her rather limited experience. He was serious, intense and still burdened by his parents' mistakes, very intelligent, very focused, and once she'd loved him more than anything. Now…now she didn't know what she felt for him.

"He's a nice guy," she said carelessly, though those exact words were the last she would ever really choose to describe him. They sounded so bland, so generic, and there was nothing bland or generic about him.

"'A nice guy,'" Rebecca repeated. "Somehow I think you're holding something back. That's okay. We'll find out soon enough."

The circa-1870 grandfather clock against the wall softly bonged the hour, and Rebecca glanced at it with a sigh. "Time to head off to work. Give my love to Katy. If there's anything we can do, give us a call."

"I will. Thanks."

As Rebecca left, Fiona tilted her head back, closed her eyes and sighed. *If there's anything we can do…* All her friends and family were willing to help, but none of them possessed the one thing—a magic wand—that could help.

She could wave a wand and make everything all right. Lacking one, all she could do was muddle through and hope and pray for the best for Katy. And for herself.

And for Justin.

Chapter 7

On Thursday Katy made it through kindergarten and day care, and went home to pout and act out the rest of the evening. On Friday she made it through both and, when she heard her cousins were spending the night with their grandparents, cried to go, too. Fiona worried over the decision until her mother made it for her.

"We've been keeping Katy overnight since she was eight weeks old," she reminded her. "We're only a few blocks away. If she needs to come home in the middle of the night, it's not a problem. We'll take good care of her, and, frankly, honey, you look like you need some good care, too. Call one of your friends and go out tonight. Have a pleasant dinner. Talk to nonmedical people about nonmedical subjects. Have a drink or two and relax." A sly look came into her eyes. "You could ask Justin. He doesn't know many people in town. He'd probably be happy for the company."

"*Ma.* You would actually set your beloved daughter up with the man who abandoned her and broke her heart?"

"I'm not talking about a setup," Delores said innocently.

"I just remember that no other man ever made you seem so relaxed and at ease. Besides, broken heart aside, he's a fine-looking young man. I'm sure he could show you a good time."

Sure, he could—right before crushing her again. "I'm not interested in going out. Besides, I haven't even seen Justin since—" yesterday morning, but if she admitted that, her mother would know she was keeping track "—well, in days. If Katy's sure she wants to go with you, I'll get comfortable, eat junk food and fall asleep on the sofa."

Delores rolled her eyes. "And my friends wonder why a pretty girl like you is still single. Katy-bug, you want to spend the night with Grandpa and me?"

Katy bobbed her head vigorously.

"Tell your mom goodbye while I pack a bag for you."

Katy climbed onto Fiona's lap and wrapped her arms around her neck. Fiona hugged her back, and for a time didn't say a word. It was sweet, touching, one of the greatest pleasures in her life—and Justin had never experienced it. He'd never gotten a hug from his daughter, or a sloppy kiss—had never heard her say, I love you, Daddy. He'd never stood in the room and watched her sleep or listened to her spin one of her tales or laughed at her jokes. He'd missed so much, and whether it was his fault or hers didn't seem to matter so much anymore.

She brushed Katy's hair back. It was so soft and silky—darker than her own but not as dark as Justin's. "I love you, Katy," she murmured, her voice thick with tears.

In response Katy puckered up and gave her a noisy smack on the cheek.

"You be good for your grandma and grandpa, okay? And if you need anything—"

"We'll be right there," Delores said from the doorway. She held out a miniature suitcase that said Goin' to Grandma's, and Katy leaped to the floor to take it just as the doorbell rang. Startled, she dropped the bag and grabbed her grandmother, who merely chuckled. "Loud noises scare you a bit, don't they? Let's see who it is."

It was Rebecca and Juliette, come to invite Fiona to the Saloon for a burger, a beer and maybe a dance or two. She looked from their matching grins to her mother's and scowled. "Gee, I smell a conspiracy."

"Don't be difficult, darlin'," Delores said. "It's not attractive. Go on. Put on your tightest jeans and your dancin' boots and remember for just one night that you're young and beautiful and *single.*"

"How could I forget with you to remind me, Ma?" she asked with a sour smile.

Delores patted her cheek. "You forgot the day you said goodbye to—" she looked at Juliette and Rebecca, then rephrased "—Katy's father. You haven't had a date in all those years. You haven't even looked admiringly at a man. Go out tonight and have fun. Be the woman you were before you met him."

An evening with friends did sound nice, Fiona had to admit. At least it would keep her from worrying constantly over Katy and Justin, and she could certainly use a break from that.

But it wasn't much of a break, she discovered fifteen minutes later when they walked into the Saloon. Colton and Steve had gone ahead and saved them a table, where Fiona's seat faced the bar.

Where Justin sat alone.

At first she thought it was an even bigger setup than she'd imagined, but Juliette and Rebecca seemed as surprised to see him as she was. The only difference was they were pleased, while she was… Hell, she was pleased, too. Just a bit.

He was the only man in the bar wearing a suit, but he somehow managed not to look out of place. He was getting more than his share of attention from the women. As she watched, first one busty blonde slid onto the stool beside him and talked for a few minutes before wandering off, then another. He apparently wasn't feeling too chatty.

"Why don't you ask him to join us?" Juliette suggested after they'd ordered a round of cheeseburgers and fries.

"I'd rather not." Remembering the look he'd given her Thursday morning, Fiona thought he was more likely to bite her head off than accept an invitation from her.

"Oh, come on," Rebecca coaxed. "He's alone, he doesn't know many people in town..."

A brunette slid onto the stool, leaned close to give him a good view of her cleavage and laughed flirtatiously. "He's getting acquainted with more of them every minute." And that was fine. She didn't have a problem with it. What he did and who he did it with meant nothing to her, as long as it didn't affect Katy, and a flirtation with some easy-virtued bar tramp wouldn't hurt Katy at all because she would never know.

Dropping the subject, her friends launched into conversation. They passed on gossip, debated topics and made her laugh and almost forget the dark cloud she'd been living under the past week. But they couldn't keep her gaze from straying back to the bar, couldn't stop her from surreptitiously noticing how long each woman who approached Justin stayed before leaving again.

They ate, the others danced, and Fiona turned down invitations to dance. Her mother was right, she thought disgustedly after sending a handsome cowboy off with a "no, thanks." She *had* forgotten she was single after Justin had dumped her. Not a single date, not an innocent lunch, not one wicked night. For six years she'd had no love life, and no lust in her life, either. She'd dedicated herself to being the best mom, the best businessperson, the best daughter and friend. She hadn't reserved any time or energy for being a woman.

It was his fault, not hers. There wasn't a man in Colorado who could make her feel the way he had with only one look, one touch, one kiss. She'd experienced the best relationship imaginable, and if all she could have now was less...well, no, thanks.

"He's hitting the booze pretty hard," Steve commented.

Fiona blinked. She hadn't noticed her friends returning from the dance floor and, truthfully, hadn't noticed the regularity with which the bartender was refilling Justin's glass. She'd been too interested in the regularity with which every damn woman in the place was hitting on him.

"Someone should probably take his keys so he doesn't try to drive in that condition," Juliette said.

All eyes turned to Fiona, who shook her head. "You're the chief of police, Colton."

"Yeah, but we have a working relationship that I'd rather not undermine if I don't have to."

"Steve, you're the surgeon who would probably get called in to put him back together if anything happened. Consider it preventive medicine."

"He doesn't like me. The one time we met, he was antagonistic. Hostile." He grinned slyly. "Jealous. He came into Katy's room at the hospital and saw me with my arm around Fiona. He didn't like it one bit, did he?"

Her face burning, Fiona tried to deny it. "He wasn't jealous. He was just...short-tempered. He thought he was going back to Washington that day and instead he got stuck here. That was all."

"He was jealous," Steve insisted. "Trust me. I know the look."

"That leaves you, Fi," Juliette said, barely able to contain her smile. "And it looks like he's getting ready to leave now."

Fiona looked to see Justin slide unsteadily to his feet. He laid some money on the bar, apparently told the bartender to keep the change, then picked up his overcoat and, on second try, slid one arm into the sleeve. Scowling around the table, she stood up, pulled on her own coat, slung her purse over her shoulder and warned, ''You guys will pay for this. I promise you.''

She crossed the few yards to the bar, caught hold of the overcoat and guided Justin's left arm into the sleeve. He pulled it on, then turned and stopped in midthanks. ''I appre— You.''

''Yeah, it's me. Give me your keys.''

''I don't need your help. I can make it home just fine.''

''If you don't give me your keys, I'm going to call Colton Stuart over here to take them from you. Don't embarrass him and yourself.''

He studied her a moment, apparently decided she was serious and pulled his keys from his pocket. She slid them into her own pocket, then gestured. ''The door's that way.''

''I'm slightly intoxicated. Not blind or stupid.''

''I don't know. You were planning to drive home slightly intoxicated. That's pretty damn stupid.'' She followed him across the bar and outside into the cold night. ''Where are you parked?''

He looked up and down the street. ''In the lot around back, I guess.''

They walked around the building and searched the full lot for his rental car. It wasn't there. He looked perplexed, then shrugged as if it didn't matter. ''Maybe I left it somewhere. Give me my keys and I'll walk home. You can go back in with your friends.''

''I'll walk with you,'' she said dryly.

''I don't need a chaperone. I can hold my liquor just fine. If there's one thing we Reeds do well, it's drink.''

She didn't doubt it. If she'd been drinking fairly steadily for the last few hours, she would have passed out an hour ago. Other than a slight unsteadiness in his gait and a haze shadowing his eyes, he didn't appear drunk at all. He could easily convince anyone he was merely fatigued unless they got close enough to smell the booze on his breath.

They walked a block or so in silence before she said, "Katy's CT scan was perfectly normal."

"I know. I persuaded a hospital clerk with access to a computer to tell me." He grinned. "Little eighteen-, nineteen-year-old girls tend to be susceptible to my charm and intimidated by my badge."

"You're not as charming as you think you are."

"You only say that because I haven't tried to charm you. Where is Katy?"

"Spending the night with my mom."

"And that was the best you could do on a Friday night? Going out for a hamburger with two married couples?"

"You have every Friday night free, and this was the best you could do? Getting drunk alone in a cowboy bar?"

"I was alone because I wanted to be."

"I noticed."

He gave her a long look. "Why?"

"Why what?"

"Why did you notice? Why were you watching me?"

She sighed impatiently. "I wasn't watching you. You just happened to be in my field of vision. When my friends were dancing, I had nothing else to do but watch."

"You could have danced, too. You had plenty of offers."

"How do you know?" She'd never caught him looking, had never felt his attention on her.

"There was a mirror behind the bar."

"If you were going to watch, you should have come over and joined us. You would have had a better view."

"Or maybe you should have come over and joined me. Unlike those other women, I wouldn't have turned you down."

There was nothing suggestive in his tone, Fiona told herself. It was just talk, nothing more. Deliberately she distracted herself with a purely business question. "Am I allowed to ask how your case is going? If you've uncovered anything new on your suspect?"

"I found out where he buried the ammo can, and I got a report back from the lab that matches the blasting caps to the caps Watkins used in previous bombs. Now I'm waiting for an okay from my boss on my plan."

"What plan?"

"To draw him back here. Using the jewels."

"You think he'll come back to steal them again?"

"I don't think he'll be able to resist the challenge."

"And when he shows up, you'll be waiting."

"Yup."

She didn't think she'd ever heard him say *yup* before. It sounded incongruous. "Why don't you take the jewels back to Washington and let him steal them there?"

His jaw tightened, and his mouth thinned. "Are you so anxious to get rid of me, Fiona? I'm just trying to do my damned job. I've stayed away like you wanted. What more can I do?"

"You haven't stayed away because I told you to," she disagreed, remembering the contempt he'd shown her Thursday morning. It still caused a sharp pain dead center in her chest. "You stayed away because you wanted to."

He'd been so angry the last time they'd talked—angry enough to hit the door, bitter enough to walk out and not come back—and she didn't even know why. Yes, she'd accused him of lying about not getting her phone message six years ago, but she'd said worse things and drawn less of a response. She didn't understand why this insult had been different.

Rather than frustrate herself trying to figure it out, instead she explained her question. "I have no problem with you doing your job, Justin. It's just... That man *hurt* m—our daughter. I don't want him coming back here. I don't want him even in the same state with her."

"He doesn't have any interest in people. She's the only one who's ever been injured by his explosives. He likes the thrill of watching things go up, of destroying rich people's property. He doesn't know Katy exists and couldn't care less. She'll be safe."

"Are you sure?"

"I give you my word…for whatever that's worth."

Last time it hadn't been worth much. He'd broken every promise he'd made her and, in the process, destroyed her faith. Should she trust him again? Could she?

They turned onto their block and, a moment later, onto her sidewalk. He walked with her up the steps and to the door. After unlocking it, she returned her keys to her bag, then faced him. She didn't have a clue what to say. *It was a lovely, if chilly, walk? I had a nice time? Come in for some coffee?* "Well…"

"Can I have my keys?"

"Your keys?"

He came closer, too close, and reached in her coat pocket to retrieve the key chain. Then he moved closer still, until his coat brushed hers, until his breath was warm on her cheek, and he brushed one hand lightly over her hair. "You know, for a long time, I dated only redheads, because they reminded me of you. And for a longer time, I couldn't even look at a redhead, because they reminded me of you. Giving you up almost killed me, Fiona."

She couldn't breathe, couldn't think, couldn't argue that he hadn't given her up—he'd thrown her away. She couldn't do anything but shiver and close her eyes when his fingertips touched her cheek, and curl her hands into tight fists so she wouldn't push him away. So she wouldn't pull him nearer and never let go.

His mouth followed his fingers, touching her cheek, her jaw, then her lips. Against her will she opened to him. Helplessly she welcomed his tongue, tasted him, remembered him. Six years, and everything had changed, but not this. Just his hands could make her tremble. Just his kiss could make her weak. And hot. Hungry, greedy, needy.

His tongue stroked inside her mouth as his hands found

their way inside her coat, underneath her sweater. He kneaded her breasts, played with her nipples, made them swell and ache. He was swollen, too, pressing long and hot and hard against her abdomen, rubbing, tantalizing, sending tiny little shocks through her.

One of them had the presence of mind to open the door—him, she thought dazedly—and to maneuver them both inside. Their coats hit the floor, and they made it as far as the sofa, where he lowered her down, then immediately followed, sliding between her thighs, grinding his arousal hard against her, stirring both pleasure and pain, satisfaction and hunger.

She was mindless with sensation that arched her body against his, with fever that heated her blood, with a desperate fear that she just might die if she didn't feel him inside her in the next instant. Her hands moved frantically, unbuckling his belt, unfastening his trousers, sliding inside to cradle him in her palms. He was so strong, so hard, and she wanted…needed…

His groan was harsh and guttural. ''Ah, damn, Fiona, baby, let me…'' He unfastened her jeans, the rasp of the zipper as loud as the rasp of their breathing. It sent a cold shiver through her and brought her back to her senses, made her realize how close they were to something they couldn't back away from, something that well might break her heart again.

''No,'' she whispered, jerking her hands free. ''No, no, no.'' She wriggled out from beneath him, landed on the floor, jumped to her feet and backed away, staring at him in the dim light. ''I—I can't—I can't do this. I can't—''

Looking stunned and disappointed, he stood up. ''Why not? You obviously want it. I obviously want it. The sex wasn't the problem between us. It was always good.''

The sex. The matter-of-fact phrase and the tone in which he'd spoken made her want to cry. ''It *was* part of the problem,'' she whispered, hating that her voice was so quavery.

"I thought we were making love, and you were just having sex."

Justin gave her an impatient look, his nerves taut with frustration. This wasn't the time to argue semantics. She could call it anything she wanted. The only thing he would call it was vital. He wanted to be inside her, filling her, giving her all she could take and more—wanted it more at that moment than air to breathe. He wanted the passion, the intensity, the incredible satisfaction he'd always found inside her.

But he wasn't going to get it tonight.

He zipped his pants and buckled his belt, then flatly asked, "What do you want from me, Fiona?"

"Six years ago I wanted everything."

"And I gave you nothing. I'm sorry. I'm so damned sorry. But what do you want now?"

"I don't know," she whispered, and he believed her. She looked too distraught to be hedging. "Wh-what do you want?"

You. In his bed for sure, maybe in his life. Provided she could ever forgive him. He wanted to be part of Katy's life. He wanted to be part of their family. He wanted... "A chance."

"To do what?"

To make up for what he'd done? To prove himself worthy of her trust? He wasn't sure either were possible. "To show you that I can be a good father to Katy."

A wounded look came into her eyes, and she visibly stiffened. "I...see. Well... Naturally, no one would be happier to see that happen than me. She deserves a good fath—"

He walked to her, made her retreat until the wall was at her back. Bringing his body into full contact with hers, he planted his hands on either side of her head and bent close. "And I want you, Fiona. I want to make love to you. I want to kiss you all over, and make you moan and whimper and plead. I want *you,* and it's got nothing to do with wanting to be a good father to our daughter. I'd want you if Katy didn't exist, and I'd want Katy if you left me cold.''

He kissed her again, thrusting his tongue into her mouth, and she gave one of those helpless little erotic moans that did strange things to him. He could seduce her, could overcome her worries and hesitations—that little moan told him so—but as badly as he wanted her, he didn't want her that way. She couldn't accuse him later of taking advantage of her.

When his need was fierce, when her entire body trembled, he forced himself away. Her eyes fluttered open, and she stared at him. She looked aroused. Confused. Relieved.

Moment after moment passed as they studied each other. When he reached out to brush a strand of hair from her face, she tensed—not because she didn't want him to touch her, but because she did. He knew that instinctively. She wanted him. She just didn't want to want him.

Stepping back, he shoved his hands into his pockets. ''Should I go home now?''

''I—I can fix some coffee,'' she offered, her voice unsteady.

''How about some hot chocolate?''

''I can do that, too, though it may have to be the instant kind.''

He grinned ruefully. ''Is there any other?''

She led the way to the kitchen, regaining her composure with each step. By the time the milk was heating on the stove, she looked as if the grope on the couch hadn't happened. Except that her nipples were still visible under her sweater and her cheeks were pinker than usual and her mouth looked extraordinarily well kissed.

And though he sat at the table as if everything were perfectly normal, he was still extraordinarily hard.

''Have you had anything to eat tonight?''

He thought about it a moment, then shook his head.

''How about a tuna salad sandwich?''

His stomach tilted at the thought. "How about something less fishy?"

"I have oatmeal cookies, banana nut bread, bagels..." Her smile was apologetic. "Tomorrow's grocery day. The cupboard's a bit bare."

"I think I can handle banana nut bread."

She unwrapped a foil packet on the counter, cut several thick slices and put them in the toaster oven before taking butter and cream cheese from the refrigerator and plates from the cabinets, and he watched her every move. There was something damned satisfying about the scene—something sweet. Familial.

Something he was finding he wanted more and more.

Removing his suit coat, he hung it on the back of a chair, then slumped comfortably in his own chair. As he settled in, his gaze landed on a photograph on the wall. It was Katy, as were most of the photos in the house, this time in a baseball uniform. In spite of it, she looked fragile and perfectly feminine.

"Were you a tomboy?"

Fiona set two mugs of steaming cocoa on the table and gave him a curious look. "Not particularly." Then she followed his gaze to the photo. "No, she didn't get her jock genes from me. Who knows where they came from?"

Justin managed to scowl at her, but it wasn't very intimidating. "I'll have you know, I run five miles every day, and I've lifted my share of weights."

"And here I thought all your workouts took place in the bedroom."

"Not many. Not since..."

"Since what?"

He shrugged. "You."

She hadn't expected that answer. It heightened the color in her cheeks and made her voice husky. "I'd be flattered—if I believed you."

"You could believe me if you'd try." Because she looked

uncomfortable, he changed the subject. "Do you have other pictures of Katy?"

"Only about a million of 'em." After leaving the table, she disappeared into the living room, then returned with an armload of albums. She set them down, slid her chair closer to his and opened the top one. "Here's the first picture ever of her. She's about two hours old. Isn't she beautiful?"

He agreed, though she was, in fact, wrinkled and red, with a disgruntled and disoriented look on her face. But the mother who held her was unquestionably beautiful, even if her hair was limp and exhaustion lined her face and shadowed her eyes. She looked so happy and awed, and he felt so…cheated. But he had no one to blame but himself.

Long after the banana bread and the cocoa were gone, they still sat at the table, flipping through albums. There were shots of Katy's first Christmas and every one that followed, her birthday parties, her Halloween costumes, her frilly Easter dresses, her softball games, her first day of kindergarten. His daughter's life, in four-by-six-inch color.

When Fiona closed the final album, he rubbed his eyes. Fatigue was setting in, from the past few restless nights or the overindulgence in booze or maybe from seeing secondhand the life he'd missed out on. He was coming to regret it more than he could say.

"You look tired."

He nodded.

"We should have stopped at her second birthday and saved the rest for later." She rubbed one hand possessively over the album. "I just assume everyone wants to share every event in her life."

"I did want to. I asked you, remember?" Rising from his chair, he stretched, then carried their dishes to the sink. "You're a good mother, Fiona. Katy's lucky to have you."

"I—" Disconcerted, she managed a tremulous smile. "Thank you. That means a lot."

"Whatever happens, I would never try to take her from

you.'' Hours after finding out the truth, he'd brought up the possibility—*What if I want custody of her?*—but he hadn't been serious. He could never take Katy from her mother or the family who adored her. He wanted Fiona to know that.

''Thank you. That means a lot, too.'' She walked to the front door with him, hands behind her back, looking younger and shyer than he'd ever been in his life. She bent to pick up their coats, but he was quicker, handing hers over, putting his on.

''Tomorrow...'' Taking a deep breath so she wouldn't have to stop even for air, she charged ahead. ''Saturday is family day for Katy and me. We go out to lunch and see a movie or go for a drive or hike into the mountains—whatever she wants to do. Then we rent a video—also her choice—and have hot dogs for supper and popcorn with the movie. Would you... If you'd like to join us for any or all of it...''

His answer came immediately, without hesitation. ''Yes.'' To be included in their family for even one day, he would sit through every kids' movie ever made. But the answer came with its own question, one he was hesitant to ask. Fortunately she offered an answer without prompting.

''I should warn you that some people know it's family day. If you're with us, they'll think there's something between us, or they might even guess that you're the mystery father.''

''They'd be right on both counts, wouldn't they?''

''There...*was* something between us, obviously,'' she said awkwardly.

''And still is. Don't make me prove it, darlin', because this time I might not stop until I've seduced you or embarrassed myself.'' He took a few steps toward the door, then turned back. ''Can I kiss you good night?''

''Do you think that's wise?''

''Absolutely. I think kissing you might be the smartest thing I've ever done.''

Her hazel gaze searched his face before she hesitantly nodded. He slowly backed her against the wall, lazily brushed her hair from her face, teasingly drew his fingertip across her mouth. She was expecting another seriously hot kiss, all tongues and hunger and heavy breathing. What he gave her was sweet, innocent, his mouth against hers. No tongues, no gropes, no grinding hips. Just a chaste kiss that could consume them both.

"Good night, Fiona," he murmured when he was finished.

Her eyes opened slowly. She swallowed hard, then touched her lips gently, as if they tingled. "Good night," she whispered.

Before he could decide he really needed one more chance to change her mind, he walked out of the house and into the cold night. The last three days might have been pretty grim, he thought as he crossed the yard, but all things considered, tonight had turned out pretty damn well, and tomorrow would be even better.

As he let himself into his aunt's house, he smiled faintly. If there was one thing Reeds were, it was optimistic. There was always another fortune, a younger or richer spouse or a wilier divorce lawyer just around the corner. He'd never cared about fortunes, trading one spouse for another or divorces. He just wanted a family, and tomorrow, for one day, he was going to be a part of one.

And he was thinking seriously about making the situation permanent.

It was snowing Saturday morning when Fiona settled at the living-room window. She'd been up for hours, had cleaned house, done laundry and bought groceries, and now she was curled up in an armchair with a cup of hot cocoa and watching the street for Delores and Katy, and the snow—and Golda's house. Justin's rental car was in the driveway once more. She wondered if he'd remembered where he'd left it or located it on his morning run, and if he was hungover this morning, and if he'd slept well or regretted, as she did, that he'd slept alone.

She wondered if it was true that he hadn't been with many women since her, and that he would want her even if Katy wasn't his daughter, and exactly how sorry he was about dumping her. Sorry that he'd missed out on Katy's growing up, sure. But was he sorry that he'd missed being with *her?* Sorry that he'd broken her heart? Sorry that she'd needed him and he hadn't been there?

Her sigh sounded forlorn in the silence of the house. She picked up the remote control and turned on the television, flipping through the channels before settling on a cooking show. The volume was just loud enough to chase away the emptiness of the house, but not loud enough to provide a serious distraction. She'd gone through a long period after Justin had left six years ago when the only voice heard in the house was her own, usually sobbing. She'd known him only ten days, but he'd filled her house, her life and her heart so completely that she'd feared she wouldn't survive without him.

Love at first sight. It was a joke, romantic foolishness, fantasy—and yet that was exactly what she'd felt. Oh, not on first sight, of course, but she'd known she was going to love him forever within hours of meeting him.

But she'd been wrong. She hadn't loved him forever. It had just felt like it.

Now she was in danger of falling in love with him again. The attraction was there. The need. The tender memories. But things were different this time. She wasn't a naive young woman willing to believe every pretty thing he said. She had Katy to consider, and just as many bitter memories as tender ones.

Last time she'd rushed into their romance with no concern at all for the risks. This time she knew the risks well and intended to protect herself—and Katy.

Slowly her gaze focused on three figures walking down the sidewalk toward the middle of the block. They were bundled against the cold and moved at a leisurely pace, as if it were a sunny summer day. Setting her cocoa aside, Fiona stepped into her shoes, grabbed a coat and gloves from the closet and went outside to meet them in Justin's driveway. "Mom, Dad." She brushed kisses to their ruddy cheeks, then scooped Katy into her arms. "Hey, baby doll. Did you miss me?"

Katy nodded.

"I missed you, too. See?" Fiona held out one arm to indicate the snow. "I cried because I was lonely, and the tears went all the way up to heaven and came back down as snow."

Katy smiled faintly before laying her head on Fiona's shoulder.

"How was she?"

Delores shrugged. "Fine. The boys got on her nerves a bit. Heavens, they got on *my* nerves a bit, with all that yelling and jumping and 'rasslin'. So Grandpa took Katy-bug in the bedroom for a few bedtime stories while I got the rascals settled in." Then her mother's eyes lit up. "Did you go out with your friends last night?"

"Yes, Ma."

"Did you have a good time?"

"Yes, Mom, I did."

"Did you dance with any handsome cowboys?"

"No cowboys, and no dances." Unless she counted the prelude to the horizontal tango on the couch with Justin.

"What are your plans for today?" her father asked before Delores could bemoan her daughter's determination to have no fun.

"The usual. Lunch, Katy's choice of afternoon activities, hot dogs, popcorn and a movie." Fiona hesitated, then said, "I asked Justin to join us."

Her mother beamed. Her father's mouth tightened. "Do

you think that's a good idea—letting him see all he wants of Katy?''

Delores smacked his shoulder with one gloved hand. ''He *is* her father, Griff. I let you see all you wanted of our three when they were little.''

''Yes, but I married you before the first one was born.''

''But you had the advantage of knowing she was pregnant.'' Justin's voice came from behind Fiona and made her jump guiltily. Red-faced, she turned to see him standing a few yards away in jeans and a sweatshirt, no jacket, and holding a bag of trash in his hand. He looked rested, and his eyes were clear. No hangover, and apparently no erotic dreams disturbing his sleep and making his night a restless one. Darn.

He dropped the trash bag into Golda's battered metal can, replaced the lid and joined them. ''Hey, Kate.'' He touched her cheek in an affectionate gesture. She smiled sweetly at him, then snuggled closer to Fiona.

''Good morning, Justin,'' Delores said.

''Good morning, Mrs. Lake, Mr. Lake.''

''Oh, please, call me Delores, and you can call Griff—'' Apparently remembering that he'd always called Fiona's dad Mr. Lake, she broke off. ''Fiona was telling us that she invited you to be a part of family day.''

''Yes, she did, and I accepted.''

Fiona was wishing she hadn't come out to meet her family or had at least had the sense to move them on over to her house when Justin shifted his attention back to her father. ''If I'd known Fiona was pregnant, I would have come back. I would have married her immediately.''

His words annoyed her no end, and she gave him a stiff, haughty look to let him know. ''You're assuming that I would have forgiven you and married you.''

Finally he looked at her, utterly confident. ''You would have. Right up until the time she was born, if I had come back and said I was sorry, you would have forgiven everything.''

She had told him that at the hospital Tuesday morning—had told him more. *But you didn't come, and you broke my heart for the second time. I swore I would never let it happen again.* Had he listened to that part, too?

''You know now,'' Griff said sternly. ''What do you intend to do about it?''

''Dad!''

''The boy's got responsibilities now. I want to know if he's going to live up to them.''

''Yes, sir, I am.'' Justin's voice was even, cool.

''Then you've proposed to her.''

Not so even or cool this time. ''Well...no, sir, I haven't.'' When Griff harrumphed, spots of color appeared in Justin's cheeks. ''I intend to fulfill my responsibilities.''

''How? By giving my daughter money to stay away?'' Griff snorted. ''Rich kid like you, giving money's not fulfilling your obligations. It's buying your way out of trouble.''

''Dad!'' Fiona exclaimed again. ''Mom, please—!''

''Now, Griff,'' Delores started, but Justin interrupted her.

''I intend to be a father to my daughter.''

''And how do you intend to do that when she's here in Grand Springs and you're back in Washington?''

''I haven't decided that yet. Probably by moving to Grand Springs.''

Fiona's parents were staring at him openmouthed, and she was, too. It wasn't the first time he'd mentioned staying in town. That first night after he'd learned the truth, he'd asked, *What if I want to stay here? Live next door? See Katy every day? You won't object to that?* But she hadn't thought...

Finally Griff harrumphed again, but before he could say anything else, Delores slipped her arm through his. ''Come on, darlin', let's go home and let the kids get going.''

''But I still have questions to ask.''

"They'll just have to wait. If you want your little girl to ever get *m-a-r-r-i-e-d* so you can have more grand-*b-a-b-i-e-s,* let's go away and let them handle things for themselves."

"Ma, we're both college graduates," Fiona said impatiently. "We can spell."

"Well, of course you can, darlin'. Come along now, Griff. They don't need us." Delores pulled Katy's suitcase from his hand, gave it to Justin, then turned Griff around and headed for home. "See you later, kids. Have fun today."

Shaking her head exasperatedly, Fiona put Katy down, tucked her suitcase into her hands and gave her a push toward the house. "Go on inside, baby, and see if there are any cartoons on." She watched until the closing door hid Katy from sight, then turned back to Justin. "There are advantages to being estranged from your parents."

"No, there aren't."

"If you never see them, then they can't embarrass you."

"My parents don't have to be on the same continent with me to embarrass me."

After an awkward moment, she said, "My father didn't mean anything—"

"Yes, he did. I don't blame him. No bastard's ever going to get the chance to do to Katy what I did to you."

"You think you can stop her from having sex before she's married?" Fiona's skepticism was heavy as she shook her head. "The only way my father could have stopped me from having sex with you was to lock me away until you were gone. Maybe it's easier for mothers to understand that children have to be free to make their own mistakes. That's how they learn. It's how they grow up."

His blue eyes darkened with shadows until they seemed almost black. "And making love with me was your mistake."

Last night he'd called it sex. Were the words interchangeable to him—merely different names for the same act? Or did he truly understand the difference?

"No," she replied quietly. "Making love with you wasn't my mistake. If I hadn't, I wouldn't have Katy, and she's the greatest treasure in my life. Falling in love with you—that's where I went wrong. That's what cost me."

After staring at her a moment, he combed his fingers through his hair, dislodging snowflakes. "Do you know how it feels when the only person you've ever had a normal, healthy relationship with tells you it was a mistake?"

The wistful, hurt look in his eyes tugged at her heart. If that relationship had been with any other woman in the world, she would sympathize with him—say she was sorry, but hey, he'd find someone new. But it hadn't been any other woman whose heart was broken. "Probably almost as bad as when the only person you've ever loved says he'll call you but never does. Says he'll come back to you, but never does that, either. Says he'll love you forever, when he never loved you at all."

He folded his arms over his chest. The posture looked defensive, but in reality, she suspected, he was just trying to generate some heat. She was pretty frozen herself, and she was dressed for the cold. "I loved you, Fiona," he said flatly, intensely. "If you never believe anything else about me, believe that."

"I wish I could," she said, and she meant it with all her heart. "But words are easy, Justin. Following through with your actions—that's the real proof." And his actions hadn't supported his words.

"Easy? You know how many people I've said those words to in my life? Two. You and Golda." His tone turned bitter. "And apparently she didn't believe them any more than you do."

She let him take a dozen steps toward the house before she spoke again. "Sometime why don't you try saying them to your daughter?"

He gave her a look that was surprised and fearful. ''You wouldn't mind?''

''Little kids need to hear often that they're loved. Otherwise, they might grow into adults who have trouble following through.'' She paused a moment, then finished. ''Why don't you come over when you're ready, and we'll go to lunch. We'll get this family day show on the road.''

Chapter 8

Family day, Fiona had neglected to tell Justin, included a nap time for Katy. After two hours on the ice at the skating rink, he was more than happy to carry her upstairs and settle her in bed. He removed her shoes, pulled a sheet over her and, for a moment, simply looked at her. With eyes so like his own, she looked back solemnly before pointing.

"What do you want, Kate?"

Raising onto one arm, she leaned past him to point again. There was a bookcase back there, filled with books and games, a lamp and several music boxes, as well as an overflowing toy chest.

"You want the lamp on?"

She shook her head.

"Want to play a game?"

Another shake.

"You want some music? Want to read a story?"

Grinning, she nodded.

He picked out a book and leaned against the bed frame. Before he'd reached the first page, though, she tugged his arm, then scooted over and patted the mattress. ''You want me to come up there?''

Another nod.

The bed was sturdy enough, though he couldn't begin to say how foolish he felt climbing up to stretch out in a tree-house bed to read silly poems. But he'd never done many foolish things in his life. He was entitled.

With a pillow under his head and Katy's small body pressed to his side, he began reading. Even when her soft snores punctuated the words, he continued a few pages further before laying the book aside. He watched her for a while before raising his gaze to the cloud-studded ceiling.

He wasn't sure exactly when the decision had been made, but he was staying in Grand Springs. His job with the ATF was great and he liked it a lot, but it couldn't compete with spending an afternoon with his daughter and her mother. Nothing in his life could compete with the possibility of creating a family with them. If he could persuade Fiona that he was worth having. Worth trusting. Worth forgiving.

He didn't have a clue how to go about it.

So maybe she could help him, he thought as she came into the room with a stack of neatly folded clothes. She smiled when she saw them side by side and softly said, ''Let me get a picture of you lying there. You could send it to your folks.''

''Harrison and Amelia aren't 'folks,''' he said absently, then changed the subject. ''Have you ever slept in the tree house?''

''Nope.''

''It's not bad. Come on up. Give it a try.''

''There's not room.''

''You can lie on top of me. I won't complain.'' He watched her roll her eyes even as spots of color appeared in her cheeks.

''No such talk in front of the child.''

"The child's snoring like a lumberjack. She must get that from your side of the family."

"What? Reeds don't snore?"

"No, ma'am. It's forbidden." He raised his hand to the railing where hers rested and touched just one fingertip to her fingers. "As I recall, your room is just a short distance down the hall. The child is sleeping too soundly to hear a peep—or a moan, or a single 'Damn, Justin, that was fantastic.'"

"Damn, Justin, I don't think so." She pulled her hand back and started out the door.

Carefully he worked free of Katy, slid down the ladder and followed her. She was coming out of her bedroom with a laundry basket when he blocked her way. "Can you imagine a more pleasant way to spend a few hours?"

"I have quite an imagination."

"I remember. Or should I say I don't remember so you'll remind me?"

Her only response was a cool smile.

"Okay, then tell me this. What do I have to do to get invited in there—" he gestured toward the bedroom behind her "—with you?"

"Catch me in a weak moment." She pushed forward, and the laundry basket hit him in the middle. He took it from her, backed up so she could get by, then followed her to the bathroom, holding it while she put away the towels it held. When that was done, she took the basket, dropped it to the floor in the linen closet, then waited expectantly.

He led the way downstairs and back to the kitchen, where she started fixing a pan of brownies, one of Katy's special treats. He leaned against the counter and watched her so intently for so long that at last she put the wooden spoon down and faced him. "Were you— You were serious up there, weren't you?"

He raised one hand as if giving an oath. "My parents aren't even remotely similar to 'folks,' the bed's not uncomfortable considering it's in a tree house, to my knowledge Katy's the only Reed who snores, and yes, I seriously want to know what I have to do to get back into your—'' taking a glance at her face, he changed words without a hitch ''—good graces.''

Her cheeks turned crimson, and an annoyed look slipped across her face. But she wasn't annoyed, he realized. She was flustered. ''You mean you want to have sex with me.''

''I do. And make love with you. And—''

''You understand there's a difference?'' she asked sharply.

He feigned hurt feelings. ''Of course I do. I've had sex with women for no reason other than that I was lonely or they reminded me of you. But you're the only woman I've ever made love with, and I want to do it again. I want—''

Last night, when she'd frozen up on him and left him aching on the couch, he'd asked her what she wanted from him. Six years ago I wanted everything, she'd said. He was six years late, but that was what he wanted, too—the passion, the connection, the emotion, the commitment. Everything.

''You want what?''

He opened his arms wide to encompass the house around them. ''To be a part of all this. A part of your family. A part of your life. So tell me, Fiona, have I got a chance, and what do I have to do?''

''This is ridiculous. You can't just decide that you want to share someone's family. Things don't happen that way.''

''Six years ago we decided that we would have a family of our own, remember? And now our little girl is asleep upstairs dreaming of whatever little girls dream of.''

She opened a drawer for a spatula, then pointed it in his direction. ''Yes, six years ago we decided to have a family. And a few days later, *you* decided to not be a part of that family. You decided I didn't deserve an explanation, or a chance to change your mind, or even a 'Go to hell, Fiona,

I don't want you anymore.' And now you've decided— What? Maybe you made a mistake back then? That if you have to be a father to your daughter, you might as well get something from her mother, too?''

This time the hurt wasn't feigned. He studied her for one long, quiet moment after another before finally asking, ''You have a lot of anger toward me, don't you?''

She tried to scrape the brownie batter from the bowl into the pan, but her hands were trembling too badly. He gently pried the spatula from her clenched fingers, pulled the bowl free and completed the task, then pushed it all aside.

Fiona breathed heavily. ''I guess I do. No one has ever hurt me the way you did. Those ten days with you were incredible. They turned my life upside down. And then you destroyed it all—my dreams, my hopes, my love, *me.* The only thing that saved me was Katy. I had to pull myself together for her sake. If I hadn't gotten pregnant, I don't know how I would have survived.''

''It was hard for me, too.''

''How could it have been? It was *your* choice. You didn't want me anymore, and so you cut me out of your life without a second thought.''

''I never stopped wanting you, Fiona. I just didn't believe I could have you.''

After putting the brownies in the oven, she moved to the other side of the island and gave him a look that was part perplexed but mostly suspicious. ''You did have me. You chose to dump me.''

''That's not what happened.''

''Then tell me, Justin. What did happen?''

He turned to look out the kitchen window. The snow was still falling—hadn't slowed all day. The fresh earth where Katy had uncovered the ammo can a week ago was covered completely. Except for the swing set and lumps where a few of her toys were, the yard was smooth, unsullied white. He wished all the mistakes of his life could be made to disappear as easily, but he lived with them, faced them every day.

"I told you my parents are overachievers in the frequent-marriage department. Time after time I watched them fall madly in love, usually about ten minutes after they met the person, and time after time I watched them after the wedding, trying to figure out who these people were and what they were doing married. It didn't take me long to realize that love didn't last and marriages made in haste ended the same way. I intended to learn from their mistakes. I swore I would never get suckered into the same sort of impulsive, disastrous entanglements they were known around the world for.

"And then I met you." He said it softly, remembering the sweetness, the innocence, of it all. He'd been about a hundred years younger, and he'd had his share of affairs, but not one single serious relationship. He hadn't believed in love at first sight—hadn't believed in love at all. Just lust, short-term companionship, good sex and nothing more.

But when he'd met Fiona, he'd fallen hard and fast. He hadn't even cared that he was making exactly the same mistake his parents always made.

"When I was here with you, anything seemed possible—falling in love, getting married, living happily-ever-after." Fairy-tale words, when he'd never been given a chance to believe in fairy tales. "But the minute I got on that airplane, the doubts set in. I had a lifetime of proof that our kind of affair couldn't last, and no reason to believe it could. I couldn't risk the inevitable breakup. I couldn't face the comparisons to my parents. And so I got out, before I got in any deeper. I convinced myself that it had all been an illusion, just a vacation romance that was doomed from the start. I told myself it was lust, not love. After all, if there's one thing Reeds know nothing about, it's love."

He glanced over his shoulder at her, but couldn't read anything on her face. Her gaze was directed away from him, and her expression was carefully blank. He turned to face her, to watch her so carefully avoid him. ''I know I should have talked to you, but the truth is, I was afraid. If I had picked up the phone, I would have begged you to change my mind. To convince me that it could last, that I really could love someone, that someone really could love me.''

''All you had to do was take a chance.''

''And risk finding out that it *wasn't* real? That, like my mother and father, I'm not capable of loving anyone? That no one is capable of loving me?'' He shook his head. ''I couldn't take that chance.''

''So it was better to pretend it was nothing and go on with life as usual—alone.''

He smiled bleakly. ''I've always been alone, Fiona. When you have all that experience at it, it's not so bad.''

With that one sad smile and those few simple words, he broke her heart for the third time. Fiona wanted nothing more than to curl up someplace private and dark and cry for the loneliness he'd endured, for the harm his parents had done him, for the hurt they—through him—had caused her.

Golda's last wish for Justin, written into her will, slipped into Fiona's mind, whispered in her old friend's grandmotherly voice and directed this time to her instead of Justin. *Mistakes can be set right, forgiveness is vital, and love is possible. Trust yourself. Trust your heart.*

She'd trusted her heart once, and she'd suffered for it. What if she tried again? Could she survive another betrayal?

Maybe a better question was could she live her life expecting another betrayal. Expect the worst, the saying went, and that was certainly one way to live. But wasn't it a sad way?

He pushed away from the counter and came to stand in front of her, one hand covering hers where it rested on the island. ''I'll go home now,'' he said quietly, a grim set to his features.

Maybe the wisest action—for herself, at least—would be

to let him go. She didn't take the time to debate the issue, but turned her hand to catch his when he started to leave. "Hey, I'm not watching two hours of talking dinosaurs with Katy by myself, especially when you cast the winning vote for the dinos over the talking pooches. Besides, I'm still considering an answer to your question."

"What question?"

"What you have to do to get back in my...good graces." Her tentative smile disappeared as she twined her fingers through his. "Please stay, Justin."

He brought his other hand up to lightly touch her hair. "I was right about one thing back then. You deserved better than me."

She shook her head. "I deserved you. We were so good together. It could have been damn near perfect."

"If I hadn't screwed things up." He smiled thinly. "That's what we Reeds do."

"Hey, I've only known three Reeds, but I've loved all of them dearly. Knock off the disparaging of their name, would you?" When the oven timer started to beep, she pulled away, removed the brownies to a rack to cool, then took two sodas from the refrigerator. "Come sit in the living room. Let's talk."

"That sounds ominous."

She took his hand and pulled him behind her through the dining room and into the living room. There she sat at one end of the sofa while he settled at the other. "It's not ominous. I just think we need to discuss a few things."

"Like what?"

"This morning you told my father you might stay here. Did you mean it?"

Regret hardened his features. "Is this the price I've got to pay for breaking my promises to you before? You're going to doubt everything I say for the rest of our lives?"

Our lives. Simple words. Didn't mean a thing. Just easier than saying your life and my life. But she had to admit that, deep down inside, some wistful, lonely, romantic part of her liked the sound of it a lot. *Our lives. Our daughter. Our future.*

Maybe, someday, *Our love.*

"Yes," he went on. "I meant it. Once I catch Patrick Watkins and see that he's punished for what he did to Katy, I'm turning in my badge and credentials and moving here. Does that annoy you?"

She imagined living with the knowledge that he was right next door, that he would be there next month and next year and every day for the next fifty years. She pictured Katy's birthdays with Justin there, Easters and Thanksgivings and Christmases with Justin in their midst. She considered the comfort in knowing that he was right there to help with illnesses and homework, with teenage rebellion and first dates, first love and broken hearts.

"No, it doesn't annoy me at all." As long as he never married, never fell in love and never made the commitment to another woman that he hadn't been able to make to her. "I think it would be good for Katy, and for you."

"And what about you? Would having me here be good for you?"

She thought about their kisses last night, and the erotic dreams and memories that had kept her tossing and turning. "I don't know. It depends."

"On what?"

"Whether you catch me in a weak moment."

For a time he looked so serious that she wondered if he'd forgotten her use of that phrase upstairs. Then slowly, smugly, he smiled. "Have you had many weak moments since me?"

"Plenty of 'em—but none of that sort."

He stared at her. "None?"

"I was pregnant for the better part of a year," she said a tad defensively. "I gained a ton of weight, and the only men interested in me were my obstetrician and the anesthesiologist at the delivery. Then I didn't get a good night's sleep until Katy was three, and by then I'd forgotten what sex was."

"Last night you obviously remembered."

Oh, yes, she'd remembered. Unfortunately she'd also remembered what heartache was. Loneliness that ate into your soul. Hurt that sucked the life right out of you. Sorrow that made it tough to get out of bed.

"And you obviously never forgot," she said dryly.

"There were some women," he acknowledged, "but, as I told you, not many. I learned pretty quickly that I couldn't replace you, so I only tried when it was too damn hard to go home alone."

"Gee, here's an absurd idea. If you couldn't replace me, why didn't you come back to me?"

"After six months or so, I figured you'd just as soon shoot me with my own gun as look at me. After three years... Let's face it. When I did come back, you weren't happy to see me. Even now, I'm never quite sure what you're feeling. Sometimes I don't think you know. You're a complicated woman, Fiona."

"I'm not complicated at all," she disagreed. "I want what most people want—family, friends, health, satisfaction. I want to live a rich, full life, and I want Katy to do the same. When I look back at the end of my life, I don't want any regrets."

"Do you have any now?"

"A few. I regret that I didn't make more of an effort to tell you I was pregnant. When I realized that something was wrong between us, I regret that I didn't get on the next plane to Washington and track you down and force you to tell me to my face that you didn't want me anymore."

"I wouldn't have done it," he said quietly, and she believed him. I would have begged you to change my mind, he'd said in the kitchen. He'd wanted to believe in them, but his parents had provided him with so many reasons not to. She could have given him more compelling reasons to believe, but she hadn't. Instead of fighting for him, for them, she'd surrendered with nothing more than a heartbroken whimper. She hadn't demanded an explanation, hadn't camped out on his doorstep or marched into his office. She hadn't even let Golda dump a load of maternal guilt on him.

All because she'd been afraid. Because, like him, she'd been troubled by doubts. But she'd damned him for his doubts, while accepting hers as normal.

"Ah, Justin," she said with a rueful sigh. "Think how different our lives would have been if you'd had more faith or I'd had more courage. Katy could have had two parents to love her. You wouldn't have missed out on her life. We could have had our happily-ever-after."

He took her hand in his, sliding his fingers between hers, pulling her along the couch until she was near enough to rest her head on his shoulder, if she chose. Part of her wanted to, but she didn't. "You think so?" he asked skeptically.

She gave a wistful shake of her head. "As much as I loved you, as much as you…loved me—" his fingers squeezed hers in acknowledgment "—it wasn't enough. If we'd been meant to stay together, if we'd had that forever sort of enduring love, there wouldn't have been any room for doubt. All the fears in the world wouldn't have been able to keep us apart."

"So what was it?"

"Life?" she responded with a shrug.

"Or maybe a prelude to this."

This. A new relationship. A chance to right mistakes, to learn to forgive, to love like committed adults, to trust each other and themselves.

Or maybe his *this* was simpler—a sweet, gentle kiss that spread warmth through her, that made heat curl in her belly and gave her the urge to rub against him and purr with satisfaction.

When he ended the kiss, he was slow to retreat—at least, until a wiry little body maneuvered onto the couch between them and forced them apart. Katy's hair stood on end, her clothes were twisted, and indentations on her cheek showed where she'd pressed against the pillow. Fiona combed her silky dark hair into some order, then lifted her onto her lap. "Hey, babe. Did you have a good nap?"

Katy shook her head crossly.

"Is that because you think you're too big for naps?"

This time she nodded. Unfolding her arms, she thrust out the video they'd picked before ice skating.

"Not until after supper, so why don't we get the hot dogs cooking now? You know your job." Fiona watched Katy wriggle to the floor, then race for the kitchen, before smiling at Justin. "Welcome to Parenting 101. Small children can actually hear their parents' hormones heating up—the little sizzle, the heavy breathing—"

"Those incredibly erotic sounds you make."

Her cheeks flushed. "I understand from Juliette that it's actually enough to awaken a child from a sound sleep."

"So you're saying if I want to actually seduce you, I should call Delores first. But if I just want to play with you and torment the hell out of myself, I can do that anytime." He grinned. "It's going to be fun learning how to be a father from you."

"I don't think that was my point," she said as he helped her up, then settled his hands on her shoulders and steered her toward the kitchen. Then again, maybe it had been.

They cooked and ate hot dogs with chili, then cleaned the kitchen. While Justin built a fire in the living room, Fiona and Katy made popcorn and hot chocolate, carried it all on a tray to the coffee table, then settled on the couch while he put in the video. He was about to sit down when Katy grunted and pointed to the lights overhead. He shut them off, sending the room into shadow, then joined them.

Fiona noticed how naturally his arm went around her

shoulders, how easily he accepted Katy on his lap when she decided to move there, how tenderly he held her as she leaned back against his middle. Just like a real family.

Justin wanted to be a real family—at least, that was what he said. What he wanted *now.* She had to believe him, had to trust that whatever happened between her and him, he would never hurt Katy. He would always do what was best for her.

And she wanted to believe him. Wanted to make a family with him, wanted to watch their daughter grow up with him, wanted everything he'd promised her six years ago.

She wanted *him.*

A half hour into the movie, Katy wandered off and returned with an armload of stuffed animals. She used a pillow to prop them up on the floor in front of the TV, then stretched out beside them. Ten minutes later she disappeared again, this time dragging in dolls, a book and the blanket from her bed. When she took off for the third time, Justin bent his head close to Fiona's. "Is this how she normally watchcs movics?"

She shook her head and whispered, "She finds it a little hard to concentrate sometimes since the explosion."

"Hmm. So does her father."

"Want to stop the tape and turn on the lights?"

He pulled her closer and let his hand slide from her shoulder, over the fabric of her shirt, until his fingertips were on her skin above the vee. "What tape?" he murmured, making her shiver when his lips brushed her ear, when his fingers brushed her skin.

It was the first of the twenty or so times she'd seen the talking-dinos movie that she could honestly say she'd hated to see it end.

She hated to see the evening end, too, even if saying goodbye was a very long, drawn-out and intimate process. Once she closed the door behind Justin and locked it, she leaned against it and sighed heavily. She hoped she wasn't making a mistake, hoped he wouldn't break her heart again, hoped that this time they really could have their happily-ever-after.

Because if he hurt her again, this time she might not get over it.

Pushing away from the door, she made a circuit of the first floor to shut off lights and close the fireplace doors. When she went upstairs, she was surprised to see a light on in Katy's room. Justin had carried their daughter to bed more than an hour ago, and they'd both tucked her in. Fiona had kissed her good-night, but he had simply stood beside the bed and looked at her as if she were fragile. Precious. A mystery.

The door Fiona had closed behind them was ajar, the lamp clamped to the head rail for a reading light was on, and Katy lay wide-awake, the stuffed bear Justin had given her clutched in one arm. Fiona rested her arms on the mattress at the top of the ladder and her chin on her arms and studied Katy solemnly. The color of her hair and eyes were the obvious resemblances to her father, but there were others. Her bone structure was similar to his, particularly in the stubborn line of her jaw. Her mouth was shaped like his, which contributed to their grins being nearly identical. Even her hands reminded Fiona of his.

She sighed softly, bittersweetly. "Having trouble sleeping, babe?"

Katy nodded.

"Probably because of that nap you took this afternoon, huh?" Fiona tugged the bear's ear. "You like your polar bear? Do you like Justin, too?"

She nodded again, then cocked her head to one side, a quizzical look on her face.

"I like him, too," Fiona admitted. "He's a nice man." *A nice man.* What a terrible way to describe Katy's father to her. She wanted to add to that description, to say, He's your daddy, Katy. But she'd kept the words to herself for so long that they wouldn't come. Soon she would have no choice but to tell the truth to Katy and the world.

But not tonight. Tonight her sweet little girl was still hers and hers alone.

The snow ended in the early hours of Sunday morning and the snowplows were out soon after. By Monday morning, the main streets were clear, and the side streets were passable. Justin had just settled in his office in the police station when the phone rang. It was George Wallace on the other end.

"Saw on the news you folks got some snow out there. It's low-sixties here today."

"Don't gloat. This front's moving your way. What's up?"

"You got your okay. Since the jewels were all insured and the insurance companies have already paid the losses, the gems are now their property. They weren't too pleased with the idea of making them available to Watkins to steal again. They agreed only after I assured them that there was no way in hell he was getting away with them a second time." George hesitated. "There *is* no way, is there?"

"Everything's locked up at the local police department. They've got good security and good officers. The chief is former DEA. He knows what he's doing."

"I'll fax a copy of the authorization to you when we hang up. What's your first plan?"

"I'll ask Chief Stuart to call a press conference, but we may have to wait a day or so. I need to find out what the roads are like in the county. We need the Denver media here, since all Grand Springs has is a small daily paper."

"So basically you're going to flaunt the jewels and say, 'Hey, Patrick, look what you lost and I found'?"

"Basically." As he'd told Fiona, he didn't think Watkins would be able to resist the challenge. After all, the gems in the evidence lock-up represented four of his biggest and toughest jobs, with a combined value in the high seven figures. Ego would demand that he reclaim what he'd stolen, and what could be more satisfying than reclaiming it from a secure police station? It would be the adrenaline high to beat all adrenaline highs.

''You want some help from the Denver office?'' George asked.

''Nah, not right now. The police department's been pretty cooperative, and if we need them, we can use the sheriff's office, too.'' He'd discussed the plan in detail with Colton Stuart last week. The chief had been skeptical of their chances for success, but he'd offered whatever assistance was necessary.

Justin hadn't mentioned that skepticism to his boss.

''You know, a police station is never empty. Someone's there twenty-four hours a day. We don't want anyone getting hurt, Justin.''

Justin understood his point. In the past, Watkins had blown up garages, unoccupied guest houses, storage sheds—even a swimming pool once. But the Grand Springs police station was so much smaller than his previous targets. Was there any way he could carry out that aspect of his ritual without risking injury to someone inside? ''We'll be on guard. We'll do the best we can.'' Maybe his target would be something reasonable—like unoccupied police cars—or his blast would be smaller, contained, more symbolic than destructive.

''How's the little girl?''

''Still not talking. She's got an appointment with a speech pathologist and an ear, nose and throat doctor this afternoon. They're going to do a complete evaluation, check her hearing, check for damage to it.'' Fiona had told him yesterday over lunch and asked if he wanted to go along. Of course he did, barring some catastrophe here.

''Poor kid. Her parents must be distraught.''

''Her mother's holding up pretty well, considering.''

''Is there a father?''

''It wasn't an immaculate conception,'' Justin said dryly. ''He's holding up pretty well, too.''

''It's a damn shame when it's not safe for a little girl to play in her own backyard.''

''Some things you can't protect against. A freak incident like this is one of them.''

''Well, I hope the kid's okay.''

''Yeah, me, too.'' If his supervisor knew how much he hoped and why, he'd be on the first plane to Denver. Justin didn't intend for anyone official to find out the truth until the case was over and done with. They could be angry with him and discipline him then. He didn't care. He'd be handing in his resignation anyway. Until Watkins was in handcuffs, though, he needed to stay on this case.

''Keep me informed. If you change your mind about wanting help, let me know and I'll get some people sent out there.''

''Thanks.'' After hanging up, Justin took the wanted flyer for Watkins from his files, then headed to the copier. He took the first copy from the tray and laid it on top of the machine to study while the others printed.

''Is this your guy?''

He glanced over his shoulder at Colton Stuart. ''Yeah. Doesn't look like a criminal mastermind, does he?'' The photo was a driver's license photo, six years old, and showed disheveled hair, a rumpled shirt and beard stubble. There was nothing remotely remarkable about the man. He could walk down any street in the country and not draw even one second look.

''Looks like a computer geek—or the sort of man whose neighbors gather after some grisly deed and say, 'He was a quiet man who kept to himself.''' Colton studied the physical description and read the text, then asked, ''How did you ID him?''

''Dumb luck. We didn't have a clue who he was until his fifth burglary. I'd been checking with neighbors and local authorities about strangers in the area and found out that his car had been parked alongside a county road a few miles from the victims' house before the robbery. A trooper had stopped to offer assistance, found a flat tire and assumed the owner had gone for help. He made a note of the tag number, then forgot about it in the excitement of the burglary and explosion. From there it was a simple matter of talking to people who knew him. Found out he'd blown up the chemistry lab in high school—took out the whole science wing and shut down the school for a few days. He'd claimed it was an accident, but the teacher had always had his doubts."

"A kid's dream—blow up the school and not get punished for it."

Justin's smile was faint. He'd been twisted enough to like school. Of course, when the alternative to being there was being home with one or the other of his parents, or alone... "We got the okay to use the gems to lure Watkins here. I want to distribute these to everyone in your department and also the sheriff's department, and I plan to take them around to all the motels and gas stations. The quicker we find out that he's in town, the better our chances of catching him."

"You really think he'll try to steal the jewels from our lock-up?" When Justin nodded, Colton shook his head. "Do you know how thick that door is? Two inches of solid steel. The walls are even thicker, and there aren't any windows."

"If there's any explosive that can get him in, Watkins knows about it, and if there's any chance in hell, he'll take it."

"What makes you so sure?"

"It's a game with him. He's not doing it for the money. He only sells the jewels when he needs cash, and apparently he lives frugally or has another source of income. He hasn't fenced even one-twentieth of what he's stolen. He has no connection to his victims, so he's not motivated by revenge or anything personal. He seems to do it because he can. He circumvents some of the best security systems in the country, outwits the authorities time and again, risks his life—and then he goes and buries millions of dollars in gems in a can. Now *we* have some of those gems. Trust me, he'll want them back. He'll feel honor bound to take them."

"And hopefully, instead, we'll take him."

"Hopefully. Because if he gets away with the jewels again, there are a few insurance companies out there that are going to be looking to string me up." To say nothing of the fact that he was hoping the only time he'd have to leave Grand Springs in the future would be to close up his apartment, quit his job and make the move back here. But if Watkins was still free, after what he'd done to Katy...

After a moment's silence, Justin glanced at the chief. "I, uh, can't remember the last time I had too much to drink in public. I think I was probably in college. Just for the record, I don't have a drinking problem. I don't make a habit of doing that."

"I didn't think you did." This time the hesitation was Colton's. "Fiona's a nice woman. I understand you knew her before this incident with Katy."

Justin felt as if the temperature had risen ten degrees. "Uh, yeah, we met years ago when I was visiting my aunt."

"I'm surprised Golda didn't try a little matchmaking. She adored Fiona and Katy. She considered them family."

Did Colton know or suspect the truth, or was he merely making conversation? A look at him gave no answer. His expression was utterly innocent—but no one was that innocent.

Justin caught himself tugging at his tie and forced his hand to his side. "I...understand she was very fond of them. She never had much in the way of decent family. I guess she felt she had to look outside the family to find anyone worthy of her affection."

"She didn't have to look far, did she?"

Not far in distance? Or not far outside the immediate family? Fortunately, before Justin had to respond, the copier spit out the last sheet and stopped. He stacked the copies, added the original on top, then said, "I'd better get started passing these around. By the way, do you know how the roads are between here and Denver?"

"Not bad for a four-wheel drive. They'll be clear by Wednesday."

"You want to set up the press conference for that afternoon?"

"No problem. You want anybody who'll make the trip or just the big guys?"

"Anyone. The more, the better."

"I'll take care of it."

Justin left with a nod. Before returning to his office, he placed a flyer in every officer's in-box, then got his coat and briefcase. He spent the next ninety minutes at the sheriff's office, telling the sheriff what he needed to know and passing out flyers there, too. By the time he finished, it was almost lunchtime and he was only two blocks from Past Times. Coincidence or subconscious planning?

The bell rang when he opened the door. There was no sign of Fiona, but her voice came from the back room. "I'll be with you in just a minute."

He approached the room quietly and found her in jeans and a sweatshirt, bending over a table. Her back was to him, presenting him with an enticing view of faded denim stretched over nicely rounded curves and clinging to her thighs. "Nice—" Startled, she straightened and whirled to face him. Aware of what he'd been looking at, she gave him a reproving look, and he immediately changed his next words. "—card table."

She continued to give him that look as she circled to the opposite side of the half-circle table. "Most people think it's a demilune."

"Nope, it's a card table. The top unfolds and locks in place." He pushed his hands into his pockets and smugly rocked back on his heels. "Want to know more about it?"

"By all means."

"The primary wood is mahogany, and the inlays are flame birch veneer. It was made in New England, probably in the early 1800s. This—" he pointed to but didn't touch a design in the center of the table "—is typical of the work of a furniture maker in Delaware whose name…I don't recall."

Fiona stared at him. "How did you know all that?"

"I grew up with antiques. Never had a piece of new furniture until I graduated from college and rented my apartment."

"So everyone who grows up rich absorbs obscure details about antiques like that?" she asked doubtfully.

"My grandmother valued things for their age and workmanship. Antiques were her passion. She talked a lot, and I listened."

"Were you close to her?"

"God, no. Even Grandfather was close to her only four times. She wasn't a particularly likable person."

"Golda's mother—that's who we're talking about?"

"The one and only. That was the first time Grandfather got close to her."

Fiona gave a disbelieving shake of her head. "My grandma Lake was as big around as she was tall, and she baked the most wonderful cookies and threw a pretty mean fast ball even though she couldn't run worth squat. My grandma Baxter raised her own kids and most of her brothers' and sisters' kids and could hammer a nail quicker and straighter than any man. She took up smoking cigars when she was trying to get Grandpa to give 'em up. Because he thought it was vulgar for a woman to smoke, he finally quit. She never did."

"And you loved them both."

"Yes, I did." Her expression was sweet and tinged with sadness. "Did you love your grandmother?"

"Sometimes I admired her. Sometimes I hated her. Mostly I was afraid of her." He shrugged, somewhat embarrassed by the conversation, and changed the subject. ‘‘Want to have lunch before Katy’s appointment?’’

She hesitated a moment, studying him over the table, then slowly smiled. ‘‘I’d like that.’’

All she’d agreed to was lunch—sharing a meal in a public place, surrounded by others. People had lunch together all the time—friends, acquaintances, strangers discussing business—and it never meant a thing. But it *felt* as if it meant something. That smile felt as if it meant something, too. Something important.

But damned if he knew what.

Chapter 9

Shortly after noon Wednesday, the common area of the police department had begun to take on the look of a television soundstage. All the major television stations within reasonable distance had sent crews for the press conference, as well as the newspapers both large and small. Justin stood in the doorway of Colton's office, running Anita Blandings's 1.2 million-dollar emerald-and-diamond necklace between his fingers, and watched as the press set up. Behind him, Colton was going over their notes. He would be the face man. Justin would merely stand in the background and be available for a question or two. Hopefully, wherever Watkins was, he would see the interview, including shots of the jewels, and the temptation would be more than he could resist.

"It's time," Colton said, coming to stand behind Justin. Before they could move, though, the phone rang. The chief answered it, listened for a moment, then asked, "Are you sure?"

Even across the room, Justin could hear the annoyance in the caller's response.

"Okay, I'll be right there."

"Problem?" Justin asked.

"Juliette's gone into labor. Her contractions are coming pretty quickly, and she wants to get out of here before she winds up giving birth in front of all those reporters. Sorry, Justin. You'll have to handle this one yourself."

Justin watched him stride across the crowded room to the records office. A moment later, he and one of the clerks unobtrusively escorted a pale Juliette from the building.

How had Fiona felt, going into labor in the middle of the night alone, driving herself to the hospital, giving birth with no one but the hospital staff in attendance? He should have been there to take her to the hospital, to hold her hand and tell her everything was going to be all right, to accept those threats she'd made and to welcome their daughter into the world. He damn well should have been there, and he regretted like hell that he hadn't been.

"Special Agent Reed? They're waiting for you."

He focused on the dispatcher, then nodded. He walked over to the table where Colton had intended to stand, where two officers stood watch over the jewels displayed, and stepped up to the podium. "Everyone ready? Chief Stuart got called away on an emergency. I'm Justin Reed, a special agent with the Bureau of Alcohol, Tobacco and Firearms." A reflection of sunlight on glass drew his attention to the doors as Fiona came in. He'd told her about the press conference, but he hadn't expected her to show. After taking a place against the far wall, she looked up, met his gaze and smiled faintly.

He opened with the prepared statement Colton had intended to read, giving the bare-bones details of the explosion and the discovery of the jewels. They'd agreed to keep Katy's name out of it and mentioned only that a five-year-old child had received minor injuries and had been hospitalized overnight. They'd also agreed not to provide a photograph of Watkins—only a physical description. If Watkins thought his face was plastered all over the state of Colorado, he might be reluctant to take the risk of reclaiming the gems, or they might discover that he was as skilled with disguises as with explosives.

"What is the ATF's interest in stolen jewelry?" the nearest reporter asked when he opened the floor for questions.

"None. The thefts of the jewelry are being investigated by the FBI. But each burglary was followed by the detonation of an explosive device, and explosives are the ATF's purview."

"Where and from whom were the gems stolen?"

"From private citizens in the Washington, D.C. area."

"What is Watkins's tie to Grand Springs?"

"Good question," he said, accompanied with an I-don't-know shrug. There were a few details he wanted to keep to himself.

"How much are the gems worth?" That one had been inevitable.

"Approximately 7.4 million dollars." There were murmurs of surprise all around the room. Even Fiona's eyes widened a bit.

"How many thefts and bombings is this man responsible for?"

Another inevitable question. "Twenty-four in eight years."

"And you haven't caught him yet."

"No," Justin said with a rueful shake of his head. Then he held up the emerald-and-diamond necklace, letting it dangle from his fingers, catching the light and damn near sparkling, and he grinned. "On the bright side, we *have* recovered 7.4 million dollars worth of gems."

"What happens to them now?"

"They're currently in the custody of the Grand Springs Police Department. I assume they'll be returned to their rightful owners once the investigation is completed. As I said, the ATF's only interest in this case is the explosives.''

He answered a few more questions, then came the one he'd hoped for. ''Is it wise, keeping such valuable jewels in the police station? Wouldn't they be safer someplace more secure?''

''The police chief believes the evidence room is secure enough.''

''But what if someone tries to steal them again?''

''Who ever heard of breaking *into* a police station?'' Justin smiled as if amused. ''Even Patrick Watkins doesn't have the skills or the audacity to attempt to take the gems out of here. They couldn't be more secure.''

He called an end to the interview, thanked them, then watched the two officers pack up the jewelry to return to the lock-up. As Fiona came to stand beside him, he held up the necklace. ''You like?''

''It's pretty.''

''Too bad you can't have it for the trouble he's caused you.''

''I'd rather have my daughter talking again.''

He handed the necklace to the nearest officer, then gestured toward the hall. ''My office is back in the corner. Want to see it?''

''Sure.''

He led the way, then stepped back to let her enter first. ''My desk. My computer. My chair.''

She made a show of looking around. ''Not an antique in the bunch.''

''Nope. And this is my door—closed for privacy.'' It clicked as he shut it. Leaning against it, he watched her. He'd first kissed her last Friday night, had spent all day Saturday with her and a good portion of each day since, and had gotten at least a kiss or two every time. But he wasn't quite sure what to expect from her this afternoon, and her expression gave him no clue.

She leaned against the table and rested her hands on either side of her hips. "I was impressed."

"By what?"

"You. You were very professional."

"You thought I wouldn't be?"

She shrugged. "That's the first time I've seen you working. It's hard to imagine you giving it up."

"Though I might do all right as a long-distance father to Katy, I can't very well seduce you from the other side of the country."

"Is that what you're doing?"

"I sure as hell hope so." His grin came and faded just as quickly. "I bet I know your next question. Is that the only reason I'm staying? No, I'm staying for Katy and for myself. Do I wish you wanted me to stay for you, too? More than you know, darlin'. More than you know."

"What if you regret it?"

"Regret what?"

"Giving up your career. Moving here. What if you make these major changes in your life and find out you hate being a full-time father, living in Grand Springs and not working for the ATF? What if you find you've given up more than you've gotten in return?"

Insecurity? Was that what he was seeing in her hazel eyes? Doubts that he could be satisfied with only them? Fear that just when they became accustomed to having him here, he'd leave?

Pushing away from the door, he slowly approached her. "What if Katy lived back east with me? You love this town. You love your house and your shop and your family and friends. But you would give it all up to be close to your daughter, wouldn't you? And you would never regret it, and you would never leave."

"Yes, but—"

When she didn't continue, he planted his hands next to hers and leaned close. "But what? You're a better parent than me? You're more willing to make sacrifices than I am?''

''I can have an antique shop anywhere. I can visit my family and make new friends and a new home.''

''I don't want to visit my family, but I can make new friends and a new home, too. I'm not a complete incompetent, Fiona. Believe it or not, I'm generally pretty capable.''

''I know that. It's just...your job has been the most important thing in your life since I've known you, and you can't do it here.''

''It's been the most important thing in my life because it's been the *only* thing in my life. My friends are people I work with. My hobby is spending my free time reviewing my cases. I've lived in the same apartment for eight years, and the only thing I've ever hung on the walls is case notes.'' He raised one hand to tuck a wayward strand of silky red hair in place. ''I'm ready for a change, Fiona. I'm not going to regret it, and I'll never go back.''

Then he kissed her.

Fiona felt as if her knees had gone weak and her body turned feverish. She wanted to cling to him but didn't, wanted to sink back on the table and pull him with her but didn't do that, either. She did wrap her fingers in the fine fabric of his lapels, and she kissed him back greedily, almost desperately.

When he ended the kiss and dragged in a deep breath, she pressed her face to his chest. It seemed she'd spent virtually all of her time lately worrying, except when she was in his arms. There she felt safe, no matter how foolish, no matter how dangerous. Apparently he knew how she felt, because for the moment he was willing to merely hold her.

After a time, he murmured, ''Why don't you ask your mom to take care of Katy this evening? I'd like to take you out someplace special.''

''Grand Springs doesn't have many special places,'' she said with a faint smile.

"We don't have to stay here. We could go anywhere. Want some Cajun food? We could be in New Orleans by dinnertime. Lobster? I know a great place on the coast of Maine. Mexican? How about San Antonio?"

Raising her head, she gave him a chiding look. "We can't go to any of those places and back in one evening."

"Sure, we can. All it takes is one phone call to Denver to charter a Lear."

"Charter a Lear? Spend thousands of dollars to have a nice dinner for two?" She shook her head. "You're going to spoil Katy rotten, aren't you?"

"I don't know. I'm not having much luck spoiling her mother."

When he grinned, he was so damn appealing. Without thinking, she raised her fingers to his mouth, as if she could capture the expression. He opened his mouth, drew in just the tip of her index finger, and she shivered. "It all sounds wonderful, especially the part about New Orleans. I bet it was warm in New Orleans today. But—" she sighed wistfully "—I can't get a baby-sitter for Katy because I'm going to be baby-sitting myself. I heard when I got here that Juliette had gone into labor. We'd already agreed that I would take care of Martin while she's in the hospital. So...how about pizza? There's a place here in town that both kids love."

She didn't tell him it was one of those places sane adults avoided at all costs, with loud music, games and waiters costumed as rodents. The food was bad, the atmosphere worse, and the only guarantees were a case of heartburn for the adults and a lot of fun for the kids.

"There's a little place in New York—" With a grin, he broke off. "Pizza right here in Grand Springs sounds fine."

"We'll be home around five-thirty. Come over anytime." She pressed a kiss to his cheek, then walked to the door.

"Hey, Fiona? Why'd you come over?"

She smiled sweetly. "To see you. To be impressed by your press conference."

"There are a lot of things I do better than press conferences."

"I know. I remember. See you tonight."

Fiona was halfway back to the shop when her father called her name. She turned to see him coming down the steps of the post office across the street. He crossed against the light and swept her into a hug as he stepped onto the curb. "How's my baby?"

"Katy's doing fine. She got her stitches removed Monday and had more tests and evaluations. Everything looks good."

"I'm glad to hear that, but I was talking about you. Katy's my grandbaby. You're my baby."

"I'm fine, too."

"Spending a lot of time with that Reed boy, from what I hear."

As they began walking, Fiona controlled her grin at the thought of calling Justin a boy. He was thirty-four years old, carried a badge and wore a gun, and she doubted he'd been very boyish even when he was one. "And where do you hear that? From nosy Mrs. Kravitz across the street?"

"Olga Kravitz isn't nosy. She's observant. Is it true?"

"Yes, Dad."

"Do you think that's smart?"

She thought back to Friday night, when Justin was leaving to go home. He'd wanted to kiss her good-night, and she'd asked if he thought that was wise. Kissing you, he'd replied, might be the smartest thing I've ever done. Now she parroted his words to her father. "Spending this time with Justin might be the smartest thing I've ever done."

"He broke your heart," Griff said.

"And gave me a beautiful daughter."

"He could break it again."

"Or maybe he'll put it back together again. Maybe he'll

give me more beautiful children. Maybe we'll live happily-ever-after.'' But even as she said the words, a snippet of Justin's conversation in his office replayed in her mind and stirred the hurt she'd hidden upon hearing the words the first time. *You love your house and your shop and your family and friends. But you would give it all up to be close to your daughter, wouldn't you?* He said he wanted to make love to her, to be a part of her life, a part of her family, but he was giving up everything and moving here only to be close to his daughter. Not to Fiona. She was just sort of the icing on the cake.

''Or,'' she admitted quietly, ''maybe he'll break my heart again. But he'll never break Katy's heart. I believe that, Dad.'' She reached for Griff's hand, the way she used to when she was Katy's age. ''I was lucky, growing up with both you and Mom. Every little girl needs a father to take care of her and protect her and make her feel safe. Justin will be a good father. Katy needs him, and he needs her.''

''What does he know about being a father?''

''I imagine about as much as you knew when you first became one. Katy and I will teach him, and Colton and Steve, Colleen and Jeff, Kerry and Matt. And you. You'll teach him, too.''

''Why would I do that? I never did like the boy.''

''Because you love Katy, and you love me, and you want what's best for both of us. Besides,'' she teased, ''the only reason you never liked him was because you thought he was going to take me away from here.''

''Better that, much as your mother and I would have hated it, than leaving you here, devastated, pregnant and alone.'' Griff frowned down at her. ''He ever give you an explanation for that?''

''Yes, he did.''

''Well?''

She returned his frown. ''Some things between a couple

should be private, don't you think? Or would you also like to hear the details of my sex life with Justin?''

Color flooded her father's face, all the way to the tips of his ears. ''Absolute— I don't— You shouldn't—'' Finished sputtering, he grunted. ''You girls have too much of your mother's sass in you. I'm your father. I'm not supposed to know you even have a sex life.''

''Then where did Katy come from?''

''She's a miracle. That's all I need to know.''

Fiona stopped in front of her shop and turned to face Griff. ''Whatever happens between Justin and me, promise you won't make it difficult for him with Katy. We wouldn't have her if not for him, and she's going to grow up loving him and thinking he's the most wonderful man in the world, exactly the way I did with you.''

He studied her for a long time, his gaze intent, searching. Whatever he found softened his features and closed his throat with emotion. ''I promise. And someday he'll find out how it feels when another man replaces him in his little girl's heart.''

Fiona's throat was clogged a bit, too, as she hugged him. ''I love you, Dad.''

''I love you, too.'' He stepped back, squinting as if the sun were responsible for the dampness in his eyes. ''Bring this boy—young man over sometime for dinner. He and I will talk.''

''I will.'' She let herself into the shop and flipped the Closed sign to Open, then returned her father's wave as he walked on. As she headed for her desk, she thought about her father's invitation. Wouldn't Justin be thrilled by that?

She waited a few hours, until they were following a six-foot mouse to a table at the pizza parlor, to mention it to him. He gave her a long, unblinking look that definitely wasn't thrilled. ''Talk about what?''

''Good question.'' In addition to echoing his response from the press conference, she mimicked his shrug, too, then grinned. ‘‘Maybe he wants to know what your intentions are toward his granddaughter.’’

‘‘More likely he wants to know what my intentions are toward his daughter,’’ he disagreed. ‘‘He never did like me, you know.’’

‘‘Only because he was afraid you would take me away from here.’’

‘‘He didn’t think I could possibly ever be good enough for you, not even on my very best days. And he was right.’’

The mouse stopped at a picnic table between two occupied tables. ‘‘Here you go,’’ he said in a bored-teenager voice. ‘‘Your waitress will be with you in a minute. Enjoy your meal.’’

As she shrugged out of her coat, Fiona said a polite hello to her sister Kerry’s neighbor at one table, then to two of her high school classmates at the other. She didn’t miss the appreciative looks they gave Justin or the speculation that fueled their curious expressions. As Katy climbed onto one bench with Martin right behind her, Fiona wondered if it would look odd if she sat beside them and left Justin the other bench. She could make the argument that Martin needed help with his dinner, but the boy was quite capable of stuffing pizza into his mouth without her assistance.

With a sigh, she folded her coat on the bench next to Martin, placed Justin’s overcoat on top, then completely covered both of them with the kids’ machine-washable coats. Sliding onto the bench, she scooted down until her shoulder brushed the wall, smiled once at the two women across from her, then turned her attention to the menu.

‘‘Friends of yours?’’ Justin asked softly as he sat beside her.

‘‘Acquaintances.’’

‘‘The kind who like to gossip?’’

‘‘Of course.’’

‘‘So are we supposed to pretend that this is strictly business?’’

Some part of her wanted to say yes, no matter how ludicrous it sounded. The stronger part gave him a dry look. "Not unless you think Molly Mole is hiding a bomb inside those big hands."

"Who is Molly Mole?"

Fiona gestured to the girl approaching their table in a mole outfit, complete with oversize hands. "Hi, I'm Molly Mole. I'll be your server this evening. Can I interest you in some chips and Molly Guacamole?"

Justin looked from Molly to Fiona, his expression utterly bemused. She ordered pizza and soft drinks all around, then gave an exaggerated sigh. "You've lived a deprived life. Before long, you'll recognize every cartoon character on sight, know the dialogue to every Disney movie by heart and find yourself watching *Sesame Street* even when she's not around."

"I can live the childhood I never had through Katy," he said cheerfully. "I've never watched cartoons or *Sesame Street* or seen a Disney movie."

Fiona sent the kids off to play, then twisted on the bench to face him. "Never? What did you do for entertainment when you were a kid?"

"I stayed out of my parents' way. I studied and read. Sometimes in the summer they sent me off to camp for a few weeks. Usually they left me with the household staff and went off on their own vacations." He shrugged carelessly. "I was alone a lot. I told you that."

It was difficult for Fiona to imagine the life he described. "Why did they even have a child if they couldn't be bothered with raising him?"

"I was the obligatory heir. My grandparents impressed on all of their children that they *would* do their part to see that the Reed name continued. Only Golda defied them. If my parents hadn't had a son first, they would have kept trying. Isn't that a scary thought?"

"It's sad. When you say things like that—" and so matter-of-factly "—it makes me angry." It made her want to smack his parents, made her ache to comfort that unwanted little boy.

"Would you prefer that I not answer your questions?" he asked soberly.

"No! I'm not angry with you. I just don't understand how parents could treat their own child like that. Kids are so easy to love, and so easy to hurt." And the hurt could go so deep—could affect their lives and decisions long after they became adults. It could make a man believe he wasn't capable of loving anyone, or deserving of anyone's love.

Sighing grimly, she returned to his comment regarding the Reed name. "Would you like Katy to start using your last name?" She wouldn't object, once he was living here. She thought Katy Reed had a nice ring to it.

"I think it would be convenient if all of us had the same last name."

The muscles in Fiona's stomach tightened, and her palms got damp. "And which of us do you propose should change?"

His dark eyes got even darker. "Interesting that you should use that word."

"What? Change?"

"No. Propose." He cleared his throat, looked away to check on the kids, then back. "Changing Katy's name is an easy enough process. After all, I *am* her father, and traditionally children have their fathers' names. Also traditionally, mothers have the same names as their children."

"We haven't exactly been traditional from the beginning." Fiona took a long drink of soda, then lifted her hair off her shoulders. When had it gotten so warm in here? Maybe it was just all the active bodies in a confined space, with every kid in the room running, jumping or climbing something.

But if that was the problem, why was she the only one who looked the least bit uncomfortable? Kerry's neighbor didn't. Her two former classmates didn't. Justin, in his suit and tie, looked as cool as the snow outside.

"No," he agreed. "We haven't been traditional. But there's no reason why we can't start now for Katy's sake. It's the right thing to—"

His next words were lost as her classmates descended on them, claiming the kids' bench. "Fiona, we were so sorry to hear about Katy," one said, and the other bobbed her head enthusiastically. "We do hope she's going to be all right."

"And you, too," the other added. "Why, you just look worn-out with worrying over her. Once this awful thing is over and you have some time to take care of yourself, things will look so much better."

Fiona was too grateful for their interruption to mind the jibe. She would have welcomed anything that would stop Justin from saying what he was leading up to for all the wrong reasons—what was surely going to bring with it more hurt than she wanted to bear. "Thank you, Betty Jane, Lisa. I appreciate your concern. Have you met Justin Reed?"

Both women turned their attention to him, and Betty Jane laid her hand over his. "Oh, Golda's nephew! We are *so* sorry about her death."

Fiona tuned out their conversation and focused instead on part of Betty Jane's statement. *So sorry.* That was a good way to describe how she was feeling at that moment.

So very sorry.

The phone was ringing when they walked into Fiona's house after dinner. She went to answer it, leaving Justin to help the kids out of their coats. Martin was telling Katy a story that made little sense, as far as Justin could tell, but she listened as if she understood every word. They were like rag dolls, letting him move them whichever way was necessary to remove their coats, hats and gloves. Once he was finished, they raced up the stairs to Katy's room, and he moved to the living room doorway.

"He can spend the night here," Fiona was saying. "It's not a problem at all." Then she added, "I understand. I'll have him ready. Give my love to Juliette."

When she hung up, Justin said quietly, "I don't suppose the 'he' who's welcome to spend the night would be me."

Startled, she looked up, met his gaze and immediately looked away. "That was Colton. Juliette had a girl. They've named her Sara. He's coming by in half an hour to pick up Martin, so I—I need to get him ready. I want to give both of them a bath and get Martin dressed in clean clothes. He's got pizza and pop all over himself, and I swear, there's pizza sauce in his hair. I—I appreciate the dinner and enjoyed the company, but if you don't mind—"

"Fiona." His voice was enough to halt the nervous flow of words. "You've been unsettled all evening. Ever since we talked about changing names."

Her attempt to smile was dismal. "I'm not unsettled. I just have things to do, and I can't do them standing here talking to you. So…if you'd just let yourself out…"

He caught her arm when she started past him. "Can we talk about this?"

She gave up her pretense that nothing was wrong. "No."

"You know I was about to suggest that we get married when your friends interrupted. Is that such an awful thing?"

Pulling free, she folded her arms over her chest. "It's ridiculous. Give me one intelligent reason why we should get married."

"Katy."

"Katy is a perfectly happy, well-adjusted child. Our not being married hasn't hurt her in the least, and that's not going to change."

"Us. We have a daughter, and we have a relationship. Getting married is the natural next step."

"We have a daughter and a sexual attraction," she said

stiffly. "Having sex is the natural next step. But getting married just so you can have sex is ridiculous."

Sexual attraction. The words left Justin cold inside. Was that really all she felt for him? Had he mistaken lust and being-friendly-for-their-daughter's-sake for something more? The way she kissed him, the way she looked at him sometimes, the way she touched him... He'd thought she cared about him. Hell, in the middle of the night when he couldn't sleep for wanting her, when anything seemed possible, he'd thought that maybe she was falling in love with him just a little.

He *knew* he was falling in love with her.

"I have an obligation," he said harshly.

"To be a good father to Katy. That doesn't give you any responsibility—or right—to me."

He slid his hand inside his jacket, rubbing the ache twisting in his gut, and tried to look away from her beautiful, cold, angry face, but he couldn't. He tried to walk away without saying anything else, with at least some measure of his dignity in place, but he couldn't do that, either. "Your parents expect—"

"My parents don't want me seeing you, even if it is just for Katy."

He swallowed hard, but it did nothing for the bitter taste in his mouth. The god-awful food at the pizza place had given him one hell of a case of heartburn. He needed to go home and take something before he got sick, though he doubted antacids would help this pain. "I—I'm sorry. I won't keep you any longer. Tell Katy... Never mind."

Picking up his coat, he walked out and closed the door quietly behind him. Just as it clicked shut, he heard her speak his name, or so he thought. But when he stood there for a time, utterly still, he heard nothing else. It had merely been wishful thinking.

At home he took a double dose of antacids as if they really might make him feel better, then changed into sweats and running shoes. He hadn't been running as regularly as he did back in D.C., and he could tell. He needed a marathon workout to burn off this excess energy and to release whatever feel-good endorphins he might have. He *really* needed something to make him feel good.

Though the temperature was in the low twenties and snow still covered many of the sidewalks, he didn't mind. He ran in the street, following the five-mile route he'd laid out his first day in town. When he came back to Aspen Street, he didn't turn toward the house but kept going, pushing through another mile, then another and another, until his heart was pounding and his lungs were bursting and he thought he just might collapse if he didn't force some small breath into his chest.

He was bent over at the waist, hands braced on his knees and struggling to breathe, when headlights slashed across him. The car came to a stop and the driver got out, but he couldn't see a thing, thanks to the blinding lights. If he had seen, he would have considered running the other way—if he could have moved at all.

"Justin? Justin Reed, what are you doing?" Delores Lake took hold of his arm and pulled him toward the passenger side of the car. He didn't have the energy to resist her. "Why, you're soaking wet. You're going to catch your death of pneumonia."

Finally he did manage to stop her forward motion. "I—I'm o-okay. Jus' need to—to catch my—" He broke off and took a deep breath.

"Okay?" she scoffed. "You're shaking all over. You get in that car right now and turn that heater to high. I swear, for an intelligent person, you aren't showing much sense."

Give me one intelligent reason why we should get married. Fiona didn't think he was too smart, and now neither did her mother. He just wasn't having much luck at all impressing the Lake females.

He let Delores push him into the seat and close the door,

then leaned his head back and closed his eyes, concentrating on breathing and slowing his heart rate. He didn't move when she got in, buckled up and turned the heat on high, and didn't look when she turned on the interior light to watch him.

"You want to talk about what's wrong?"

"No, ma'am."

"Does it have to do with my daughter or granddaughter?"

Finally he did look at her. "I don't mean to be rude, but which part of 'no, ma'am' did you not understand?"

"Ah, so it does. Katy's far too young to cause this sort of foolish behavior in a man, so that means it's Fiona. What did my stubborn youngest daughter do?"

"Mrs. Lake—"

"Delores."

"Delores, I'm tired, and I still have some work to do, so if you're offering me a ride back to the house, I appreciate it. But if you expect some sort of confidences in return, it's not going to happen."

In response she shut off the light, then pulled away from the curb. He didn't relax too much, though. He knew she wasn't likely to give in so easily. After all, Fiona got her stubbornness from Delores.

She gave him two blocks of peace before speaking. "You know, Justin, you hurt Fiona very deeply. I'm not saying that to criticize. It's just… Something like that is hard to get over. When someone's broken his promises, it's not easy to trust him again, no matter how much you might want to."

What happened tonight had nothing to do with trust and everything with wants. He wanted love, marriage, a family, and she wanted sex and a father for Katy. But that was hardly the sort of thing he could tell her mother, so he said nothing at all.

After another two blocks, she spoke again. "Sometimes when a person's been hurt, she says things she doesn't mean. She might want to punish the other person, or she might just want to protect herself from more pain. Maybe it's petty, but we humans *are* petty, and foolish and afraid. But even petty, foolish hurts can be set right."

As she turned onto Aspen, he faced her and saw that all the lights were off at Fiona's house except the porch light and a dim lamp in her bedroom. "I appreciate your concern, but it's misplaced. I just went for a run and overdid it. There's nothing to set right between Fiona and me." As far as Fiona was concerned, there was nothing between them at all but Katy.

And sex.

Delores turned into his driveway, then squeezed his hand. "How are you on patience?"

"I have my share," he said guardedly. "Why?"

"Every parent of a five-year-old needs his share and then some. And any man dealing with Fiona needs it in bunches, too. But the result will be worth it."

He gave a shake of his head at her insistence on believing her daughter was the reason he'd damn near run himself into the ground and, at the same time, wondered how her intuition could be so dead on target. Was he so transparent? Did she know Fiona too well?

"Thanks for the ride, Delores." He pulled free of her grip and got out of the car. His muscles were tight and protested every step. That was what he got for ending his run so abruptly. He should have refused her ride, should have walked back and given himself a chance to cool down gradually.

Despite his talk to Delores about having work to do, his only plans were to take a hot shower, then go to bed. Alone.

He was so damn tired of going to bed alone.

After the shower, he wrapped a towel around his waist, then went into his room next door. He turned down the bed, set the alarm, shut off the lights…and walked to the side window. A half twist on the rod, and the blinds opened wide enough to give him a view of the side of Fiona's house while still providing him with privacy. It also gave him an unexpected view of her.

Her bedroom window was directly across from his. The lace curtains were parted, and she was standing there, gazing in his direction. Her expression was pensive, her manner vulnerable. With her pale red hair falling past her shoulders and her nightgown—light green, lots of ribbons and lace, perfectly modest and surprisingly enticing—she looked beautiful, womanly, approachable.

But not by him. Unless he was willing to accept only what she wanted, their relationship would never be anything more than single parents sharing a daughter.

Why shouldn't he accept what she wanted? It was more than he had now. Just because he'd gotten greedy and wanted still more was no reason to settle for nothing. If she was willing to go on as they had been—spending time together, acting almost like a family, getting intimate with no hope of anything more—why shouldn't he be, too?

Because she was spending time with him only because of Katy, getting intimate only because she'd been celibate for so long. Not because of any feelings for him. Not even because of lust for him. Any man she saw enough of would likely do as well.

After a time, she lowered her head and covered her face with her hands. Even across the distance he could see the shudders rocking through her and knew she was crying. More than anything in the world, he wanted to hold her and assure her that everything would be all right, but he would be lying to one or both of them. "All right" for her would be pure hell for him, and he imagined she thought the same of his version of "all right."

Wishing he really was the coldhearted bastard most people believed him to be, he twisted the rod, closed the blinds tightly, then went to bed.

But it was a long time before he slept.

Chapter 10

After cleaning house Saturday morning, Fiona got out the wrapping paper and tape and settled at the kitchen table to wrap the gift she'd picked up the day before for Juliette and Colton's new baby. She'd chosen the frilliest of little dresses with matching booties and tiny lace socks—the sort of prissy-little-girl outfit that she'd hoped Katy would always wear. She had, right up until the time she'd learned to undress herself. She'd preferred wearing nothing over wearing anything fussy, a fact Fiona had reluctantly accepted after finding her naked at church one Sunday.

Now, wearing denim overalls with a white T-shirt and a red baseball cap, she looked exactly like the tomboy she was. She sat on her knees in the chair across from Fiona and solemnly watched her work.

As Fiona began cutting the baby-themed paper, Katy plopped her polar bear in the middle. When Fiona brushed it aside, Katy put it back. "I see your bear," Fiona said, "but it's in my way there. Move it, please."

Katy lifted it for a moment, then put it down in the scissors' path again. Fiona moved it. Katy put it back. Fiona moved it again. "I see the bear, Katy. What about it?"

Her daughter just looked at her.

"I can't read your mind, sweetie. What do you want?"

Her only reply was another long look, edged with frustration.

Fiona returned to her task. The pediatrician had called the day before and told her that the speech pathologist's report was perfectly normal. The audiogram showed no problems, and neither did the tympanogram. The ENT exam was also normal. The only exams left were the neuropsychiatric evaluation and the EEG, scheduled for Monday. If the results were all right, then all that was left for diagnosis was post-traumatic stress disorder, and all she could do was wait.

Waiting with Katy's silence was driving her crazy.

She was trimming the last edge of the paper when the polar bear hit her square in the face, then tumbled to the tabletop. Picking it up, she scowled at her daughter. "What was the purpose of that? You do not throw things at people. Do you understand?"

Katy simply scowled back, picked up her place mat and threw it.

"Katy!"

Before Fiona could stop her, she reached for the glass of chocolate milk left over from breakfast, dumped it on the wrapping paper, then threw the glass, too.

Fiona snatched up the gift box and the roll of paper, jumped to her feet and headed for a towel. "Kathleen Hope, you get your butt up to your room *right now,* and don't you dare come out again until I give you permission. *Move!*"

Looking belligerent and totally unrepentant, Katy stomped around the table and down the hall.

Fiona mopped up the milk, set the tumbler in the sink and carried the towel into the laundry room. While in there, she heard Katy's door closing and knew she'd slammed it to be sure Fiona heard. She leaned against the washer, hugging herself tightly. She couldn't begin to imagine how difficult this entire situation was for Katy. Her daughter was scared, frustrated, and must feel incredibly helpless, because Fiona felt the same, plus she felt guilty as hell for the frustration. She just didn't know how to cope too much longer with it.

She forced herself to take a few deep breaths, to calm the panic that sought to escape. When she felt in control again, she returned to the kitchen, washed the table and cleaned the floor where the milk had pooled. She spread out the wrapping paper on the island and quickly cut it and wrapped the box. Once its pretty yellow bow was affixed on top, she took another deep breath, then headed upstairs to talk to Katy.

She was surprised to find Katy's bedroom door wide-open, and even more surprised that the room was empty. She checked in the closet, the bathroom, her own room, then took the stairs two at a time. The living room was empty. So were the dining room, the kitchen, the laundry room, the bathroom. The dead bolt lock on the door to the garage was locked. The back door was locked. The front one...wasn't.

She jerked the door open, checked the porch, the yard, the sidewalk. There was no sign of Katy. She was heading back inside to call her parents when she remembered the plush bear hitting her in the face. *Justin?* Was that the message Katy had been trying to get across to her—that she wanted to see Justin?

Without taking time to get a coat, she ran down the steps and across the yard to the Reed house. Just as she raised her hand to knock, the door opened and Justin and Katy came to an abrupt stop.

Even as overwhelming relief swept over her, Fiona was all too aware of the ache in her chest. It seemed as if she hadn't seen him in years instead of three days. She wanted to absorb every detail about him, wanted to throw herself into his arms and beg him to forget the marriage business so they could go back to the way things were...or to love her, so she could accept his proposal.

He didn't look as if he cared to do anything for her.

"I—I sent her to her room for behaving badly, but she—she slipped out without my knowing it."

He didn't speak, and his expression didn't change one bit. As long as Katy was unharmed, she suspected, he had no interest in her explanations or excuses. She turned her attention from him to her daughter instead. "You think you were in trouble before, sweetheart, you are in *serious* trouble now. Come on. Let's go home." She reached for Katy's hand, but the girl backed away behind Justin.

Fiona expected him to pull her forward and hand her over. Instead he moved so she was hidden behind him. "We were coming to tell you that we're going out for lunch."

"But—" Today was family day, *her* special time with her daughter, and he knew it. He couldn't just claim it for his own. "No," she said flatly. "Katy is coming home with me."

His eyes darkened and cooled. "You misunderstood. We weren't coming to ask. Just to tell."

"No. She can't be rewarded for running off like that."

"She didn't run off. She came to see her father, which she hasn't been able to do lately."

Shame flooded Fiona's face and made her feel ridiculously warm, considering that she stood in twenty-five-degree cold in short sleeves and jeans. "That's your fault, not mine. You could have come over anytime. I didn't make you stay away."

"Really? Somehow I missed that open invitation." His thin smile disappeared, and his expression turned granite-hard. "But I didn't miss the part about nothing between us but lust, or putting up with me only for Katy's sake."

The shame increased a few miserable degrees, leaving her unable to meet his gaze. "This is hardly an appropriate conversation to be having in front of her."

"No, it's not," he agreed. "So why don't you go away and we'll stop having it?"

"Not without my daughter."

"She doesn't want to come with you."

"She's five years old. She doesn't get to make that decision." Frustration made her voice tremble. "Damn it, Justin, I know you're angry with me, but you cannot use Katy to get back at me." When he gave her the same unwavering, solemn look that Katy so often used, she threw up her hands in surrender. "Fine. Take her to lunch. Teach her she can get away with doing anything she wants. I'll deal with the results when she gets home."

She was halfway down the steps when the door closed, at the bottom when he spoke again, his voice bold, mocking, filled with challenge. "If sexual attraction is the only thing between us, why aren't we having sex?"

She froze in midstep before slowly, reluctantly, turning to face him. He stood alone on the porch, hands shoved in his jacket pockets, looking as if the question he'd asked wasn't at all important but waiting for the answer just the same. "Wh-what?"

"If we don't have a relationship, if the only thing between us besides Katy is the mutual desire to have sex, why haven't we done it?"

"I—I—" She didn't have a clue how to answer, short of admitting that she hadn't meant anything she'd said Wednesday night. She'd simply wanted to stop him from talking about marriage as if it were a matter of convenience, as if love, or the lack of, played no role in it. She hadn't wanted to hear such an unromantic proposal, hadn't wanted to face the fact that, with all his reasons for wanting to get married, the most important one was missing. He wanted to do it because of Katy, because he'd never had a real family, because her parents expected it—for every reason except loving her. Wanting her. Needing her.

And she couldn't do it for *any* reason except loving, wanting and needing him.

"Well?"

She found momentary distraction when a horn sounded as a car passed. She waved at the driver, one of her best customers, then anxiously glanced back at Justin. "You—you haven't exactly tried," she said defensively.

"Well, gee, there was that time on your couch, when I had my tongue in your mouth and your hands were wrapped around my—" He broke off when she made a choked sound and turned beet-red. "Ah, you remember. Your nipples looked just like that that night."

She folded her arms across her chest and wished she'd taken the time to put on a bra this morning, or a heavier top, or had zipped her thickest parka to her chin. "I—I— Why are you doing this?"

"You're the one who said it was nothing but lust. I'm just trying to understand."

"I'm going home," she said stiffly. "Please bring Katy over as soon as you get back."

He moved quickly, catching her arm before she'd made it across his driveway. "Oh, come on, Fiona. You've already rejected me for marriage or any kind of relationship. Don't I deserve to get laid at least once for my efforts?"

She couldn't have been more stunned if he'd slapped her. Tears welled in her eyes, blurring her vision as she stared at him. He looked pretty stunned himself as he stared back.

"I'm sorry." All the sarcasm and mockery left his voice, and his hand dropped away from her arm. "I didn't mean to say that. I swear, I didn't mean..."

Funny thing—she believed him. He wasn't a cruel man. He only struck out when he was angry and hurt, and Wednesday evening she'd given him good reason to be both. She had lied to him, had hurt him to protect herself, and now he'd repaid her in kind. Now it was her turn again. Did she punish him for it and keep their emotional insecurities whirling in a vicious cycle until they'd destroyed any chance for a future? Or did she act like an adult?

Mistakes can be set right, forgiveness is vital, and love is possible. Fiona wasn't so sure about that last one, but Golda had certainly been right about the first two. With effort, anything could be fixed, and there wasn't a relationship in the world that could survive without forgiveness.

Justin swore in a low voice, then reached out without touching her. "I'm so damn sorry, Fiona. I don't know—"

She forced an unsteady smile as she took his hand tightly in hers. "It's all right."

"No, it isn't—"

"We all say things we don't mean sometimes. I know you, Justin. I know you didn't mean it." She took a deep breath and wiped her eyes with her free hand. "You'd better get back inside. There's no telling what Katy's up to. Enjoy your lunch."

She tried to leave, but now he was holding on. "Come with us. It's family day. I know we're never going to be a real family, but... Come with us."

Hearing the wistfulness that crept subconsciously into his voice, she wanted to point out that traditionally fathers in real families loved the mothers, wanted to ask if there was even the slightest possibility that he might ever love her—really love her, the way her father loved her mother. But what did he know about that kind of love?

And what was she doing to help him learn?

She managed another smile, stronger this time, and shook her head. "I think this should be a father-daughter lunch. You two will do fine together." And maybe this evening *they* could have some father-mother time.

"Fiona—"

She closed the distance between them and pressed a kiss to his mouth. "You want to come over for dinner tonight? About seven?"

He nodded.

"Good. Have fun." She tugged free, then hurried across their yards and into the house. Shivering fiercely, she had trouble holding the telephone receiver to her ear and dialing the numbers, but her voice was steady when the call was answered. "Hi, Mom. I have a favor to ask. Can Katy spend the night with you this evening?"

It wasn't easy communicating with a five-year-old who wasn't able to speak, but Justin finally determined that Katy wanted a fast-food burger under the golden arches for lunch. At least, he thought as he pulled into a parking space, he hoped that was what that particular grunt meant. His original decision to take Katy to lunch had been a selfish one, he was ashamed to admit—so that Fiona *couldn't* take her. Now that he was faced with actually walking into a restaurant, figuring out what Katy wanted and sharing the meal with her, he really wished Fiona had come with them.

He stopped at the back of the car to wait for another car to pass. When they started across the traffic lane, Katy slipped her hand in his as naturally as if she'd been doing it all her life. It made him feel clumsy. Awkward. Intimidated.

As they took their place in line, he swung her into his arms. "What do you want, Kate? Let's see, they have hamburgers, hamburgers and for something a little different, hamburgers."

She giggled but didn't speak. He wished she would, wished just once he could hear his daughter's voice. If she didn't start talking soon, he was taking her to the top experts in the country—hell, in the world. One of these days she was going to call him Daddy.

The line moved forward pretty quickly. Before he was prepared, it was their turn to order. "You've got to tell me what you want, Kate, because I don't have a clue. A hamburger?"

She nodded.

"Great. That narrows it down." There were only a half dozen or so to choose from. He scanned the menu above the counter, where a familiar item caught his attention. On his first night in town, he'd asked Fiona where to get a good burger. We like Happy Meals, she'd replied. "You want a Happy Meal, Kate?"

Once again she nodded.

"One Happy Meal and a hamburger and fries," he told the kid behind the counter.

"What kind of burger, sir? What size fries? What kind of soft drink with the Happy Meal?"

Justin shrugged. "Surprise us."

The kid took his money and served up a tray. Justin tried to balance it one-handed, then put Katy down and followed her to a table. "So, Kate… Is it okay if I call you Kate?"

Swinging her legs hard enough to shake the table, she stuck a French fry into her mouth.

"I've never had lunch alone with a little girl before. What would you like to talk about? I could tell you about my job, but you'd probably find it boring. Your mom always did. She never could work up much interest in RDX, booster explosives, det cord or lead azide. Or you could tell me what you did at school this week, but I'm afraid that would be an awfully short conversation."

Already he'd lost her attention. Still swinging her legs, she was looking around the restaurant, her gaze pausing on every kid in the place. She apparently knew some of them—he saw the waves—but he never would have guessed it from her expression. For a time she stared at the playground equipment out front, coated with snow. Then she dug out the toy that had come with her meal and played with it while she ate.

He felt like a failure, though he had to admit that she was often just as inattentive with her mother. Fiona was simply better equipped to deal with it.

He'd finished his meal and was watching her distractedly eat hers when a familiar voice boomed, "Katy-bug!"

Twisting around in her seat, she lit up with a big smile and raised her arms. Griff Lake picked her up, swung her around, then gave her a loud, smacking kiss that made her giggle. When he set her back in her seat, he gave Justin a less than friendly look. "Where's Fiona?"

"Home, I guess."

"She let you bring Katy out without her?"

"I didn't kidnap her, Mr. Lake."

"Why would she do that?"

"Maybe because—" Justin watched the older man's jaw clench and finished with a shrug. They both knew the answer to his question. There was no reason anyone around them should know.

Yet.

"Fiona says you want to talk to me."

"When the time and place are right."

Meaning when they had some privacy. Justin thought about mentioning that, in his opinion, there had been more than enough privacy. Then he considered the likely topic of Griff's conversation—his intentions toward Fiona and Katy—and decided it was best put off. A few days ago he'd had an easy answer—he'd wanted to marry Fiona and be a father to Katy and the other kids they would have. Since then, he'd been reminded—*again*—that there was nothing easy about Fiona.

But wasn't it true that the things you worked hardest for were the most satisfying? And it wasn't as if he had better things to do.

After a few more stilted words, Griff kissed Katy again and left. Justin waited until he'd driven out of the parking lot, then he and Katy also left. When he took her home, he accompanied her only as far as the corner of their yard that abutted his. He thanked her for lunch, and she gave him a kiss, then ran across the yard to the porch. He was still standing there, his cheek literally tingling, when Fiona stepped out on the porch. She didn't say anything, but she smiled and raised one hand in a tentative wave.

He returned the smile and the wave, waited until she went inside again, then went inside his own house. He wandered through the quiet rooms, studying photographs, picking up knickknacks and replacing them. None of Golda's friends mentioned in the will had contacted him yet about picking up their bequests. The Gustav Stickley set she'd left Fiona still filled the dining room. Katy's jewelry was still upstairs in Golda's bedroom. The teapot, music box and Hümmel collections were gathering dust on the shelves, and the Lladró was unappreciated in its glass-fronted cabinets.

He wondered what Fiona would do with the Stickley. Put it in her shop and sell it for the small fortune it was worth? Store it somewhere for Katy to have when she was older? He wished she would use it in her own dining room—he had a few good memories of meals at that table—but he didn't have a clue about her plans.

Too restless to hang around the house until dinnertime, he grabbed his keys and coat and headed for Denver. His first stop was a florist, his second a car dealer. By the time he began the return trip to Grand Springs, he'd turned in the rental car, bought a four-wheel-drive sport-utility vehicle better suited to Colorado winters and paid an exorbitant price for a bouquet of orchids. He got home in time to shower and dress for dinner, and rang Fiona's doorbell at precisely seven o'clock.

She opened the door wearing a long sweater over a flowing skirt that reached practically to the floor. Her hair was secured back from her face with gold combs, and she smelled of exotic perfume and baby powder. "Hi."

"Hi." He stepped inside, then presented the tissue-wrapped orchids.

Her eyes brightened as a smile of pure pleasure swept across her face. "Oh, Justin, you remembered! They're beautiful! Where on earth did you find orchids in Grand Springs?''

''In Denver. While I returned the rental car and bought a truck, the florist tracked down every orchid in the city.''

''They're perfect. Thank you so much.'' Rising onto her toes, she kissed his cheek, just an innocent peck, and started the same tingle Katy had. A gee-that-was-sweet and damn-that-was-special sort of tingle. ''Come on back to the kitchen while I put them in water.''

He followed her into the kitchen, expecting the fragrant aromas of dinner cooking but instead smelled only exotic perfume and baby powder.

She filled the vase with water, added the flowers, then carried it to the kitchen table with a remarkably satisfied smile. ''I can't believe you remembered all these years that I love orchids.''

''I remember everything about that time.'' How much he'd loved her, how happy they'd been and, later, how badly he'd hurt them both.

After a moment she looked from the flowers to him, and her smile became unsteady. Uncertainty entered her eyes. ''Dinner won't take long to fix. I wasn't sure whether you'd want to eat now or...later.''

Justin studied her a moment, then quietly asked, ''Where is Katy?''

A blush colored Fiona's cheeks and she shifted from foot to foot. ''She—she's spending the night with Mom and Dad.''

''On family day?''

''They're family, too.''

''Are you planning to seduce me?''

Her blush deepened. ''I— You— Yes.''

The part of him that wasn't incredibly turned on by the idea was disappointed. ''Is this because of what I said outside this morning?''

He half expected her to take offense. Instead her discomfort disappeared and a womanly smile took its place, making him ache, as she slowly approached him. "Don't be foolish. This is because I've never wanted any man the way I've always wanted you. I'd waited all my life for you, and when I lost you, I still waited. I've met other men. I've gone out on dates. But none of them kissed me the way you do. None of them made me feel the way you do. None of them made me want..."

Her words were lost in a kiss, her mouth brushing his, her tongue sliding inside his mouth. He thought about pointing out to her that they were standing in front of a window in a well-lit room, where the neighbors in back could clearly see, and then she pressed her body against his and suddenly he couldn't have cared if they were standing in the middle of Main Street at high noon. He slid his arms around her and pulled her hips hard against his, rubbing against her. When she ended the kiss, she whispered one word with the power to bring him to his knees.

"Please."

"Yes." Yes, he wanted her. Yes, dinner could wait. Yes, he would please her.

Smiling primly, almost shyly, she took his hand and led him down the hall and up the stairs to her bedroom. The covers were turned down, the blinds closed and only the lamps on the night tables burned. "You were pretty sure of me, weren't you?" he asked with a grin.

"Not sure. Hopeful." She released his hand, drew her sweater over her head and dropped it to the floor, then stood naked to the waist in front of him. "I've always been hopeful with you."

The sweater had tousled her hair. He smoothed it, then, for a long time, simply looked at her. She was beautiful, with skin as pale and fine as his mother's best china, nicely rounded breasts, rosy nipples swollen with the need for his kisses. Her body was strong, yet gave the impression of delicacy, along with her shy smile and angel's face.

He ached to reach for her, to draw her near and take off his clothes and the rest of hers, to lower her to the bed and arouse her, take her, please her, brand her, make her his forever. But all he did was slide his index finger inside the waistband of her skirt and move it from side to side, making her incredibly soft skin pebble and ripple in response. "Tell me it's not just sex."

Her smile was hazy, sensual, full of promise. "It's sex and lust. Need. Hunger, arousal, love, bliss, necessary, vital, right. So right."

Love. Had she used the word to placate him? Or had her subconscious slipped it in?

She reached behind her to unfasten her skirt, but he stopped her. "Let me." With his hands on her bare shoulders, he turned her so her back was to him—and what a back—long, muscled, enticing. He pressed a kiss to her shoulder, left another on her spine and one on her neck before sliding his hands around to cup her breasts. "When I went back to Washington," he murmured, his mouth just above her ear, "I used to dream about you—about kissing you, touching your breasts, dying inside you—and I'd wake up, impossibly hard, and in those moments before I opened my eyes, I could taste you. I could feel your body against mine. I could smell you on my skin and my sheets. I wanted you so much that I hurt."

He gently pinched her nipples and she gasped, then twisted her head around for a greedy kiss. They'd made love like this once—both of them partly dressed, him entering her from behind—but instead of her bedroom, they'd been in the kitchen. It was the day after they'd met, and she'd been at the sink, rinsing their breakfast dishes, when he'd taken his coffee cup to her. Simply being that close to her had made him instantly hard, and he'd unzipped his jeans, lifted the hem of her nightshirt and slid inside her, and she had welcomed him, wanted him, come for him.

He'd known then that he'd never met a woman like Fiona

and never would again. She was special. He'd cautioned himself not to lose her.

Of course he'd managed to anyway.

He toyed with her nipples, kneaded her breasts, stroked her stomach, then finally found his way back to her skirt. The button slipped free with a tug, and the zipper glided silently to its end. He slid his hands inside, pushing the skirt over her hips, then leaving it to fall on its own while he explored warm skin, cool silk and delicate lace.

"Please," she whispered again, her voice strained and thick.

His was no better. "Please what?"

"I want you."

"You've got me, darlin'." For as long as she wanted. He hoped for forever, but he could settle for now. Maybe.

She twisted in his arms and yanked his shirt over his head before planting a hot, wet, openmouthed kiss directly over his nipple. Every taut, sucking draw of her mouth sent a jolt of need straight through him, making his muscles tighten, sending blood and heat and need to his groin, pulling a harsh moan from deep inside him. At the same time, she unfastened his jeans as quickly and efficiently as he might have, slid her hand inside and made him groan with need that was quickly becoming desperate.

Forcing her back, he shucked the rest of his clothing while she did the same, then he joined her on the bed, settling between her thighs, sinking inside, pushing, filling, bearing down hard against her until she'd taken every bit of him. Her hips cradled his, and her legs wrapped tightly around him, holding him as if he might try to leave. Not a chance. He'd never felt so wanted, so safe—so hopeful—as when he was inside her. He just might stay there forever.

She moved underneath him, sending shocks of sensation through him. His muscles strained as he held himself rigidly still, letting her torment them both with her lazy, taunting strokes. After a moment, when the sensation was too much, when one more tiny movement was going to make him explode inside her, she became still. Opening his eyes, he saw that she was staring up at him with a tenderness that was normally reserved for Katy. She brushed his hair back, then cupped her palms to his jaw and pulled him to her for a kiss. "Welcome back," she murmured. "I don't have the words to tell you how much I've missed loving you."

Who needed one more movement? Just that admission, that sweet, husky whisper, along with that sweet, tender look, was enough to steal his control, to make him empty inside her and push her over the edge, too. His last coherent thought, before emotion turned everything hazy, was that they'd both been right.

She was special.

And this was right. So damn right.

Fiona could count the number of men she'd been with on less than one hand—two before Justin and none after—but at the moment she couldn't remember their names, or what kind of lovers they'd been or anything else about them. With lazy satisfaction, she acknowledged that he had ruined her for other men. He might want her only because of Katy—even now, the thought stirred an ache in her chest—but she never would have guessed it from the way they'd just made love.

She wondered if he'd guessed that she had fallen in love with him again.

Some time ago, he had collapsed on top of her, then moved to lie face-down, half on the bed, half on her. Now he lifted his head from the pillow and shifted, pressing his knee harder against the hot, damp place where her body had sheltered his. For the first time since she'd seen him at Golda's funeral, he looked totally, utterly relaxed, handsome enough to make a grown woman swoon and appealing enough to break her heart.

Was he patient enough to put it back together?

"You look like a thoroughly satisfied woman, and I know because I'm a—"

"Thoroughly satisfied man." She raised her hand to gently touch his face. "You're incredible."

He turned his head to kiss her palm. "Thank you. All my women tell me that."

"All?" she scoffed. "There were some, but not many."

His dark blue gaze locked with hers. "You sound awfully sure."

"I am. You told me."

"And you believed me." He sounded surprised, relieved and so touched that Fiona was ashamed of her lack of faith.

"I believe you about a lot of things. I believe you'll be the best father any little girl could ever want. I believe Katy's life will be richer for having you in it."

"What about you, Fiona? Can I make your life better?"

"You already have. You gave me Katy."

"And maybe a brother or sister for her." He turned onto his side, resting his head on one hand, laying the other hand on her stomach. "Unless you've done something I don't know about, we didn't use any protection just now."

Smiling faintly, she shook her head. They'd made love twice this evening, and a quick scan of her mental calendar suggested she was in the middle of her cycle. She very well could get pregnant.

"You don't look worried. It wouldn't bother you?"

She shook her head once more. "I love being a mother. I love Katy. I love—" *You.* "We talked about having lots of babies, remember?"

"Yes. But we also talked about getting…" With shadows darkening his eyes and his mouth thinning into a taut line, he trailed off.

"Married," she said gently. "You can say it."

"If you got pregnant, would you marry me?"

She still remembered the exact words he'd spoken the first time they'd talked about marriage. *I love you, Fiona, and I want to spend the rest of my life with you. We'll build a house on top of a mountain and make love and fill it with the happiest, best-loved kids in all the world.* It made the memory of the last time they'd discussed marriage—for Katy's sake, for convenience, because it was "right"—shabby and even more painful in comparison.

"No, Justin. I wouldn't marry you just because I was pregnant."

Tension made the lines of his face harder, harsher. "What do I have to do to change your mind?"

"I don't know," she murmured, though it was a lie. She wanted to shriek, You have to love me—Fiona Frances Lake! Not Katy, not some unborn child who might not even exist. He had to love *her,* want her, need her, more than anything else in the world. He had to match that first proposal or maybe even top it. He had to make her believe in her head, her heart and her soul.

But she couldn't tell him any of that. If she did and he said, Of course I love you, she would never be able to believe him again.

And she really needed to believe him.

Feeling suddenly modest—and fearfully anxious—she tugged the sheet over to cover her, then sat up, the headboard at her back, and clumsily changed the subject. "I think it's time we told Katy the truth about you two."

He sat up, too, facing her, but he didn't bother with modesty. He looked exquisite—broad shoulders, straight spine, impressive…er, muscles. And he looked so serious. "Do you think that's a good idea?"

"People who knew I was dating you six years ago are going to do the math before long. People who didn't know are going to see you and Katy together, with your dark hair and matching blue eyes and identical grins, and they're going to figure it out, too. I'd really prefer that she hear it from us than from the kids at day care."

"What if she doesn't want me for a father?"

"She'll be happy. She likes you."

"How do you know that?"

"She treasures the stuffed bear you gave her. When I asked her if she liked you, she said—nodded yes. This morning she defied me and sneaked out to see you. She sits on your lap. She lets you carry her. Believe me, she likes you." She hesitated, then reached for his hand. "Don't you want her to know?"

"Of course. I want everyone to know the two of you are mine."

Though his macho boast was as hurtful as it was amusing, Fiona chose to ignore the hurt and smile dryly instead. "Gee, maybe you could have T-shirts made that say Property Of Justin Reed, with different colors for each day of the week."

"Would you wear them?"

"Watch it, or you might be wearing the imprint of my palm on your cheek."

"Assaulting a federal agent is a serious crime. I'd have to handcuff you and lock you up."

"Hmm..." She gave him what she hoped was a wicked grin. "Might be fun."

Rising onto his knees, he pulled her down to the bed until she was on her back, caught her wrists and pinned them to the mattress, then settled between her thighs. Already he was hot and swollen. Already she was aching and needy.

He slid inside her and easily found the rhythm that raised goose bumps on her skin and made her muscles tighten. She tried to meet his thrusts, but he used his greater weight to press her to the bed. She tried to touch him but couldn't free her hands. The pleasure built quickly, as if her six years of celibacy hadn't ended a short while ago in this very bed. Of course, the celibacy had nothing to do with it. It had always been like this between them—sizzling, combustible, incredible.

"Let me touch you," she gasped, twisting her wrists as the pleasure threatened to become unbearable. "Please..."

"Let *me* touch *you.*" He ducked his head to take her nipple into his mouth, dragging the rough surface of his tongue across it, slowly, lazily sucking it even as he took her faster, harder, deeper. A soft, helpless cry escaped her, followed by another. His intense gaze caught hers. "Come on, baby," he said, his voice rough and raw. "I want to hear those little sounds you make...those damned erotic sounds that always..."

And she did.

Chapter 11

Justin wasn't sure exactly what awakened him Sunday morning—the lack of sunlight in the room, maybe the hunger that came from skipping dinner last night, the certain knowledge that he wasn't home and wasn't alone. It certainly wasn't the well-rested feeling that came from a good night's sleep. For starters, he hadn't slept more than a few hours—not that he was complaining. The things he and Fiona had done through the night were worth giving up sleep forever.

Without opening his eyes, he knew she was next to him, lying on her side, her back to him. He moved his hand fractionally and felt smooth, warm skin. The innocent touch stirred a not-so-innocent response in his body, and he rolled onto his side, fitting his body to hers. He was deciding whether to kiss her awake or merely slide inside her and see how long that took to awaken her when the mattress sank behind him and something small and bony, like an elbow or knee, poked him in the back. It was more effective at dampening his desire than a cold shower could ever be.

''Fiona?'' he murmured directly into her ear.

''Hmm.'' She found his hand where it rested on her ribs and guided it to her breast, forming his fingers around her nipple, urging him to squeeze it the way she liked. The instant she let go, though, he pulled back.

''Fiona, someone's in bed with us.''

That woke her up. She half sat up, remembered she was naked and caught the sheet, then turned over. ''Hey, baby doll. Where's Grandma?''

He scowled at her. ''How about a polite 'Please leave the room, Kate, and close the door on your way out'?''

She gave him a sleepy smile in return. ''If you intend to spend many nights in this bed, you'd better get used to the fact that Katy's going to come in from time to time. Don't be so modest. You're perfectly decent.''

''Katy!'' Delores called from the stairs. ''Did you wake your mama and tell her I'm fixing breakfast?''

''Thanks, Mom,'' Fiona called. ''We're hungry.''

''We?'' Delores came to an abrupt stop in the doorway, blushed and quickly looked away. ''Good morning, Justin. I didn't know— Of course I should have guessed— Come on, Katy-bug. You can help me in the kitchen.''

Katy hopped down from the bed and left. A moment later, the door closed firmly.

''Well…'' Justin's voice sounded awkward. ''That was embarrassing.''

''No, darlin', 'embarrassing' would have been if they were ten minutes later, because they would have found us like this—''

Letting the sheet fall, she moved to sit astride his hips. Her hair was disheveled, her nipples swollen, her body beautiful and perfect in the thin morning light. Despite his discomfort at having been caught in her bed by both their daughter and Fiona's mother, his body responded to hers, to the slow, wet, heated slide of her flesh against his. He halfheartedly protested, catching hold of her hips, intending to stop her movement. "Fiona, we can't— Your mother— Kate—" But his argument was less than convincing, and he held her still only long enough to thrust inside her.

She leaned forward, her breasts brushing his chest, her mouth brushing his as she huskily replied, "My mother will keep Katy busy downstairs. As long as we're quick and reasonably quiet..."

"You? Quiet?" He slid his hand between their bodies, stroking her in just the right place to make her moan. "You've never been quiet unless I do this." Sliding one hand to the back of her neck, he yanked her close and took her mouth. As he filled it with his tongue, he thrust into her and continued to rub that slick, hot place. He brought her to orgasm within minutes, her frantic gasps and moans muffled by his kiss, and he was only seconds behind her.

Her entire body quivering, she collapsed on top of him, then raised her head to give him a chastening look. "You are a wicked man."

"And you are an incredibly sexy woman. Any chance your mom will take Katy to church with her this morning?"

"So we can stay here and be wicked together? I don't think she would approve."

"Damn," he said, but he wasn't really disappointed. There was always Katy's naptime, and bedtime rolled around every twenty-four hours like clockwork.

With a sudden burst of energy, Fiona jumped out of bed. "I smell coffee and bacon. Want to take a quick shower with me?"

"You and me, naked and wet and soapy together?" he asked dryly. "There wouldn't be anything quick about it. Trust me."

"Yeah, but we wouldn't have to be quiet. Give me five minutes, then the shower is yours."

Expecting five minutes to really be twenty, he stretched out. Before he got too comfortable, though, she came back, wrapped in a towel with another around her hair. ''Go ahead. Make it quick.''

Though he obeyed her and took one of the shortest showers he'd ever had, when he walked back into the bedroom, it was empty. But it smelled of her perfume and baby powder, of his cologne and especially of steamy, hot, incredible sex. If he intended to spend many nights in this bed, he'd better get used to the idea of Katy walking in on them, Fiona had said. He would have to try, because he intended to spend every night in this bed, at least until they built their house on top of a mountain.

When he went downstairs, the television was turned to cartoons in the living room and Delores's and Fiona's voices were coming from the kitchen. He glanced at Katy, surrounded by stuffed animals and dolls on the sofa, then headed for the kitchen—and came to a stop outside the doorway when Delores spoke. ''You're avoiding the question, Fiona. *Has* Justin asked you to marry him?''

There was a moment's silence, then Fiona impatiently replied, ''Yes, Ma. And I said no.''

''Why?''

''Because he asked for all the wrong reasons.''

''And did you explain that to him?''

''No. He has to figure it out for himself.''

''That's ridiculous,'' Delores said. ''Half the time men don't have a clue what they want until we tell them. And how could he be asking for the wrong reasons? He doesn't want to marry you for your money. He certainly didn't propose because of your bright and sunny nature. You can be as prickly as a porcupine, you know. And obviously, you still enjoy sex with him.''

''Ma!''

''I saw that grin this morning. You didn't even have the decency to be embarrassed that you got caught.''

''I was covered from neck to toe. I didn't have anything

to be embarrassed about. Besides, Justin was embarrassed enough for both of us.''

There was a moment's silence, then Delores said, ''He was, wasn't he? It's so cute to see a grown man blush.'' After another silence, she asked, ''Do you love him?''

Justin's breath caught in his chest, and from the sound of her sigh, Fiona's had, too, for a moment. ''You know, Ma, some things between two people need to *stay* between them, at least for a while.''

''If he hurts you again—''

''I'll survive.''

Feeling an intense gaze burning into his back, Justin turned to find Katy standing a few yards away, watching him with an accusing look in her eyes. He held one finger to his lips, then realized the foolishness of it. She wouldn't talk. She couldn't.

Picking her up, he settled her on his hip, then spoke in a heartier voice than necessary. ''Hey, Kate. I hear you spent last night with your grandparents. Did they spoil you rotten?''

She nodded as he carried her into the kitchen. He set her on a chair at the table, but she continued to stand, one thin arm wrapped around his neck. His face warming again, he said hello to Delores and got a smile from Fiona, who was taking a stack of plates from the cabinet.

''We're going to tell Katy about Justin today,'' Fiona said as she spread the plates across the island.

Delores dished up portions of fried potatoes and peppers. ''Don't you think she already knows? We've talked about it in front of her for two weeks.''

''I don't know exactly what she understands.''

''Well, don't go into a lot of detail. She doesn't need to know all that stuff that went on six years ago. Just keep it simple.''

''How simple, Ma?''

"Say, 'Katy-bug—'" Delores turned to face her granddaughter. "Did you know that Justin's your daddy?"

Grinning shyly, Katy nodded, shook her head, then nodded again.

"He is," Delores assured her, "and you can start calling him— What do you want to be called, Justin? Fiona calls her father Dad, except when she's whining, and then she says Daddy. What do you call your father?"

"Sir, until I turned eighteen and he instructed me to call him Harrison, as any other adult of his acquaintance would."

Delores stared at him with dismay. Fiona gave him a sympathetic look. "What about your mother?"

"I always called her Amelia. She didn't want anyone to think she was old enough to have a child, especially after her fourth marriage, when she'd knocked fifteen years off her age. It would have been harder to pass for thirty if people had known she had a twenty-year-old son."

Whipping off the apron that covered her dress, Delores came to the table and patted his arm. "Don't worry. We'll show you what a *real* family's like. Katy-bug, call him Daddy, and do it in your sweetest voice with your sweetest smile—" Delores demonstrated "—and there's nothing he won't do for you...because then he'll have to answer to Grandma. Fiona, I'll see you later."

"Thanks for the breakfast, Ma. And for last night."

Delores got in her parting shot before leaving the room. "Thank Justin for last night. He's the one responsible for that grin. And you'd better hold onto him, because there aren't too many men who can inspire a grin like that. Fortunately, your father's one of them."

A moment later, with the closing of the front door, she was gone.

For a moment the room seemed unusually quiet, then all three of them sighed at once. "I love my mother dearly,"

Fiona said, ''but it can certainly seem peaceful when she leaves.''

''Don't whine,'' Justin said as he helped her carry the plates to the table. ''Sometime I'll take you and Kate to meet my mother. She's the reason London is chilly and damp. Even the sun doesn't want to come out around her.''

Fiona agreed in her sweetest voice. ''Fine—but not until I teach Katy to say Granny Millie. You know, Amelia can just be so difficult for a five-year-old to pronounce. And then we can whip on over to Paris and say hello to Pawpaw Harry—or do you think he'd prefer Papaw Hank?''

The thought of his parents' reactions to the nicknames was enough to make Justin laugh. ''I think he'd hate them both equally, darlin'. But it's a deal. Teach away.'' Just as soon as they were married.

Just as soon as he found the courage to ask for all the right reasons.

Wednesday was Valentine's Day—a perfectly useless holiday, Fiona had always thought, reasonably enough since she'd never been in a relationship when the day rolled around. She didn't know what she was in this Valentine's Day—besides love—but she'd certainly appreciated the surprise of awakening to a bouquet of yellow roses on the nightstand...and another on the dresser...and yet another on the kitchen island. She had been touched—had almost cried—and admitted to Justin that she hadn't given a thought to the holiday. Then she'd seduced him and he'd said that was exactly what he'd wanted for Valentine's Day. Just her. Forever.

She'd wanted to ask him to define ''just her'' and ''forever.'' She didn't, though, for fear of what he might say.

Besides Valentine's Day, Wednesday was also another day at the hospital for Katy, this time for a neuropsychiatric evaluation and an EEG. Fiona had paced the waiting room. She'd watched part of a game show on TV and read part of a magazine. Now she was sitting quietly on the couch, her head on Justin's shoulder, his arm around her. "How do you stay so calm?"

"I'm a federal agent, ma'am. It's part of my job." Then he grinned and murmured, "Truth is, this woman I've been seeing is keeping me up half the night. I don't have the energy to pace."

She gave him a wry look, then sighed. "I hate this, Justin. Every day I think maybe this will be the day she starts talking again, and every night I tell myself, well, maybe tomorrow. She's just so smart and funny and entertaining, and this silence is so unnatural and unnerving. Sometimes I think I can't bear it one more day, and then I feel so selfish because it's so much harder for her."

"You're not selfish, Fiona. You're worried, frustrated and frightened, and that's perfectly natural. Listen, when all this is over, let's go away somewhere—just you, me and Katy. We can take a cruise or go to the beach."

She rested her hand on his chest, where she could feel the steady, reassuring beat of his heart. "The beach would be nice. Katy and I have never seen the ocean before."

"My family's got a place on Nantucket and another off the coast of Georgia."

"What exactly are you calling a 'place'? A twenty-room cottage?"

He looked and sounded uncomfortable when he answered. "The Nantucket house is something like that. I believe there are four or five houses at the Georgia place. It's a, uh, private island."

"A private island, huh? With private beaches and no one else allowed? Where clothing could be optional?" Closing her eyes, she envisioned herself naked on a pristine beach with the Georgia sun beating down and chasing away every memory of Colorado winters from her bones—or, better yet, making love on the beach with Justin while the warm ocean waves gently washed over them. Giving a great sigh, she plaintively asked, ''Could we take along a baby-sitter for Katy?''

''Darlin', we can do anything you want.'' As he kissed her forehead, his cell phone rang. He fished it from his pocket and answered.

Fiona felt the tension streak through him, and a knot of worry formed in her stomach. He listened a few moments, then said, ''I'm at the hospital. I'll meet you at the front entrance.'' After returning the phone to his pocket, he stood up and pulled her up, too. ''That was Colton. The manager of a motel outside town said a man matching Watkins's description just checked in. Colton and the sheriff are going to pick me up and we're heading out there. Take the keys to my truck—'' he pressed them into her hand ''—and I'll give you a call when I'm finished.''

''Be careful.''

He started to walk away, then came back and kissed her mouth. ''Of course I'll be careful. I still intend to marry you.''

She smiled, but as he disappeared into the elevator, it faded sadly. ''Not unless you fall in love with me,'' she whispered.

Great. Now she had two reasons to worry. She paced the waiting room for a while, wandered the length of the hall a time or three. She'd finally taken a seat and was forcing her way through the rest of the magazine she'd started earlier when Dr. Hunter, the neuropsychiatrist, came into the waiting room with Katy.

''We're through for the day,'' he said as Katy skipped over to Fiona. ''I'll need her back here tomorrow at nine. We'll start the tests then.''

''We'll be here.''

Katy looked around the room, then back at Fiona, an obvious question in her eyes. Fiona smoothed her hair. ''Your daddy had to go to work. We'll see him later, okay?''

Her face falling, Katy nodded and slid her hand into

Fiona's. They bundled up at the hospital doors, then crossed the parking lot to Justin's truck. It had every luxury—even heated leather seats—and cost more than many small houses, was twice the size of her car and a dream to drive. It must be nice to decide one afternoon to buy such a vehicle, pay cash for it and drive away the same afternoon, she thought, then regretted it. Money couldn't buy happiness. It couldn't make people love you.

She loved Justin for free. Too bad she was afraid to tell him so. Maybe soon. If he stuck around. If neither of them blew it again.

They were halfway to the day care center when, on impulse, Fiona made a right turn instead of a left. "We're going to go by your father's office before I drop you off at day care, okay? We'll see if he's back and can have a late lunch with us."

Katy shook her head mutinously, meaning, Fiona knew, that she didn't want to go to day care. For that reason, she ignored her response.

She parked in front of the police station, then she and Katy went inside. "Hi," she greeted the desk sergeant. "Is Special Agent Reed back yet?"

"No, ma'am. Would you like to leave a message for him?"

"Um..." As Fiona debated what she would say, a blast of cold air blew in. She glanced at the double doors and the man standing just inside. He was a stranger, though the time when she'd known everyone in town was long past. Turning back to the officer, she said, "Yes, I think I would. Could I borrow a pen and paper?"

The officer slid both pen and paper across the counter to her, and she moved toward the end so he could help the stranger. She wrote Justin's name, then stopped. What could she say? *Sorry I missed you?* Or how about, *Sorry. I missed you?*

While she tried to decide, she couldn't help but overhear

the stranger's request. "I'm looking for the ATF agent who was on the news last week. Reed's his name. Justin Reed."

"Isn't everyone?" the officer asked dryly with a look at Fiona. "He's out at the moment. Would you like to leave him a message, too?"

The man looked at her, then smiled at Katy. It was a simple gesture, but it made Fiona's skin crawl, made her want to grab Katy and pull her to the other side where he couldn't see her. "Oh, he'll get the message all right. You see..." He set the gym bag he carried on the counter and reached inside, pulling out first a gun, then a device that looked horribly like a bomb to Fiona, and then he smiled again. "I'm Patrick Watkins. I'm the man he's looking for."

Justin stared out the side window of the sheriff's patrol unit as they headed back into town. He was accustomed to leads that went nowhere. They were a part of the job. But something just didn't feel right about this particular one.

With backup consisting of about half the sheriff's and police departments, they'd approached the old motel with caution. They'd stayed some distance back and set up a perimeter, had run the license tags on the cars in the parking lot and tried to reach the manager by phone. Turned out the cars belonged to him and his wife, and they weren't answering the phone because they were both hard of hearing and too stubborn to wear hearing aids. They insisted they hadn't rented a room to anyone matching Watkins's description—not to anyone at all today—and they both swore they hadn't placed a call to the police department.

But someone had. Why? For the juvenile pleasure of sending them on a wild-goose hunt?

Or to draw as many cops out of town as possible?

He leaned forward, tapping the police chief on the shoulder. "Colton, try to raise your dispatcher on the radio."

"Why?"

"Just do it."

Trading curious looks with the sheriff, Colton keyed the microphone and called in. He got no response, not in three tries. At the same time, Justin dialed the number on his cell phone, but it rang endlessly. He swore furiously as he disconnected. "Watkins is in town. He's the one who called in the report, to get us away from the police station."

Taking the microphone, the sheriff called his own dispatcher, then flipped on the lights and siren and floored the accelerator.

Justin leaned back in the seat, silently berating himself. If he'd been paying closer attention to his case than to his love life, he would have been expecting something like this. It was classic—draw the cops to the wrong location while carrying out the crime where they should have been. Damn it, he should have known, should have focused solely on Watkins, shouldn't have let Fiona distract him.

But Fiona wasn't just his love life. She and Katy were his *life.* Without them, he had nothing.

By the time they reached the police station, the few remaining officers and deputies in town had blocked off the streets on all four sides. Most of them were on crowd control, but one young deputy excitedly met them as they passed through the barriers erected to keep people back. "He's inside, sir. He's armed, he's got explosives, and he's got hostages—about nine of 'em, as far as we can tell."

Colton did a mental count. "Eight of them should be mine. The other one—"

Dragging his hand through his hair, Justin glanced around, passing over, then coming back to, a brand-new sport-utility vehicle parked in front of the police station. Letting loose a stream of curses, he started for the building, but didn't get far before Colton Stuart jerked him back. "What the hell are you doing?"

"The ninth one is Fiona! That's my truck. I left it with her at the hospital. The son of a bitch has Fiona!"

‘‘And your busting in there isn’t going to help her. Has anyone gone in or come out?’’

The deputy shook his head.

‘‘What’s the number at the day care center?’’ Justin demanded.

The sheriff and his deputy looked at him as if he were crazy. Understanding turned Colton’s expression grim as he gave it from memory. Justin’s hands trembled as he dialed the number, but his voice was steady when he identified himself. He asked about Katy, then numbly disconnected without another word. ‘‘Katy’s with her,’’ he whispered. ‘‘She’s inside.’’

Colton walked to the nearest police car, parked at an angle across the street, picked up the microphone and switched the siren to the public address system. ‘‘Mr. Watkins, this is Colton Stuart, chief of police. I’m going to call you on the phone so we can talk in private, all right?’’

He dialed the number and waited patiently. Justin counted off the seconds, stopping abruptly when Colton spoke into the phone. ‘‘I understand you’ve got some of my people in there. Why don’t you let them go, so I can come in and we can talk?’’

Predictably Watkins refused.

‘‘At least send the civilians out, especially the little girl. You don’t want to risk hurting a little girl.’’

His little girl, Justin thought, coldly furious. He’d sworn to make Watkins pay for what he’d already done to Katy. If he hurt her again, if he did *anything* to her or Fiona…

Colton talked for a few more minutes before hanging up. ‘‘He’d planned to be gone before we got back here, but he’s having some trouble with the steel door. He said everyone’s all right. He’s got all the exits from the building wired and has a nice little package set up just inside the front doors that will go off if anyone tries to gain entry.’’ Colton directed his next words to Justin. ‘‘I could hear Katy crying in the background. He said she’s just scared. He’s going to figure out a plan of action and give me a call. We'd probably better do the same.''

''I have a plan of action,'' Justin said bitterly. ''I'm going to kill the bastard.''

Fiona's head ached. Her back ached. She was hot, hungry and scared, but she didn't focus on her discomforts. She didn't consider stopping the side-to-side rocking that had helped put Katy to sleep. She didn't think about how much she hated Patrick Watkins or the harm she wished him. All she could let herself think about was keeping Katy safe, and Justin. He was surely outside now, working on a plan to free them.

''Want me to hold her for a while?''

Fiona smiled at Mariellen, one of Juliette's two records clerks, and matched her whisper. ''Thanks, but I'd better hang onto her. I'd rather not wake her if I can avoid it.''

''Poor kid must be scared to death—'' Mariellen blanched and rephrased it. ''Must be scared out of her wits. To tell the truth, so am I. This is *not* how I imagined spending my Valentine's Day.''

''We'll be okay. He's never hurt anyone before. There's no reason for him to start now.'' *Please, God.*

''How do you know that?''

''Justin told me.''

''Justin. Special Agent Reed.'' Mariellen's smile was regretful. ''I knew he was seeing someone, but I couldn't figure out who. Sheesh, he wouldn't even give me the time of day.'' Her gaze turned speculative as it moved to Katy. ''Looks like he gave you a whole lot more.''

Fiona shushed her as Watkins glared at them. He had them all sitting on the floor in the center of the room, with the police officers handcuffed together. She was grateful he'd left her, Katy, Mariellen and Faye, the other clerk, free, or Katy really would have had fits.

"What are you talking about?" he demanded, careful to stay out of sight of the glass doors.

"I asked if she wanted me to hold her daughter," Mariellen replied. "You know, you're going to have to let us go to the bathroom soon. We're also going to need food. We were supposed to go to lunch two hours ago."

"Shut up, or I'll have to gag you."

Mariellen opened her mouth to retort, then closed it again and smiled sarcastically.

Watkins pointed his pistol at Fiona, making her breath catch in her chest. "What's her name?"

"K-Katy."

"How old is she?"

"Five."

"Where's her father?"

Her mouth went dry, and it felt as if her tongue were permanently glued to the roof. "G-good question."

"What's Reed to you?"

"He—he's my neighbor and—and friend."

He raised his other hand so she could see the folded sheet of paper clasped between two fingers. "Try again."

It was the note she'd written Justin and left on the counter when Watkins had ordered them to the middle of the room. If something went wrong, if for the first time, one of his crimes ended in tragedy, she'd wanted at least a chance for Justin to know the truth, and so she'd scribbled it on the notepad. *I love you.*

She smiled and was surprised she could. "We're very *close* neighbors."

"Is that his kid?"

Another smile. "He's only been in town a couple of weeks. That would be some miracle, wouldn't it?"

"She's a cute kid. You want to lay her down on that couch over there?"

She looked at the vinyl sofa fifteen feet away, then shook her head. "Thank you, but I'd rather not."

He fell silent, and Fiona went back to rocking Katy, watching her sleep and listening to the clock on the wall tick off the seconds. She figured about six hundred of them had passed when the phone rang, startling them all.

Watkins listened for a few minutes before swearing. "Apparently, Chief, you don't take me seriously. Let me talk to Reed." He paused for a moment, then said, "Listen up, Reed, make those people understand that I'm not playing games here. They've got ten minutes to have one of these bubbas unlock that door for me. If they don't do it by then, I'll have no choice but to blow it, and who knows what kind of damage that could do?" He paused again, then grinned at Fiona. "Hey, Reed? Don't forget I've got your pretty little redhead and Katy in here. Be real persuasive, or they might get hurt."

As the line went dead, Justin handed the phone back to Colton. "Does one of your people in there know the combination to that lock?"

"Sergeant Hamilton does."

"Tell him to open it and let Watkins take what he wants."

"You can't do that!"

Justin turned to look at the stranger who'd spoken. He wore a suit, glasses and a boring tie, carried a briefcase and looked like a damn insurance salesman. "Who the hell are you?"

The little man puffed up. "I'm Howard Madden. I'm the authorized representative of the insurance companies which own those jewels. It's luck that I was changing planes in Denver and heard about this on the news. I came straight here."

"We don't need you here," Justin said dismissively.

"You can't let that man walk out with 7.4 million dollars worth of *our* property."

Justin leaned menacingly close. "*That man* has my family inside. I'm going to let him walk out with anything he damn well pleases!"

The man backed up a step, then turned to Colton. "Chief Stuart, be reasonable. Patrick Watkins has never harmed anyone in his life. He's not going to hurt these people. You can't just hand over a fortune like that. There's no reason to."

"Mr. Madden," Colton began. "Patrick Watkins has never been in a situation where he had to take hostages. He's never been trapped, never come so close to getting caught. We don't have a clue in hell what he's going to do. We do know he's got a gun and enough explosives to take out an entire city block, and we know he's got eight police department employees, a woman and her five-year-old girl in there. Our primary goal is to get those people released safely. If it means letting Watkins go, fine. If it means giving him your jewels, that's fine, too. Surely you don't want to explain to the families of those ten people that you'd rather let them die than risk losing a few diamonds and emeralds. You can start with Special Agent Reed here."

Justin scowled at the man. "Go ahead, Mr. Madden. The woman and the five-year-old girl are mine. Tell me the jewels are more important than their lives." And after he'd punched some sense into the little bastard, he would call Watkins back and tell him he'd won.

"I— Of course— Nothing—"

Colton gestured to an officer nearby to escort the man away, then checked his watch. "Call him. Tell him to put Hamilton on the phone."

Justin did as directed, handed him the phone, then turned away, rubbing his eyes with the heels of his hands. When he opened them again, there was a cup of coffee in front of him, offered by the sheriff.

"You look like you could use something stronger, but this is the best I can offer." The sheriff leaned against a parked car and sipped his own coffee. "You give him the jewels, and then he'll want a car. He'll release the hostages, though he'll probably keep one for insurance. Then what?"

"He'll head out of town."

"Driving a car we can identify. Every law enforcement agency within five hundred miles will be looking for it before he reaches the city limits."

Justin sipped the coffee—strong, black, bitter—and waited for the sheriff to go on.

"My men who've been out patrolling reported there are cars parked alongside the roads. Now, people do that all the time up here—leave the car on the shoulder and go hiking. Kids go into the woods to drink or fool around. People can't wait to get to the next bathroom to take care of business. But these cars... There's one on every highway leaving Grand Springs, and each one's parked around a curve, where you don't see it until you come around the curve and there it is."

"Watkins's cars?"

"Seems reasonable to me. Ditch the one we can identify. Take off in a different one. We wouldn't have any idea what to look for."

"Sheriff, tell your men—"

The older man's grin stopped him. "I've got some pretty good mechanics working for me. Those cars aren't going anywhere."

Colton joined them, rolling his head from side to side. The sheriff gave him a sympathetic look. "Brings back memories, doesn't it?"

Colton nodded, then explained to Justin. "A few years ago, a local businessman ordered the murder of Grand Springs's mayor—my mother. It took nearly a year for the police to build a case against him. When they got too close, he took Juliette hostage and held her for thirty-six hours. She was unharmed, but he died when we rescued her." He rolled his head again, then gestured across the street. "That blue sedan is Watkins's car. Hamilton's opening the lock-up for him now. He said he'll leave the hostages inside, except for one, when he has the jewels. Hamilton volunteered to be that one.'' Colton looked past them, nodding to someone out of Justin's sight, then said, ''You've got company, son.''

He looked over his shoulder as an officer moved a barrier to allow Delores and Griff Lake through. They both looked as sick as he felt. ''Is it true, Justin?'' Delores asked, her voice shaky but her grip painfully strong as she squeezed his hand. ''Is a man with a bomb holding Fiona and Katy hostage?''

''Yes, ma'am, but they're all right, and he says he's going to release the hostages soon.''

''What the hell are they doing in there?'' Griff demanded. ''Katy should be at day care, and Fiona's supposed to be at the shop. Why in hell were they at the police station? Because of you? This is your fault?''

''Griff,'' Delores admonished, but he ignored her and stared Justin down.

Was it his fault? Justin wondered bleakly. He'd been suckered in by Watkins's ploy. Fiona and Katy had probably gone to the station to see if he was in. He hadn't kept them safe. Hell, yes, it was his fault. ''Mr. Lake, I swear, we'll do everything we can to keep them safe.''

''Truth is, you can't do anything but wait, can you?''

''At the moment,'' Justin admitted. ''Just wait and pray.''

''Justin,'' Colton called.

He gently freed his hand from Delores's and joined the chief. ''He's got the jewels. He's coming out, and he's got two hostages with him. The rest of them are handcuffed inside. He said he's disarmed the bomb at the front door, but I'm not inclined to take his word for it. I'm ordering everyone to stay away from the building until you've checked it out.''

His gaze locked on the glass doors, Justin absently nodded. Wait out a hostage situation, disarm a few bombs—all in a day's work. And Fiona thought he might actually miss this job.

Slowly one of the doors swung open, and Justin's heart stopped beating. The two hostages the bastard had chosen were Fiona and Katy.

He didn't realize he'd moved forward until Colton grabbed his arm. Justin shrugged him off and moved as close as the sidewalk. "Hiding behind a woman and a small child, Patrick? What kind of hotshot serial bomber does that?"

"One who knows where you've been spending your nights. Fiona and Katy are going with me."

"No. Leave them here, and I'll go with you."

Watkins smiled. "I don't think you'd make such a great hostage. I don't think anyone would be as concerned for your safety as you are for theirs. You do everything the way I say, and you'll get them back unharmed. And don't test me. Don't see how far you can push me before I take action. Now...move away from the car."

Justin moved a few yards into the grass, and Watkins headed for the car. He held Fiona around the shoulders with a pistol in that hand. The black bag he carried in his other hand, presumably, held the jewels and at least some of his explosives. Because his hands were full, he couldn't hold onto Katy, too. Fiona's hand rested on her shoulder, guiding her. They both looked terrified. Hell, *he* was terrified, and he'd been through years of training to deal with this sort of thing.

All they could do was wait and pray, he'd told the Lakes. He'd never been much for praying, but he'd never had anything worth praying for before. Please, God, he silently pleaded, keep them safe.

Keep my family safe.

Chapter 12

Fiona felt as if she were being choked. The weight of Watkins's arm over her shoulders was oppressive, and she was practically paralyzed with fear. But she was also very hopeful. When he'd announced he was taking her and Katy with him, she'd gotten a moment to whisper in her daughter's ear. How well Katy would obey remained to be seen. She might not have understood. She might be too scared. She might…

They drew even with Justin, and Fiona gave Katy a push in his direction. She almost wept with relief when her daughter took off running, yelling, "Daddy! Daddy!" She almost collapsed with gratitude when he grabbed Katy in his arms and held her tightly, kissing her face, murmuring to her, holding her protectively, possessively, against him. Her daughter was safe with her father. What better Valentine's Day gift could she ask for?

The pressure around her throat made Fiona gasp. Watkins pulled her back so far that she stumbled. "You're smarter than I gave you credit for. That's okay. Let him have the kid. I've still got you."

He walked her to his car, shoved her in on the passenger side, then ordered her to slide across to the driver's seat. He started the engine, then gestured with the pistol for her to move. Feeling Justin's gaze burning into her, she raised her left hand in a hesitant wave, thinking, please, God, don't let this be goodbye. Then she twisted around to see behind her as she backed out of the space.

"Wh-where are we going?" she asked as she slowly drove through the opening where grim-faced officers had moved the barriers.

"Just keep going straight on this road."

Denver was his destination, she guessed—a big city, an easy place to get lost. Main Street turned into a highway that, after a beautiful drive through the mountains, ran into the interstate. From there it was a breeze to reach Denver or any number of places, provided he could avoid the police.

"I wish you wouldn't do this," she murmured as they passed the city limits sign. "My daughter needs me. She's been through a really tough time. Her emotional state is fragile right now, and I don't know what it'll do to her if anything happens to me."

"You lied about her being Reed's kid."

"Don't take it personally," she said, unable to control the sarcasm that crept into her voice. "I've lied to everyone about it. Justin didn't know himself until a few weeks ago." Glancing in the rearview mirror, she saw what looked like the sheriff's patrol unit, a big sport-utility similar to Justin's, some distance back. Behind it was a number of other units. They made up some sort of bizarre parade.

Seeing where her attention had strayed, Watkins glanced behind them, then reached into his bag for the radio he'd taken from Sergeant Hamilton. "You there, Reed?"

There was a moment's static, then Justin's voice. "Yeah."

"Like I said, do what I tell you and you'll get her back. That's a nice distance you've got there. Don't come any closer. I assume from the lack of traffic on the road that there's a roadblock somewhere up ahead. Am I right?"

This time it wasn't Justin who replied but the sheriff. "Yes, sir. It's about two miles ahead."

"Not a problem. Of course, as we approach, you'll radio your officers to let us pass."

There was a long silence, then a grim response. "Of course."

Was there anything she could do? Fiona wondered desperately. Drive the car into the side of the mountain? Simply stop and refuse to go on? Get out of the car and force him to either continue his escape alone or shoot her? *Would* he really shoot her, or would he figure he was better off without her and get the hell out? Justin said he'd never hurt anyone before Katy, and he hadn't intended to do that, but could she risk her life on that? Didn't most criminals start out as petty criminals before graduating to the heavy-duty crimes? This could be the crime that moved Patrick Watkins up a giant step from jewel thief and bomber to murderer.

And she had two wonderful reasons for not becoming his first victim.

They were on a downhill grade with mountains on the left and a two-thousand-foot drop on the right when the roadblock came into sight ahead. Two sheriff's cars were parked at angles across the road, and the two deputies stood behind them, rifles with scopes at the ready.

"Stop here," Watkins directed. "Let's see if the sheriff's true to his word. If not, you'll get to see how much fun it is to ram a couple of police cars."

"You know this from experience?" she asked dryly.

"Actually, no. I've had very little contact with law enforcement. I'm too good for them to even come close."

She couldn't resist giving him a sidelong look. "We're

sitting on a highway with cops in front of us and cops behind us. Are you sure you're not just a little overconfident?''

The two deputies ahead moved, getting in their cars, backing up, pulling to opposite sides of the road, and Watkins laughed. ''Good call, Sheriff,'' he said into the radio as he gestured to Fiona to go on. ''Special Agent Reed, you see that curve up ahead? We're going to slowly drive around that curve and stop. I want you and all your people to stop at the roadblock. If you do, if no one follows us around the curve, I'll let Fiona go. Do you understand?''

''I understand,'' Justin said. The worry in his voice made Fiona ache, made her long to grab the radio from Watkins and tell him she was sorry, she loved him, and she would be thrilled to marry him even if he didn't love her. She didn't move, though, other than to flex her hands that ached from gripping the steering wheel so tightly. ''How long do you want us to wait?''

''Until you hear my signal.''

''And what will that be?''

''Oh, you'll recognize it. Trust me.'' He laid the radio aside and pulled a pair of handcuffs from his bag. Before she could even wonder, he'd snapped one cuff around her right wrist, looped the chain through the bottom section of the steering wheel and fastened the other around her left wrist. Next he whipped out a bandanna, folded it in fourths lengthwise and efficiently tied it around her head, completely covering her eyes.

''What are you doing?'' she demanded, hearing the helplessness and fear in her voice.

''This curve here is only the first in a series of curves. You probably know that, living in the area. You may have guessed that I have a vehicle parked on the other side, one that no one can identify. I can't very well let you see it and give them a description or the tag number. That wouldn't be very smart, would it?''

Fiona took a couple of deep breaths, swallowing her

panic. ''But letting me drive blindfolded, with that huge drop-off on the right?''

''I'll do the steering. Ease off the brake. Don't give it any gas. Just let it coast down the hill. Damn, I'm just too good to be believed.''

He sounded as if he were having the time of his life.

''What the hell is he doing?'' Colton demanded.

Justin lowered the binoculars. ''He blindfolded her. So she can't see his getaway car.''

''What do you think his signal is going to be?''

Ignoring the sheriff's question, he got out and walked a few feet past the roadblock, staring at the place where Fiona and Watkins had disappeared from sight. It was colder out here than it had been in town, and Fiona hadn't been wearing a coat.

Then he gave himself a mental shake. She was being held hostage by a career criminal who was armed to the teeth and had a fondness for blasting things to smithereeens. Being cold was the least of her worries.

You'll recognize the signal, Watkins had said, which suggested it was something Justin would associate with him, or something he would associate with Justin, and since they were both in the explosives business…

He took a few halting steps toward the curve, then started running. He was only a hundred feet from the place where he'd last seen Fiona when a series of explosions shattered the air. The ground shook violently under his feet, knocking him to the pavement, and small rocks and dirt cascaded down from the hillside above him. On his feet again instantly, he raced around the curve and skidded to a stunned stop.

Watkins had brought half the mountainside down onto the roadway. The road was buried in a seventy-foot-wide swath of dirt and rock, and his getaway car was up to its roof in rubble. Justin didn't give a damn about that, though he hoped the bastard was dead. It was the other car that concerned him—the sedan Fiona was in. The sedan precariously balanced on rubble and guard rail, with the front half teetering in thin air.

"Oh, damn." Colton stopped beside him and raised the radio he'd thought to grab. "Get the sheriff's truck down here. Anyone have a towing chain in your car, we need it. Get a wrecker out here *now* and call EMS, too."

Justin scrambled over the dirt, working his way as close to the driver's side as he could. "Fiona? Darlin', can you hear me?"

"J-Justin?" Her voice was weak, tearful. "Where are you?"

"I'm over here to your left. Are you hurt?"

"Not yet."

"You want to take the blindfold off?"

She ducked her head in an odd gesture, then raised it. "I can't reach it."

"Why not, babe? Are your arms pinned?"

"I'm—I'm handcuffed to the steering wheel."

Justin looked at Colton, who'd heard her plaintive words and looked as grim as he felt, and he echoed his earlier words. "Oh, damn." Forcing as much calm into his voice as he could muster, he said, "It'll be okay, Fiona. We'll get you out."

"It feels like the car's suspended in air."

He took a deep breath, then said, "It—it kind of is, so don't move, babe. Just—just be as still as you can, okay? We're going to get a chain on it, and as soon as it's secure, I'm going to come in and get you, okay?"

"Okay."

"I'll be back in a minute." He climbed over the rubble to pavement as the sheriff parked his Tahoe as close to the landslide as possible. A deputy pulled up behind him and brought a towing chain from the trunk of his car, and he and another officer went to work securing one end to the rear axle of the sedan, the other to the towing hook welded to the Tahoe's frame. Once that was done, the sheriff backed up until the chain was taut.

"It's not perfect, but the Tahoe outweighs the car by a ton or so. It should hold until we can get a wrecker here," Colton said. "A couple are on their way. You have a handcuff key?"

Handcuffs used a universal key, and Justin kept his on his key ring, even when he didn't have the cuffs with him. "Yeah—no. I gave my keys to Fiona this morning."

Colton handed his over, then added a second one. "Just in case you get in there and drop one. We don't want you scrambling around trying to find it." He hesitated, then went on. "One of my officers volunteered to go in. He's smaller than you—lighter."

Justin shook his head. "I'll do it."

"I'd prefer you didn't. What about—" Breathing deeply, Colton looked away, then back. "What about Katy? If anything happens—"

He meant if the chain broke, if the blast had weakened the road, if it gave way, if the car tumbled two thousand feet to the bottom of the gorge with Fiona in it.

He meant if Fiona died.

The possibility sent a stab of pain through Justin so sharp that he barely managed to keep from doubling over with it. "Nothing's going to happen."

"Justin—"

"When Juliette's life was in danger, did you stand out on the sidewalk and watch while someone else went in to rescue her?"

"No. But Juliette and I didn't have a child."

Justin thought of Katy and how he'd felt when she'd called him Daddy, about leaving her, never getting the chance to talk to her again, never getting to know her or watch her grow up. The idea was almost more than he could bear.

Losing Fiona *was* more than he could bear.

"Fiona's life is in danger because of me. She was at the police station to see me. He chose her because of me. I have to do this for her."

Colton laid his hand on Justin's shoulder. "Why don't you go over and talk to her? Keep her calm. Promise her a Valentine's dinner to remember."

He returned to the driver's side, working as near the edge as he dared. "Fiona, I'm back again. Hey, did you hear Katy back there in town? She was talking, darlin'."

"She called you Daddy."

"Yeah. I—I left her with your mom and dad. We'll pick her up as soon as we get back to town, and then I think we need that vacation we talked about."

"Your family's island in Georgia sounds awfully good right now." After a moment's silence, she asked, "Did Watkins get away?"

"No. One of the deputies had disabled the car."

"The explosion—what was that?"

"He'd planted charges on the mountainside and brought it down across the highway. He intended to be long gone and to keep us from following. Unfortunately for him, he set off the blast before discovering that his car wasn't going anywhere. And unfortunately for us, either the mountain was more unstable than he thought or he miscalculated how much explosive he needed, and you got caught in the slide."

"Is he alive?"

Justin glanced over his shoulder. A number of officers were at work, digging out his car, but they had a long way to go before they could get him out. "I don't know, and I don't care. If he isn't, it's no more than he deserves. Hey, remember that day in your shop when you showed me your phone bill and I said there was something important about that date?"

"The date I left the message that I was pregnant?"

"Yeah. I remember what it was. We had one hell of an

electrical storm that night, and my apartment got hit by lightning. It zapped my television, satellite dish, computer, VCR, stereo, the phones—just about everything."

"Including the answering machine." Underneath the bandanna, her pale lips curved in a smile. "How in the world can you remember that?"

Though she couldn't see him, he shrugged. "It was my birthday, and I remember thinking only a Reed could mark his birthday by frying about ten thousand dollars' worth of electronics."

Fiona would have shaken her head in dismay if she weren't too afraid to move. August 17, he'd muttered that day in the shop. *Why does that date seem important?* Not once had he ever mentioned that it was his birthday! Of course it was important! "Oh, Justin," she said with a sigh. "Your birthday will always be important from now on—and it won't have anything to do with electronic equipment...though there might be a few sparks."

He was silent for so long that she panicked. "Are you there?"

"I'm not leaving you, babe."

"If...if something goes wrong—"

"Don't even think it," he said fiercely.

"Promise me—promise me you'll take care of Katy." Tears seeped into her voice and into the bandanna that covered her eyes. "Please, Justin."

"Nothing's going to go wrong."

"Please..."

"I promise I will take care of you *and* Katy for the rest of my life." He was trying to smile—she could tell it in his voice. "I've waited forever to be part of a family. You think I'm going to let it break up before we even make it official?"

"Justin? We're ready." That was Colton's voice, and it came from somewhere behind the car.

"Okay, babe. The tow truck's here. They're getting another chain on the car now. We're going to break the back window, and I'm coming in. Stay as still as you can, but don't be afraid. I'm not going to let anything happen to you, okay? You ready?''

She nodded, unable to speak for the lump in her throat. She'd never been so scared in her life, had never prayed so fervently, had never been so terrifyingly aware of her own mortality, or of Justin's. What if the chains couldn't hold the weight of the car and both of them? God help them, what if it went over the side with him inside, too? Who would raise Katy then? Who would take care of her and teach her and love her?

''Justin!'' she cried. ''Please don't come in here! Just—just throw the key to me! Let me come out by myself!''

He ignored her pleas and soothingly replied, ''I'll be there in a minute, darlin'.''

''You ever use a window punch?'' Colton asked. ''It's spring-loaded. Just put it against the upper or lower corner of the window, and it does all the work.''

Fiona cursed the blindfold that kept her from seeing what was going on, but she couldn't raise her hands more than a few inches above her lap and the space was too cramped to bend over that far. She couldn't even try to rub it off using her shoulder. All she could do was listen. Wait. Pray.

There was a small, sharp report, followed by the faint cracking of glass, then the car shuddered as someone—not Justin, she prayed, please let it be someone besides him—climbed onto the trunk. Then came the horrible shriek of steel bending and collapsing, and the car tilted sharply to the left, throwing her against the door.

''It's okay, Fiona,'' Justin said, his voice coming through the windowless back. ''The guard rail gave way, and some of the dirt and rock under the car slid over the edge, but they've got two heavy-duty chains attached to it. We're not going anywhere, babe. Let's just give it a minute to settle, then I'll come up there.''

"Justin, please, just throw the key up here. Please, for Katy's sake—"

"How are you going to catch the key when you can't move your hands or see?" He sounded amused, when she knew damned well he wasn't. *She* certainly wasn't.

"She's your daughter, damn it!" she shouted. "You have a responsibility to her!"

"And I love you, damn it!" he shouted back, emotion making his voice ragged. "I have a responsibility to you, too!"

She sat motionless, his words echoing in her mind. If he'd said he loved her a few minutes ago, in private where no one could hear, she would have assumed he was just trying to give her reassurance and support. She certainly wouldn't have held him to any declaration made under stress. But to shout it in front of everyone, to lose his composure and give in to emotion with most of the cops in the county listening…

In spite of her fear, in spite of her tears, she smiled. "Well," she said mildly, "I love you, too. Though I'd hoped to have a little privacy when I told you so."

He sounded half amused, half chagrined. "We don't have too big an audience. Just thirty or forty or so." He exhaled heavily. "I think the car's stabilized for the moment. I'm coming in after you. Just a word of warning, though—when I get you out, I'm going to hold you to it. That vacation just became a honeymoon."

The car shifted and rocked as he climbed into the back seat. She smelled his cologne when he drew near, then felt his hands, cold but steady, on hers. One cuff opened, then the other, and her hands were free. While he unfastened her seat belt, she yanked the bandanna away. "Come on, babe," he said. "Let's get the hell out of here."

She crawled into the back seat, then onto the trunk, where Colton grabbed hold of her and lifted her away. Justin jumped to the ground and pulled her into his arms, kissing her long and hard. When they were both breathless, he ended the kiss, but he didn't let her go. "I meant it, Fiona. I love you, and I intend to marry you."

She gently touched his face, then rose onto her toes to brush her mouth over his. "I love you, too, Justin, and I intend to let you. Just remember—you've got to stay with me forever."

Taking a blanket from a nearby paramedic, he wrapped it around her shoulders, then, still holding onto her, started walking away from the landslide and toward all the cars back at the roadblock. "Forever," he repeated wondrously. When he looked at her, his dark blue eyes were filled with satisfaction, tenderness and pure sweet love. "That's exactly what I wanted for Valentine's Day. You, Katy and me—together forever."

"Who was St. George?"

Justin glanced at Fiona as, hand in hand, they followed a sandy trail between sea oats to their favorite beach on St. George Island. "Who knows? Definitely not one of my Reed ancestors."

"Let's not knock your Reed ancestors. One of them had the sense to buy this wonderful place, and generations of them have had the sense to keep it."

"Not sense. It belongs equally to all the family, and selling it has to be a unanimous decision. Since they've never all agreed on anything in my lifetime, the island will probably stay in the family a few generations more."

They climbed a sandy slope and stood for a moment staring at the ocean. At least, Fiona did. Justin stared at her instead. In the six weeks since her Valentine's Day adventure, she had somehow become more beautiful than ever. Today she looked incredible. Her red hair was pulled back from her face, and her skin had taken on a pale golden hue in their week on the island. She wore a long slim skirt that reached her ankles and was unbuttoned to high on her thigh, and a sleeveless white cotton top that clung tightly, enticingly, to her breasts and midriff. It was partly unbuttoned, too, and revealed a tantalizing bit of skin. He would soon see a lot more. Every day they made love on the beach, and every day she sighed and said how incredible it was.

As he spread the quilt he carried on the sand, she opened her arms wide and turned in a slow circle, breathing deeply of the salty sea air. He stripped down naked, then stretched out on the quilt, leaning back on his elbows. Just watching her made him hard, and having her only made him want her more. He didn't think it would ever change.

"Did I mention that there's two feet of snow on the ground in Grand Springs right now?"

"A time or two."

"And here we are being wicked on a sunny warm beach." She unbuttoned her blouse and let it fall to the ground, then twirled again.

"Come sit on my lap, pretty girl, and I'll show you new meanings for 'wicked.'"

Stepping over him, she gracefully lowered herself to her knees. Her skirt puddled around her, until she undid the few remaining buttons and tossed it aside. She took him inside her so easily, so smoothly, then leaned forward to cup his face in her hands, suddenly intensely serious. "I love you. How did I ever live without you?"

"You'll never have to again."

They made love, fast and hard the first time, then long and hard the second. Long after, Fiona lay back on the quilt, her body slick with sweat, smelling of him and tasting of him, and gave a great sigh. "This is incredible."

"Will you miss it when we go home?"

She gave him a puzzled look. "Miss it? We're going to do it at home, too, sweetheart—at least for a while."

"Make love on the beach? How can we do that when there's no beach in Grand Springs?"

Laughing, she rolled over close to kiss him. "The incredible part is the making love, not the beach, you foolish man. *You're* incredible, no matter where."

"Oh. And what do you mean—at least for a while?"

She dug in her skirt pocket for her watch, then began lazily getting dressed. "It's time to meet Katy. And what I mean by 'for a while' is there comes a point when a woman's pregnant where she has to stop indulging in love-making until the baby's born."

Justin stared at her numbly. "P-pr-pregnant? You're pregnant? We're going to have a baby? Another baby?" He was overwhelmed. Excited. Too touched for words, and so he didn't try to find them. He simply, tenderly, kissed her.

They dressed, shook the sand from the quilt and walked along the beach toward the southern end of the island. By the time they reached the dock, Katy was running toward them, leaving her baby-sitter behind.

"Hi, Mom!" she said excitedly, then began pulling shells from her plastic bucket. "Hey, Daddy, look what I found. That's a sand dollar, and that's a sand dollar, and that's a real live, dead seahorse, and that's a—I don't remember, but isn't it pretty? And look at this. It's a crab with its own little house on its back, but I'm not keepin' it, cause it would die, and if I leave him here, then maybe I can see him next time we come. And here's another sand dollar, and this is what's inside one if you accidentally step on it because you didn't see it until it was too late, and—" She stopped for a breath and tilted her head to one side. "Why're you lookin' like that?"

He lifted her into his arms. "I was just thinking how nice it is to hear you talk and how much I love you."

"Well, of course you do. I love you, too." She kissed his jaw, then wriggled down to empty her bucket onto the wood planks.

Fiona slid her arm around his waist, and he pulled her close. "I love you, too," he murmured.

''Well, of course you do,'' she mimicked Katy, then asked, ''Are we worth it?''

''Worth what?''

''That day on the mountain you said you'd waited forever to be part of a family. Are we worth the wait?''

He didn't need to think about his answer, but he did anyway. Patrick Watkins was in prison. The jewels had been returned to the insurance companies. He'd quit the ATF and had been immediately hired by the Grand Springs Police Department. They'd started construction on their house on top of a mountain a few weeks ago. Fiona had married him, Katy's name was now legally Reed, and they were going to have a baby. He couldn't have dreamed a better life for himself—if he'd been able to dream. Now he didn't have to. He was married to a living, breathing dream come true.

''Oh, babe,'' he said confidently. ''You were worth the wait, and a whole lot more.''

* * * * *

CHECK IT OUT!

Silhouette®

INTIMATE MOMENTS™

PRESENTS THE LATEST BOOKS IN TWO COMPELLING MINISERIES

BECAUSE SOMETIMES THERE'S NO PLACE LIKE HOME...

by Kathleen Creighton

LOOK FOR **THE AWAKENING OF DR. BROWN** (IM #1057)
On sale next month
and
THE SEDUCTION OF GOODY TWO-SHOES
On sale July 2001

♥♥♥♥♥♥♥♥♥♥♥♥♥♥♥♥♥♥♥♥♥♥♥♥♥♥♥♥♥♥♥♥♥♥♥♥♥♥♥

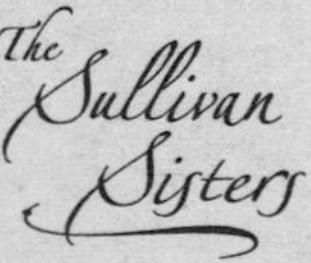

LOVE IS AN UNEXPECTED GUEST
FOR THESE REMARKABLE SISTERS!

by Ruth Langan

LOOK FOR **LOVING LIZBETH** (IM #1060)
On sale next month
and **SEDUCING CELESTE**
On sale March 2001

Available only from Silhouette Intimate Moments at your favorite retail outlet.

Visit Silhouette at www.eHarlequin.com

SIMCHECK